Jenny Pattrick is a writer and jeweller who lives in Wellington, New Zealand. She has written fiction and commentary for radio and, with her musician husband, Laughton, songs and musical shows for children. Her three previous historical novels, *The Denniston Rose*, *Heart of Coal* and *Catching the Current*, are all New Zealand bestsellers.

THE WANGANUI · New Zealand's Scenic River

Pipiriki House, Pipiriki

Landings

JENNY PATTRICK

"The Home of the Maori"

Brett Printing Co. Auckland, N.Z.

BLACK SWAN

National Library of New Zealand Cataloguing-in-Publication Data

Pattrick, Jenny, 1936-
Landings / Jenny Pattrick.
ISBN 978-1-86941-970-7
I. Title.
NZ823.3—dc 22

A BLACK SWAN BOOK
published by
Random House New Zealand
18 Poland Road, Glenfield, Auckland, New Zealand
www.randomhouse.co.nz

Random House International
Random House
20 Vauxhall Bridge Road, London, SW1V 2SA
United Kingdom

Random House Australia (Pty) Ltd
20 Alfred Street, Milsons Point, Sydney
New South Wales 2061, Australia

Random House South Africa Pty Ltd
Isle of Houghton
Corner Boundary Road and Carse O'Gowrie
Houghton 2198, South Africa

Random House Publishers India Private Ltd
301 World Trade Tower, Hotel Intercontinental Grand Complex
Barakhamba Lane, New Delhi 110 001, India

First published 2008

Random House New Zealand uses non chlorine-bleached papers from sustainably
managed plantation forests

Typeset by Anna Seabrook
Cover design: Matthew Trbuhovic, Third Eye Design
Wanganui map: Janet Hunt
Printed in Australia by Griffin Press

To my sister and brother, Dinah and Nigel

Acknowledgements

I WOULD LIKE to acknowledge the advice and help I received from the Whanganui Riverboat Centre, especially from David McDermid; also from Carla Perdue, archivist at the Whanganui Regional Museum. The Raetihi Museum provided excellent material, as did the Alexander Turnbull Library. The website Papers Past (paperspast.natlib.govt.nz) was useful in locating relevant newspaper items.

Several fine books were invaluable to my research: Arthur P. Bates' excellent *Pictorial History of the Wanganui River*; David Reid's memoir *Paddlewheels on the Wanganui*; David Young's

Woven by Water; Merrilyn George's *Ohakune: Opening to a New World*; and Charles Spicer's *Policing the River District* are some of these.

I salute the canoe party who paddled downriver from Taumaranui to Pipiriki with Laughton and me over five challenging and wonderful days — Jan Bolwell and John Schiff, Delyse and Paul Kitteridge, Andrew Mason and Jim Austin, and John and Liz Lee.

Thanks again to Harriet Allan and the Random House New Zealand team, especially sharp-eyed Claire Gummer, and to my editor, Rachel Scott.

Grateful acknowledgement is made to the following for the photographs used:

• cover (girl) — Georgia Nickless; cover (*'Manuwai'* with *'Waione'* in the background at Pukitarata [sic], 279/5, WR/C/125a) — Whanganui Regional Museum

• inside front and back cover and page 5 (staff of Wanganui Sash and Door co. on their annual picnic, with Trinity Young Mens Institute, WR/C/125) — Whanganui Regional Museum

• title page (Pipiriki house letterhead) — Whanganui Regional Museum

• page 13 (boat on the Whanganui, F-140001-½, B Webster Collection) — Alexander Turnbull Library

• page 133 (Captain Kenny Stuart aboard a steamer on the Whanganui River, 1900–1910, C-8847-½, McIntosh Album) — Alexander Turnbull Library

• page 221 (People aboard the steamer *Ohura* alongside a bank of the Whanganui River, F-4 9536-½, Field Collection) — Alexander Turnbull Library

• page 263 (Bill Webb sculling near Upokangaro and onlookers, 1908) — Whanganui Regional Museum

Truth and Fiction
Author's note

THIS IS A WORK of fiction. The fabric of the novel, however, is laid over a framework of real events, places and situations (the excerpts for the chapter headings, for example, and from historical records).

In 1907, the time of this book, Alexander Hatrick's fleet of shallow-draft steamers and motor vessels battled their way up and down the Whanganui River between the town of Wanganui on the coast and the inland railway town of Taumarunui. They encountered 239 rapids in the 144-mile journey. The government-sponsored River Trust had the responsibility of keeping those treacherous rapids navigable — no easy task.

Hatrick, a brilliant entrepreneur, marketed the three-day scenic trip to the world as 'the Rhine of Maoriland'. Posters and postcards trumpeted the beauty of the scenery, the tranquillity and elegance of Pipiriki House, the picturesque novelty of Maori settlements. The many thousands of tourists travelled by train to Taumarunui, then by small screw-steamer to Hatrick's forty-berth Houseboat moored downriver; next day to the modern hotel, Pipiriki House, at Pipiriki, and finally, on the third day, by paddle-steamer to Wanganui. The reverse journey upriver was not quite so popular with tourists, but the steamers also, most importantly, served the many river settlements with a mail service and a means of transporting wool, stock and supplies. The river service was a gateway into the hinterland of the King Country, in the days when roads were few and the north–south railway line not quite completed. Scenic coach trips from Pipiriki via Raetihi to the Volcanic Plateau were also a popular route made possible by Hatrick's river steamers.

Hatrick himself, Captain and Mrs White at the Houseboat, Father Soulas at Jerusalem (Hiruharama), are historical figures and appear as minor characters in the book. All the main characters — the staff at Pipiriki House, the river captains, the farmers and sawmillers — are fictional.

At the time this novel is set, both river and town were spelt Wanganui in all books, articles and posters. I have chosen to use the more correct Whanganui for the river, as this spelling is commonly accepted today.

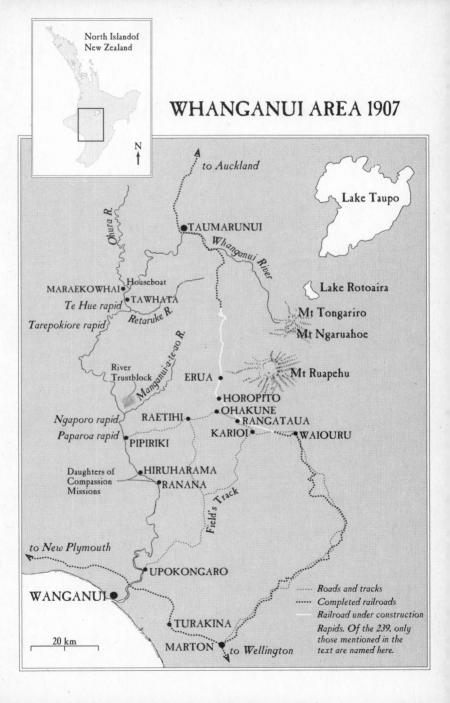

WHANGANUI AREA 1907

North Island of New Zealand

N

Lake Taupo

to Auckland

Ohura R.

TAUMARUNUI

Whanganui River

Houseboat

MARAEKOWHAI

Te Hue rapid   TAWHATA

Retaruke R.

Tarepokiore rapid

Lake Rotoaira

Mt Tongariro

Mt Ngaruahoe

Manganui-a-te-ao R.

River Trustblock

ERUA

Mt Ruapehu

HOROPITO

OHAKUNE

Ngaporo rapid   RAETIHI   RANGATAUA

Paparoa rapid   KARIOI   WAIOURU

PIPIRIKI

Daughters of   HIRUHARAMA
Compassion
Missions   RANANA

Field's Track

to New Plymouth

UPOKONGARO

WANGANUI

TURAKINA

20 km

MARTON   *to Wellington*

Roads and tracks
Completed railroads
Railroad under construction
*Rapids. Of the 239, only
those mentioned in the
text are named here.*

Winter 1907

The River

SAMUEL BLENCOE HAD lived on the river for fifty-odd years. His hut stood on a flat bank just above high flood level, looking out onto a calm stretch of river, below the fearsome trio of rapids — mighty Ngaporo and its two lesser neighbours. Samuel came upriver on foot, in 1856, walking day after day, the plod of his feet gradually stilling the chaos inside his head. When he was sure no sound of the sea would ever reach him again, he stopped, built his hut, scratched a small vegetable garden and, over the years, became rooted himself. He had a certain reputation among the river people — for wisdom perhaps; certainly he was respected. He could always be found near his hut or down at the river. People would sit with him and begin to talk. Samuel offered no advice, seldom even spoke unless to himself, but the river people went away eased from their unburdening, and so the old man was labelled wise.

Before coming to the river, Samuel had been incarcerated in the dreaded Norfolk Island prison for hardened criminals. To casual observation that island was idyllic — sandy beaches, towering pines, gentle climate. But to poor Samuel, the treatment was so harsh; the dank stone cells by the sea were so crowded, so foul, their guards so insanely cruel, that the sound of crashing surf brought back, ever after, the horrors of that time. Samuel, deported at fifteen to Australia, sent to Norfolk Island for insolence at eighteen, was released when the penal colony was closed in 1855. He was twenty-five years old then, looked twice that, no longer insolent or spirited, wanting nothing from life, hoping for nothing.

Samuel's river — the Whanganui — rose in the great mountains of the Volcanic Plateau. Everything about this river was momentous: the names of the mountains whose snows and glaciers fed it rolled off the tongue like an incantation — Tongariro, Ngauruhoe, mighty Ruapehu. Even the tributaries incited awe. Maunganui o te Ao, named Great Mountain of the Dawn for the volcano Ruapehu that fed it, ran through a deep and beautiful fern-lined trench until it poured off the plateau and flowed, wide and smooth as oil, into the Whanganui River.

From the mountains in the east, from the convoluted folds and peaks of dark bush in the west, rain filtered through the spongy soil, gathered into small streams, ran swiftly down steep valleys into the many tributaries until finally all this water — sometimes clear, often clouded by the soft papa clay of the banks

16

— spilled, or gushed, or rolled, or fell in long silver fingers to swell the one great river.

UPRIVER OF SAMUEL Blencoe — a day's journey by river steamer or three by foot — Danny and Stella, loved and pitied by all who knew them, farmed land beside the Ohura River, close to the place where that river joined the Whanganui. Or tried to farm. The land was sulky and strong-willed. You could imagine Danny and Stella being successful farmers: energy radiated off them in waves. Danny's gurgling laugh had anyone in range joining in, and Stella sang whenever she had the breath; knew all the river songs — Pakeha and Maori. You always knew when Stell was on her way up the track. But after five years of back-breaking work Danny still could not wrench a good living from his farm. The sharp hooves of his sheep broke up the soft soil, destroying his newly planted grass and opening the way for pig-fern and tussock, which the sheep would not eat.

'You must get in cattle to settle the land,' said older and more successful farmers downriver. 'Cattle will eat the pig-fern.'

But Danny was too proud — or too shy — to admit that he could not afford to buy more stock. (Mr Feathers down on the River Trust block might have offered a heifer or two, maybe even a bull calf, had he known.) So Danny worked harder, laughed a little less often, and endured the heartbreak of seeing Stella, the love of his life, go to work on Mr Hatrick's Houseboat to earn the money for the flour and sugar and tea that his effort should have been providing.

Much closer to Samuel, a few minutes upriver, Charlie Chee grew vegetables in neat, prodigiously successful rows. He supplied Mr Hatrick's establishments — the Houseboat and Pipiriki House — and anyone else who had money to pay for them. No one knew his age or where he came from or even if Charlie Chee was his correct name. Charlie Chee kept to himself. He dressed strangely, in loose trousers and tunic, and even in winter, when the tracks were deep in mud, would never put on a decent pair of boots. As Charlie Chee trotted upriver and down with his baskets of vegetables slung at each end of the pole across his shoulders, his long black pigtail would swing from side to side. An odd sight. Sometimes children from the kainga or the farms along the bank would run along beside him and tweak the swinging tail and shout: 'Chow! Chow!' Charlie Chee would frown and shout back sometimes, but never break stride. Those heavy baskets of beautiful vegetables kept their steady bobbing rhythm in time with his slapping dusty feet.

ON THE RIVER itself, captains of the riverboats earned their fearsome reputation. Theirs was a tough life. Hundreds of rapids to navigate, wild white water around every snaking bend, with no help for miles if trouble struck. Down they would charge, past Samuel Blencoe's, then, once they had navigated the treacherous Paparoa rapid, they brought their travellers to Pipiriki. Here was a settlement. Maori whares, a store, a church, the clanking, groaning water-operated generator, a landing with several canoes and usually a river steamer or two tied up. Also that great marvel — the jewel in Mr Hatrick's empire — beautiful Pipiriki House.

Ruvey Morrow lived here — cook and sometimes housekeeper at Pipiriki House. A plump, kind-natured lady on a good day, but strict with her kitchen staff, and sharp-tongued with any who took a drop too much. Ruvey Morrow and strong liquor were not to be mentioned in the same sentence. Ruvey had come upriver from the town of Wanganui to marry Albert Morrow, her Maori husband, and learned to love the river and to respect not only her husband but, in particular, that fine entrepreneur Mr Alexander Hatrick.

Three times a week, and sometimes more often, you could take Mr Hatrick's paddle-steamer downriver from Pipiriki on the leisurely trip to the coast. You would stop at Jerusalem to collect wool, maybe, or cherries from the nuns' trees, or to buy their secret herbal remedies. Perhaps Father Soulas himself would come aboard, off to visit souls in need further down. This was a busier part of the river — farmers' settlements thick and fast — the steamer zigzagging from landing to landing. As you neared the sea the views widened, the river slowed, the rapids lacking the bite of those up near Danny and Stella. Here the river captain would shout and joke with the people on the landings, then back his steamer away, easy as driving a dog-cart, and be off.

Down past Upokongaro you would thrash, usually with some kind of shouted altercation between the paddle-steamer captain and the captain of the cross-river ferry, who was generally accused of holding up a more important service with his creeping and antiquated flat-bottomed barge. Down at last to Mr Hatrick's own wharf, above Taupo Quay, where all was bustle and noise, goods piled up ready for the next trip, sightseers marvelling at the black-belching monster that had arrived safely at the modern port-city of Wanganui from the wild bush-clad reaches upriver.

Danny and Stella upriver, the Morrows at Pipiriki, Samuel Blencoe and Charlie Chee in between, the nuns at Jerusalem, the heroic river captains — all had their place on the river. All lived their lives, in some way or another, according to the orderly timetable of Mr Hatrick's river steamers. And all suffered a disruption to that order the day red-bearded Angus McPhee, with his narrow ways and his sharp nose for a bargain, came upriver with his family.

Samuel Blencoe

OUR BRIDIE WOULD often sit with me. Would pad up silently, bare feet and bare head, her shift loose, for she could never bear tight dresses. Even the Sisters at Jerusalem had given up trying. If I were down by the river, which mostly I was, she'd smile and sit close for warmth or comfort, and the two of us would watch the water making its quiet way past. Sometimes I'd point out a floating branch or a reflection.

'Clouds in the water,' I might say, and if she felt like it she might echo me.

'Clouds.' Or 'Water.' Never more than the single word.

Mostly neither the one of us spoke, though. I'd had more than enough of all that long ago. And our Bridie didn't know no better, poor sweet soul.

She were a McPhee before. Bridget McPhee, so the Sisters said. But when the Sisters took her in they called her 'our little Bride of Christ' and she smiled and seemed to like the sound of it. Later, when her belly swole and the name didn't fit like, it were too late. Bridie she was.

Always she knew when the riverboat was coming, her ears much sharper than my old ones. Upriver or downriver, morning or evening, she always knew. She would clamber to her feet, the smile slipping a mite but not in any panic. In those early times I never saw our Bridie in a fluster. She'd walk, sure-footed, away up the bank to my little hut. Round behind of it she'd sit with her back against the rough planks, fernery leaning low over her and she'd hum. Generally I'd go up too; the sight of that beast, black smoke billowing and engine racketing, is not pretty to me, though some think it a marvel. If I would go round in back to see where she hid she would smile at me through the green ferns, humming the while. She would not show fear, like, nor cry out, but there must have been some shadow of memory in that empty head. I never once saw her and any riverboat in sight together.

I reckon she liked the quiet stretches of river, same like I did. I would never live next to rapids. The rushing water reminds me of the hell time. Here the water lies calm and easy, a greenish-yellow colour like a woodpigeon's back-feathers. Below a ways it boils all to white over rocks, casting itself down the narrow passage in a trice. Sometimes I can hear the riverboat grunting and churning to get up over all that madness. For hours sometimes if the river is low. I would give in, turn back downriver, but the river captains would never. When the boat finally comes puffing up my quiet stretch you can see the captain — Jamie usually

— standing high and proud on the top deck, hands firm on that giant wheel, grinning like he knows he's won the game. The gents in their smart hats looking up at him there as if he were some god, and the ladies peeping out the windows at the sights, their pretty faces pink with all the excitement. Then they are all gone, grinding up around the bend and we are left in peace again.

Me and my hut were on our Bridie's beat, if you like, as she walked upriver and down. She stopped with me more than any other, though. I were the favourite. Charlie Chee might say different.

Sometimes you'd find her with the river Maori. They were kind to her, like unto me. Fed us both when in need. Often she'd be with the Sisters at Jerusalem — Hiruharama I should say but I can never get my tongue around the Maori, even though I seem to understand most what they say these days; the language has finally wormed its way in through my old ears but the tongue knots up and won't let it out again. The Sisters wanted our Bridie to stay put with them but she wouldn't. She'd walk the six mile up to Pipiriki House if she had a mind, and then on up to me. Or stop on the way. But she were never in any danger, or none I saw, except the once, though the Sisters worried.

We all kept an eye on her. Charlie Chee was good that way. He was on the move as much as her. Up and down with his baskets of vegetables bobbing at each end of his pole; you often saw them walking together, our Bridie a few steps behind, munching on one of his carrots.

Charlie Chee was what I call an upriver man. There are those spend their lives fighting the current, clawing on upriver to make a better life or more money or a bit of fame for themselves. Charlie Chee worked every daylight hour and some of the night; in his gardens and then selling what he grew. But a good man, Charlie Chee, for all that some might rail against the Chows.

Mr Hatrick, now — there's a true upriver type, with his fleet of riverboats and his finger in every other business pie on river and down Wanganui way. Mr Hatrick would fight upriver to his last drop of blood.

Then there are downriver folk like me and Bridie, who have maybe let go on life; we drift with the current willy-nilly, the slower the better. It is a good and a sweet way to be. Time to think. Time to keep your eye on one thing — a pigeon growing fat on ripe berries like. A river Maori mending his eel-trap. A brown trout, waiting still as a stone against the current in the sunlit water. Watch it start to finish. Some call it lazy. I call it sweet.

Sometimes I wonder about our Bridie back when she were Bridget McPhee. Did she run about and chatter? Were she quick and sharp then, or did the accident only change her nature a small degree? It's a funny old mystery, the inside of your head. There's me myself. What kind of lad were I back in England before the deporting? I can remember no shred of that life. No shred. The years of hell wiped the lot. Maybe I were a true upriver lad that got turned into what I am now by Captain Price and those other damned henchmen of Satan back on Norfolk.

Not much sense wondering when you won't find no answer.

Bridie now. Charlie Chee and me knew most what happened. Not all. Back then, after the accident, the constable come upriver on his horse asking all manner of questions, words like hammers, pencil poised. I said naught. The sight of the law clamps my jaw like unto iron. No word can pass even if my life hangs on it. I reckon Charlie would have kept mum too. None knew her whole tale — how could we? But her accident affected more folk than she ever knew, poor soul.

Wanganui to Pipiriki: 55 miles, 42 rapids

DOWN AT HATRICK'S wharf daylight is just breaking,
black smoke billowing from the *Waimarie*'s tall funnel and the
engineer signalling up to the captain on top deck that steam is
up. But on land Mr Angus McPhee is still arguing. His finger
stabs at the loading manager as if he would drill holes in that
poor hassled man.

'I need both horses *and* the cart,' says McPhee. He is not
shouting but his voice, high-pitched nasal, cuts through the
general morning hubbub to add to Scotty Dwyer's headache.

'See for yourself, sir. We have twenty head of sheep aboard, forty passengers and a full load of goods, much of it yours. You did not advise the horses and cart.'

'I did.'

'You did not, sir, not to me.'

The engineer gives a blast on the steam whistle, which stirs the sheep into a frenzy of baa-baa-ing and stamping while pretty Bridget McPhee claps her hands over her ears and screams in competition.

'Papa, Papa! Come aboard! You'll be left behind!'

Still McPhee will not board, but stands by his horses on the wharf.

Scotty Dwyer has already given in over the cart, which is stowed on the foredeck with the sheep, but he cannot manage the horses. In the end he has to run across the road to fetch Mr Hatrick himself.

That notable entrepreneur is sitting in his spacious office cutting a deal with a coal merchant. He is not pleased at Scotty Dwyer's interruption.

'Mr Dwyer, I am discussing an important business contract. Can you not deal with the matter?'

The Westport coal merchant watches with interest. He takes a breath as if about to join in, thinks better of it, stands and fidgets with his time-piece.

'I'm sorry, Mr Hatrick,' says the flustered Dwyer, 'but Mr McPhee insists he was promised transport for his horses. I never did, sir, and we can't.'

Hatrick lowers his famous eyebrows. Turns to the merchant. 'Mr Jericho, you will excuse me for a moment?'

Jericho taps his stubby fingers on the counter to indicate that his time is precious, clears his throat, attempts to look put out. But no one seriously passes up a chance to do business with Mr Hatrick. Both men know this. The coal dealer decides to stay and watch the scene.

Alexander Hatrick is a match for any man. Hatless, even on this cold early morning, in shirt sleeves and waistcoat, the big man strides across from his offices, where he has been at work since before dawn. His black moustache bristles around a glowing cigar; bushy black eyebrows are drawn low. He would carry twice the weight of Angus McPhee, who is tall but whippet-thin.

Even the sheep seem to quieten when Hatrick's voice booms out. 'Mr McPhee, will you board, please. You are holding up my river service.'

In the presence of this imposing man, who is known to run half of Wanganui and other interests abroad, McPhee becomes querulous rather than bullying. 'My horses . . . I said to you I wanted them aboard . . .'

'And I said to *you* that we had a full load and you should get your man to walk them up the river track.'

'But I need to reach Raetihi tomorrow. I have business waiting there . . .'

Hatrick clears his throat ominously. 'And your business here in Wanganui is another matter, Mr McPhee. Rumour says that you have offered a high price for any logs floated down from upriver. *Floated*, Mr McPhee!'

McPhee looks uncomfortable. 'I have my business, you have yours.'

'And the River Trust has its business. Floated logs are bound to damage our carefully, *expensively* prepared rapids, not to mention my fleet of riverboats. I will have you prosecuted, Mr McPhee, if my river captains set eyes on one single floated log.'

'You have no right . . .' McPhee's words tail away. He knows that Hatrick has the ear of government and, as former Mayor of Wanganui, the city authorities in the palm of his hand.

'Now,' booms Hatrick, 'ride your horses up yourself or step

26

aboard. My service has a timetable, Mr McPhee. Tourists have travelled a distance to enjoy this service; whole communities are waiting for their mail and their goods and we are already ten minutes overdue.'

Hatrick dodges around the waiting horses to shout up to the captain. 'Order your men to cast off, Bill. If Mr McPhee is not aboard immediately, leave him behind.'

Bill Henderson, standing relaxed on the top deck beside his big wooden wheel, removes the pipe, waves it amiably at his employer, then gives the nod to his deckhands. Ropes are cast off, the whistle screams again and slowly the two great side-paddles begin to turn.

Not an auspicious beginning to McPhee's new venture upriver. He is forced to scramble awkwardly aboard as the plank is being lifted. Douglas McPhee, watching from the lower deck, smiles to see his father bested, then turns away before the lack of loyalty is noticed. McPhee is still shouting instructions to the wharf hands, who clearly cannot hear above the clanking engine and the thrash of the side-paddles.

Douglas is more interested in the boat than the fate of his father's horses. He peers down through the open hatchway to where the engineer is swearing at the vagaries of his boiler and exhorting the stoker to keep the fire roaring. The sweating man heaves open the fire-box door, throws on another shovelful, bangs the door shut, all in one quick movement. He checks the pressure gauge and then hangs out of the hatch for a breath of cool air.

Out into the river they swing, under full pressure. Douglas would like to touch the controls, to see how it all works, but is afraid to climb down uninvited. The two men are so sure of themselves, so quick. The stoker, a wiry little man with a soot-streaked face, grins up at him.

'Eh lad, want to have a go then?'

Douglas nods quickly, but the man is only joking.

'Well then, there's not many envy my job. Most want to be river captain. Or run the Houseboat.'

Douglas shakes his head. 'I like engines.'

'Well, you won't want to have anything to do with this pig. A Yarrow boiler she is, shipped out from the mother country. Ship her back any day of the week, I say. You fight her like a wild horse the length of the river. Pressure up, pressure lost; never know where you are with the bastard.'

The engineer shouts something and Douglas's new friend winks.

'See? Pressure dropped already. I got to shovel two ton of this black stuff before we reach Pipiriki. Four shovels every ten minutes. Best be about it.' He ducks back below.

Douglas wanders to the other side of the boat, keeping clear of his father and his noisy sisters. The river is wide and lazy here and grassy paddocks line the bank, though they say there will be rapids and dark bush later. They pass a Maori encampment — dozens of canoes pulled up on the bank in front of an array of low tents and brush huts, the dogs going crazy at the racketing boat. Aft, the big side-paddles churn, round and round, flaying the water into foam, driving the loaded steamer up against the current. Douglas crouches and leans down. He can touch the water as it slides past, muddy and smooth.

This steamer is slender like a trout, built to slide through narrow channels and bucking rapids. Her length and shallow draft are custom designed for this river, which doubters had said could never be negotiated but which John Stewart of the River Trust insisted could. Douglas strokes the paintwork, feels the vibrations under his fingers and is happy.

Suddenly his father is at his side, a hand dropped heavily onto his shoulder. Douglas can't control his nervous jerk.

'I see you had words with the stoker,' says McPhee, watching his son sharply.

'Aye, Father.'

'Was he asking nosy questions?'

'No, Father.' Douglas glances up quickly then down again. 'What sort of nosy?'

'About logs, maybe? Floating logs, if you get my meaning.' McPhee's fingers bite more deeply into Douglas's shoulder.

'No Father. I don't know your meaning.' Douglas feels the panic rising. Something will be expected of him and he will fail.

'You were at the mill last week when I spoke with Morrow. You were listening — I saw you.'

'Morrow.' Douglas tries hard to remember. 'Morrow.' There was a tall stranger at the mill last week. Was that Morrow? 'Ah. I think I remember . . .'

His father makes a sound like a rusty hinge. 'Ech . . . I need take no mind. Your head's a fug and remembers no skerrik. Well then, lad, keep mouth tight if there's questions about logs and floatings. Understand? Just report to me. Can you remember that at least?' The fingers dig again.

'Yes, Father.' Douglas has no idea what his father means. He's desperate to get away.

The steam whistle whoops just above their heads. Douglas is pleased to feel even his father jump. They move apart to watch as the *Waimarie* eases up to a landing and quickly offloads several passengers, two sheets of corrugated iron, a couple of dogs and a quantity of food supplies. Greetings and farewells are shouted back and forth. The captain and deckhands join in the banter. Douglas understands none of it. He is not allowed to play with natives. The laughter and the warmth of it all draw him, though. He would like to join in.

Belching black smoke, chuffing and clanking, the riverboat heads into the current again. The next landing is already in sight. By now they have passed the furthest Douglas has been upriver — the settlement at Upokognaro — and the first of the forty-five rapids is yet to come. This is an adventure! His sister Bridget careers past, screaming, followed by his little brother and sister. Douglas ducks out of the way. Up on the top deck he edges closer to the captain and stands there quietly, feet apart like the captain. His hands twitch. In his mind he also controls a mighty steering wheel.

IN THE LADIES' saloon Mrs Evangeline McPhee sits back against the lovely purple velvet cushioning and tries to ignore her nausea. This faint bucking movement already unsettles her stomach, yet here the river is smooth. They say there is worse to come. At least the family are only going by boat as far as Pipiriki. Travel of any sort is a trial to Mrs McPhee but water travel is by far the worst. She can hear Bridget screaming again, and Gertie, bossy and angry, shouting at her to stop. Two other women in the saloon are chatting happily, exclaiming at the sights, taking tea when it is offered, but Evangeline remains silent, eyes closed, one arm holding little Jonty tightly to her. Her son is happy to sit quiet at her side, solemnly regarding the new sights from the safety of his mother's skirts. Jonty is a good boy, not wild like his brother and sister; not at all like the wilful older three, whose mother died nine years ago and who have run rings around their stepmother ever since. Angus is constantly urging her to exercise more influence on the older three, but Evangeline, with three of her own and now a new household to establish in a wild, unknown part of the country, has no energy to spare. She would like to argue back to her husband: they are your children not mine, she would like to say, discipline them yourself. Usually, though, she simply turns away, or closes her eyes.

Outside Bridget screams again. The ladies in the saloon wince and glance towards Evangeline. Such rowdy behaviour! Most unbecoming in a grown young lady. Clearly they expect the mother to take some action. Evangeline McPhee closes her eyes again. Little Jonty hears her faint moan and pats his mother's hand. She hugs him closer.

FROM THE TOP deck Bridget can see the curling white water of the first rapid up ahead.

'Oh look!' she shrieks. 'Surely we'll drown!' She seizes the arm of a perfect stranger in her excitement.

Her father reaches a long arm to disentangle her from the embarrassed tourist. 'Behave yourself, Bridget. I have my eye on you.'

Bridget smiles sweetly and slips out of his grasp. She knows she is her father's favourite, the prettiest; that he will let her behave as she pleases, while Gertie and Douglas seem to incur his displeasure whenever they are in sight.

The steamer shifts and bucks as it enters the rapid. Bridget screams again, clutching her cheeks, enjoying every thrilling moment.

Gertie gives her a painful dig in the ribs. 'Stupid! Everyone's watching you. Don't be such a baby.'

Bridget pokes out her tongue and runs upstairs to stand by the captain. 'Oh, it looks so dangerous!' she cries. 'Will we get through?'

Captain Henderson smiles and nods. 'Auohina. She's an easy rapid.'

'The rapid has a name?'

The captain looks sideways at her, laughing, 'Every one is named. All two hundred and thirty-nine. They all have their personalities, too. And their moods — just like people.' He swings the great wheel and the pounding boat heads directly into the roughest part. Bridget wants to ask why he doesn't choose the calmer water near the bank, but nervously holds her tongue. Below them, on the lower deck, the Maori deckhands take up their long poles and calmly walk forward.

Bridget screams again, shrill with excitement as the *Waimarie* bucks and slews in the rough water. The men plant their poles deep, brace their feet wide and thrust to add their weight to the straining engine. For a moment the *Waimarie* seems to stand still, then she inches forward. The deckhands lift the poles and thrust again. The rhythm of it and the strength of the men excite Bridget. She wants to hold on to the captain, to feel the strength of his arm as he pulls at the wheel. For a moment she dares to touch his hand and he turns to smile at her. Oh! She can feel the blood rise to her cheeks.

Steadily the boat mounts the rapid. Once there is a terrible clanking as a stone rattles through the flanges of the paddle-wheel. Bridget gasps in alarm but the captain seems unconcerned. Then they are through and into calm water. Bill Henderson nods over to Bridget.

'Forty-three more to go and then we're home for the night.'

Bridget gives a little shriek. 'Forty-three! How can we ever manage?'

'No need to be afraid, Miss. The river's up. When it's low the rapids are tricky. We won't be hitting bottom this trip.' He frowns. 'Or any damn foresters' logs, please God.' He calls for half speed as another landing appears, with a man waiting. The boat drifts towards the bank and the man leaps aboard. They are back in mid-stream without ever tying up.

Gertie's head appears around the corner. 'Leave the captain alone, for heaven's sake, Bridget. He has better things to do than answer your silly questions.'

Bridget looks quickly at the captain to see if this might be true. He is looking ahead steadily. Perhaps he didn't hear. Perhaps she is being a nuisance. Gertie always makes her feel unsure. Then they plough into the next rapid and both girls are flung against the rail. Gertie herself shrieks and Bridget laughs at her. She takes the captain's arm, though the rail would be a firmer stay. Bill Henderson grins at her but disengages his arm gently.

'I need my eye on the rapid, not a pretty girl,' he says. 'Off you run.'

But he says it in such an amiable way Bridget is only pleased.

LATER THE SUN sinks behind the crowding hills and the bush darkens. Bridget jumps as the steam whistle announces the marvel they have all been watching for. There on the riverbank ahead is a great mansion, the fabulous Pipiriki House, renowned worldwide as a tourist destination *non pareil*. Its two storeys are studded with rows of brightly lit windows. A splendid verandah stretches all along the upper level; below it an equally fine balcony, prouder than any city hotel, parted by a flight of steps flanked by potted ferns. Ornate posts topped by urns stand proud at the gate. On the upper balcony women are gathered to watch the approach, while down at the crowded jetty a horse and cart wait, along with several men.

On board there are now only a small number of people, but all are awed by the sight. For once Bridget McPhee stands silent and open-mouthed. It is so improbable. Since they pulled away from the Jerusalem landing in fading light, they have been thrashing their way upriver with nothing but bush and wilderness on either side, and here, around the bend, is this glowing palace!

'Half ahead,' calls the captain down to the engineer.

'Half,' echoes the engineer.

The pounding pistons slow. The drive-shaft hardly revolves. Now Bridget can hear the plash plash of the paddles as they thrash the water more and more slowly.

'Dead slow.'

Bridget smiles to see that her brother is now down in the engine-room, holding some lever as the engineer instructs him.

'Dead slow,' comes the reply from below. Now the chuffing of the smoke-stack, which has pounded like a heartbeat all day long, has at last stopped. In the sudden silence, as the *Waimarie* drifts in towards the landing, captain Bill Henderson, still awed by the familiar sight, speaks quietly.

'Welcome to Pipiriki House, ladies and gentlemen. Mr Morrow is waiting to transport your valises and other goods up to the House. You may ride too, but I suggest a gentle walk up will be rewarding. In a moment the birds will have recovered from our noisy approach. We are, I hope, not too late for the evening birdsong.'

The *Waimarie* sighs its last escaping steam. Peace ripples outwards over river and bush. A last tui farewells the light. Even the little McPhees are quiet as they walk up the road in the sweet-scented dark. Bridget and Douglas run ahead, eager to explore.

'Wait for me, sillies,' orders Gertie, but they are too quick for their lumbering sister.

Down at the landing the peace is soon shattered by Angus McPhee's high-pitched complaints. Bert Morrow and the deckhands are manoeuvring McPhee's cart from deck to land. Bert, looking to sky and bush, has remarked that it would be wiser to store it under cover, in Hatrick's shed, for the weather may turn bad in the next few days.

'My good man, I will be away to Raetihi at first light. My cart will not be standing idle any few days.'

Bert Morrow gives the rude man a straight look. 'You will not be moving anywhere with that cart. The road up to Raetihi is washed out in two places, and blocked by a mud-slide in the gorge besides. And more rain to come.'

McPhee explodes. 'Why wasn't I told?' He turns to shout back at the captain, who is coming ashore, his overnight bag slung across a shoulder. 'You saw my cart! Your loading man never mentioned blocked roads!'

Captain Bill Henderson shrugs. 'You will get used to blocked roads and mud if you are to live up this way, Mr McPhee. They are a fact of life. No one at Raetihi will be expecting you tomorrow. Besides, your horses will be several days themselves. Bert here says the river track down to Koriniti is blocked too.'

'God almighty!' McPhee glares at the dark bush as if sizing up an enemy. 'Well. We will see in the morning. I expect I will discover a way.'

Bert and the river captain exchange a smile. McPhee, who has caught the look, turns on Bert. 'Bring my cart up to the house. And have it ready for tomorrow.'

'I will see to the passengers' cases,' says Bert, 'and my other duties. Later I will see to your cart. If there is still time.'

He turns his back on the fiery man, slaps his patient horse on the rump, then walks away beside the quiet beast, up to Pipiriki House.

CHEAP COUNTRY

1120 acres; 500 grassland, balance bush, most hill
country, wintering 900 sheep and 20 head of cattle.

Price £5.7s 6d per acre
including stock and furniture.

This is the cheapest place we have handled for some time.

Apply sharp.
Lewis and Co., Land Agents, Wanganui

Wanganui Herald, *August 1907*

STELLA O'DOWD WALKS the three miles back home.
Today Danny needed the horse for farm work. Dark clouds
that have threatened all day have sunk lower to drift through
the bush on the hills ahead. It will rain soon. She plods along,
humming a tune that one of the deckhands taught them last
night. Danny will enjoy it — he loves to hear a new song. She
ignores the Ohura Falls, which are such a marvel to visitors, but
to locals like Stella only a hindrance to travel. If only they could
travel up and down to the landing by canoe, life would be much
simpler. Danny and Stella don't own a cart and must beg the use

of a neighbour's when the wool is ready or (rarely these days) supplies arrive for them.

Stella grins to herself, remembering the cheeky gentleman on the Houseboat who had offered to take her downriver to Wanganui and marry her there. It's not the first offer she's had. Stella laughs at the advances, enjoys the compliment to her good looks and cheerful nature. It's one piece of news, though, that never reaches Danny. He has trouble enough with her absence three nights out of seven when she stays with the Houseboat captain and his wife — and the rowdy crewmen — to do the tourists' breakfasts and tidy the cabins after they leave. Stella loves every crowded minute of her work on the Houseboat; loves to watch the ladies in their smart dinner clothes and to listen, as she hands around plates of mutton and vegetables, to the talk of life outside the river. News of the north and south arms of the great railway creeping ever closer to each other — a traveller voiced gloomy predictions that tourists would soon choose rail over dangerous river journeys. Stella laughed at *that* nonsense. Recently a tour party of men talked excitedly of the fabulous exploits of a New Zealand football team over in England; then of Wanganui's own Billy Webb, who has won world champion at rowing in Australia. Stella clapped and cheered at that news, earning a black look from Captain White, who likes his staff to be seen not heard. But pretty Stella, born and bred on the river, daughter of Ruvey and Bert Morrow, who also work for Mr Hatrick, finds it hard to keep silent. She must ask a question when there is a puzzle in front of her lively dark eyes, and will always answer back, even to a drunken proposal of marriage.

The first drops of rain fall, heavy and cold. Stella covers her head with a sack and tramps on. The track beside the river turns to mud before she has gone ten yards. The Ohura, their river, now curves past the old marae, past a deserted farm, the owner gone mad and hanged himself last year, past the abandoned flourmill, which was never finished or operating anyway, and finally past their own farm, where the sheep huddle wetly among stumps and patches of scrub. She turns off the track and walks up through the sad paddocks, which Danny has wrested from the bush, and which the scrub and pig-fern constantly try to claim back. Stella notices a fencepost that has tilted in the soft soil and heaves it upright, chiding it like a naughty child. Stella likes to make fun even of disaster.

She heaves a cabbage from the claggy soil of the kitchen garden, shaking the dirt and wet from its greenery. At least the cabbages grow here. Under the shelter of the porch she scrapes mud off her bare feet — better not to ruin good shoes in weather like this — and pauses, smiling, to listen. She hears a gust of laughter and then the door is flung open. Danny stands there grinning, his face flushed from the fire, his arms open.

'Here's my darling!' he shouts. 'Wetter than a drowned sailor. Quick, sweetheart, come inside before a month of winter drives in with you!' He whips the sack away from her head, spraying the water from it like a wet dog, tosses it on the bench and pulls his sodden wife into the warmth of the room, where he gives her a smacking kiss.

'Ah, that's better,' he murmurs into her hair, and then, 'But Lord above, you're colder than death. Get in by the fire — there's the billy brewing. Warm up before you're on to our dinner.'

Pita is there by the fire. A worry. Stella can smell his liquor, and knows why he has come. But holds her peace for the moment, steaming in front of the open fire, cradling her mug of sweet tea.

Pita grins at her; raises his mug. 'Will you take a drop, sister? This wowser husband of yours will have none.' He is teasing her and they all know it. Danny and Stella do not drink — have never needed it. They are cheerful as drunkards every day of the week.

'Leave off, Pita,' says Stella, sharply enough. 'The room stinks like a brewery as it is.'

Pita laughs and drinks deeply, ostentatiously, replenishing his mug unsteadily from the jar at his feet.

Danny gently strokes his wife's wet hair. Stella knows what he is going to say and wants to delay the moment. Nestling in the deep pocket of her skirt are several surprises. The best she will keep until later. Now she brings out a truly enormous carrot and two parsnips. 'But look at this!' she cries. 'Can you believe these? The size? Charlie Chee gave them.'

Danny gives her a quick look. 'In return for what? Charlie Chee gives nothing for free.'

Stella dares to tease her husband. 'Oh, well now, a kiss or two behind the Houseboat. He is a lonely man.'

Danny growls and waits for a truer answer. No one would give Charlie Chee a kiss.

'I tell him English words,' says Stella, adding with pride, 'and show him how to write them. He wants to bring a wife from China and needs English words to arrange matters.'

But the sight of the glowing vegetables has put them all in mind of the evening meal. Stella, warm again, happy to be in her own home, sings the men her new song as she peels potatoes and onions from the garden, slices the cabbage and Charlie Chee's prize roots, adds strips of smoked mutton and sets the pot of stew on the hook over the fire. Danny, the good man, has already seen that boiling water is waiting on the hob. Stella, knowing she cannot ignore the reason for Pita's presence much longer, decides against apple pie. Cheese and raisins will have to serve. And now, while the stew bubbles, another strong mug of tea.

Danny watches her, waiting for the moment.

STELLA MARY MORROW, named for the stars in the crown of the Blessed Virgin Mary, was just seventeen years old when she met Danny. A crowning joy, she was, to her parents, the Morrows of Pipiriki. An infant daughter and a stillborn son already in their little graves, but this precious one lived. It was no effort at all to put stars and Stella in the same sentence. She won the Star of Achievement every year down at Jerusalem, where the Sisters taught her to read and write and love the Good Lord. She was 'a little star' at Pipiriki House too, in her pretty muslin dress a favourite with the guests when she sang to entertain them of an evening. She would sing with the Sisters, even in Latin, her voice rising to the stars they said with little sighs of pleasure. The Sisters hoped Stella would join Mother Aubert's order, and for a while that seemed likely, as she was a devout child, happy to live with the Sisters and help with the little orphans in the school.

But as she grew tall and beautiful, less holy aspirations enticed her away from a life as a Bride of Christ. Stella enjoyed the growing attentions of the many single men in the district. In frontier land there is always a shortage of women. Single men arrive to break in a block of bush, but then, when they have time to lift their heads and scan the horizon for a suitable wife, they find they are in a male world. Stella, half Pakeha, speaking good English, was an obvious choice. She learned to flirt, to widen her wonderful dark eyes and toss her long curling hair, which her mother tried to keep tightly plaited but which seemed to break loose at the slightest pretext. Unlike her brother Pita, who looked as Maori as his father, Stella's skin was light — the colour of well-milked tea — and the bones of her face were fine.

Her mother was secretly relieved to see Stella spend less time with the Sisters and more laughing with the young men at Pipiriki. Ruvey had only two children still living. The son Pita, wild and unpredictable — who knew where he would end up?

What mother didn't hope for grandchildren, and a daughter nearby to lend a hand when aching joints became a problem? Ruvey hoped that a marriage with a river captain might be arranged, though most of them were married already. Bert would be in favour of a river captain. Or Mr Frampton's son on that nice block of land downriver near Ranana.

But when Pita brought laughing Danny O'Dowd home one evening, flirting and fine prospects came to a sudden end. From that moment on Stella had eyes only for the blue-eyed Irishman whose only wealth was an abundance of optimism.

PATRICK DANNY O'DOWD, known up and down the river as Dannyboy, was born on Great Island, County Cork, his father a steelworker in the shipyards there, his mam a hardworking mother of seven. At fourteen Danny left home on a ship, the *Mary Emanuel*, whose steel rivets bore the marks of his father's hammer. According to Danny, his mother wouldn't have noticed he was gone. Hard to believe that: Danny is definitely noticeable. Pale-skinned but with a thatch of jet-black hair, Danny turned the ladies' heads in New York and Sydney before he landed up in Wanganui and turned a few there.

He is slight and wiry, Danny O'Dowd, good-looking and cheeky, but was not one to settle. At sea or on land he skipped from one line of work to another — deckhand, galley-hand, wharf-hand, dray-man, but never a task that required letters or figures, for Danny never learned those skills. For the three years he attended school back in County Cork, Danny fooled the nuns with his charm and quick wit. He could hold a piece of paper in front of his eyes and read off a 'story' he said he'd written, while all along his mates would snigger, knowing the page to be blank. Half of those school years were spent at home helping his mam with the little ones — running errands or wiping noses. Danny is embarrassed by his lack of letters now, for his wife loves to read and write, but in the early days he got by comfortably enough. He never stayed more than a few months in the one place. Until he met Stella Mary Morrow.

After a spell on the wharves at Wanganui, young Danny fancied a foray inland. When he applied to the River Trust for work upriver, clearing channels for the passage of river steamers, Mr Stewart looked doubtful.

'This is tough work, young man. Most of my men would be twice your size.'

'I am stronger than I look, sir,' said Dannyboy, puffing out his chest, 'and not afraid of hard work.' Which was stretching the truth somewhat.

'Do you understand the native tongue? Most of my upriver gangs are Maori.'

'I have a smattering,' said Danny: a downright lie, but said with a grin that had the stern Mr Stewart grinning back.

That positive attitude earned him a place on a snagging punt, earning one and a penny ha'penny an hour, working out of Pipiriki, where Danny met Stella and fell in love with her and the river both. It was a fine, roaring kind of life with the river gangs. Danny and Pita Morrow worked together on the snagging winch. Neither of them had the strength or stamina for shifting the river boulders and building stone groins, but they were quick and clever with the winch, snaring the clogging debris of branches and logs that came down after every storm, then swinging them onto the bank, using the long arm of the snagging pole as a fulcrum. Danny was popular with the Maori workers for his easy nature and his joking ways. True enough, he soon picked up a smattering of the language and would sit around the campfire of an evening, happy to join in where he could and to laugh it off when he lacked the understanding.

That time in the bush – the rich leafy smell of it, the glorious cacophony of birdsong in the mornings, the wild moods of the rapids that they struggled endlessly to tame worked some kind of hook into Danny's restless soul. And when he met Pita's beautiful sister, who could sing like the very birds, and loved river life as happily as he did, Danny O'Dowd decided it was time to marry and settle down.

'But have you any idea of farming?' asked Bert Morrow, suspecting that his daughter's future with this likeable lad was less than secure.

'Give me the chance and I'll learn,' said Danny, confident as ever in his ability, and Bert, charmed by the smile and his daughter's evident love, gave him a piece of the family land bordering on the Ohura River. A wilderness area, a day's journey by river steamer above Pipiriki, but beautiful, full of promise, so they thought; a romantic place to settle and bring up a family.

But Danny found he couldn't charm the land as easily as he could people. And Stella's hoped-for crowd of laughing children failed to arrive. In five years no children and little to show for the hard work on the farm. When Captain White finally roped and winched the great Houseboat downriver all the way from Taumarunui to settle at the junction of the Ohura and Whanganui Rivers, it was a godsend to Danny and Stella. Civilisation on the doorstep! Stella earned much-needed money working as housemaid, and Danny suddenly found many reasons to visit the landing. A matter to discuss with the riverboat engineer; a message to send downriver to friends; the possibility that seed might have arrived. Stella could have run all these errands, but Danny went anyway. The farm sank even deeper into debt as Danny sought companionship and laughter down at the Houseboat.

It was there at the landing one day that he heard news that Angus McPhee, of McPhee and Sons Timber in Wanganui, would pay top prices for prime totara logs floated downriver direct to his yard. Pita and he had hatched the plan, pleaded their case to the elders of the Morrow hapu and won the right to cut three logs and try floating them down. Stella was dead against it.

SHE LOOKS, NOW, at her brother over the rim of her steaming mug. She knows why he is there and has thought of a way that might prevent their plan. She slips a little packet wrapped in brown paper from her pocket, lays it on the table in front of Danny and waits for him to notice. Frowning, he leans down to riddle the fire again. Won't look at her.

'Danny!' says Stella, all grins now. She stills her husband's hand. 'Dannyboy, look. I have brought you a heifer and a bull calf!'

That certainly catches Danny's attention. He looks down at the little parcel and then slowly up at his wife. He smiles. 'Doesn't look much like cattle flesh to me, sweetheart.' But he is wary, guessing perhaps.

'Open it, open it! It's a present. Open it!' Stella's bare feet dance on the wooden floor.

Danny picks up the parcel, feels the weight and the jink of it and sighs. 'Stella, I don't need any more of your money . . .'

'No, love, no, this is extra, not my regular pay. The foreign visitors sometimes leave a coin or two in the cabin. It's for me, if they like me . . . what I do . . .' Her voice is failing under her husband's stern gaze but she struggles on. 'I have saved it all this year. One gentleman left half a guinea! I kept it for a surprise.'

But she has misjudged the strength of his own need. Danny

pushes the packet towards her without opening it. 'This is your money.'

'But listen! I want the farm to do well, just like you do. We need the cattle. *I* want the heifer too.'

'And I will provide it.' Danny growls the words, tossing his thatch of unruly hair. His face is flushed but he will not look up at her. His fingers trace the knots in the rough wood of the table-top. 'You provide food for the table. That is bad enough. I will see to the farm.'

Stella opens the parcel herself, spread the coins proudly. 'But see! There is enough here . . .' She jumps as Danny's fist pounds the table.

'Put that away, Stell. I don't wish to see it. I don't wish to hear how you earned it. The logs will pay for the cattle. And for a proper coal oven for you. *I will see to it!*'

'Ah, Danny!' Stella is angry at his stubbornness and his rough denial of her gift, but knows his pride will not let him change his mind. She gathers the coins. For once she can think of no cheerful reply.

Pita chuckles. 'If he don't want it I can find a use, sister.'

Stella turns away from them both. Bangs the kettle of stew on the table and ladles it out. Perhaps food will settle them all. It is unlike Danny to be so terse.

Over the meal the men discuss the river. 'It's high enough now,' says Pita. 'We should go tomorrow. Another cloud-burst and the river will turn sluggish. Or a torrent. Neither will suit.'

Danny nods, then looks across the table quickly at Stella, knowing her opposition. 'Tomorrow, then,' he says. He lays his hand on hers. 'It must be done, Stell. The logs are ready, lashed and waiting. Pita has arranged for his cousin Hone to come up and feed the animals while we're gone. Now is right.' His quick smile is a kind of apology. 'We need this, love. And your grandfather may give the logs to someone else in the hapu if we do not move soon.'

Pita, steadier now that he has food in his belly but still over-loud and too free with his hands, hauls his sister close, holds her against his chest longer than is brotherly. 'A new dress for the little lady? A pretty nightdress to entice her husband?'

Danny gives him a slap that is more than playful, though he smiles as he delivers it. Pita knocks the hand away and for a moment real anger threatens. But Danny laughs and pulls Stella to him; the danger passes. He is on edge tonight. His blue eyes have darkened; they glitter in the low light of the lamp. It is the excitement of the coming trip. A change after all these years of fruitless farming.

'Can you be sure of the riverboats, though?' asks Stella, not for the first time.

Pita shrugs away the question. 'Ae. You worry too much, sister.'

But Danny turns to her and answers carefully. He needs her blessing. 'There is no downriver boat to Pipiriki tomorrow, Stell, you know that, and the *Wairua* will be slow coming upriver in the strong water. She won't reach the Houseboat till evening.'

Stella nods, uneasy. She has heard it all before.

'We'll float on down till we judge the *Wairua* is close, or till we hear her — she is a roaring beast and we will be silent. We'll have time to pull in under trees or beach on a shingle bank. When she is past we will continue.'

'You sound so sure you can control a raft of logs . . .'

Pita claps his chest like a champion. 'I *am* sure! I can manage that river. Any mood, any craft. The river and I, we are twins.'

'You are proud and stupid to make such a boast. And drunk. You know Mr Hatrick will not have loggers on the river.'

Pita growls. 'Mr Hatrick does not own the river. What can he do?'

'He can set his gangs of River Trust men on you. They will be right wild if you destroy any of their careful training walls with your banging great logs.'

'The River Trust gangs,' says Pita, 'are mostly related to us, as you know well, Stella O'Dowd. They will not touch us. The trees are given to us by our own grandfather from the hapu's own land on *our* river. They are waiting on the bank of *our* river on family land. We have every right to cut them and to float them down. Don't shake out your Pakeha ways against me.'

The words anger Stella, but worse is her husband's restless pacing. For the first time in five years he is going away without her. Clear to see he can't wait to be off. She fears the outcome of this adventure. That her sweet man might be tempted, down in Wanganui town, by the taste of freedom; might walk away. The farm is a failure and there are no children to call him back.

Then, as if he has heard her thoughts, he leaves his pacing and holds her tight.

'Don't worry yourself, my darling,' he says. 'It will all be grand. We will come back with money, and the farm will blossom like paradise. You will sing the night away at the good fortune of it all. Eh, Pita?'

You would think he was the drunk one, but Stella smiles, comforted despite herself by his absurd claims. 'I'll cut some bread and mutton,' she says lightly. 'You will need to start early.'

IN THE END Stella walks the two hours to the riverbank with the men — to help carry the supplies, she says, just down to the logs. The truth is that now the journey is under way she wants to be part of it. Stella swims like a fish, is as skilled as a man with paddle or pole, has lived all her life on the river and knows this section of it nearly as well as Pita does. But she also loves her work on the Houseboat and they cannot afford to lose that income.

'Just as far as Pipiriki,' she pleaded as they set out. 'I could visit Ma and Pa and come up on the next boat. They would love to see me.'

But Pita was adamant. 'Just the two of us. Two is right. We have worked together on the snagging punts and know how they buck in the rapids. Not you, Stell.'

Danny nodded. 'I would be worrying were you still aboard, instead of watching the current. Not this time, Stell.'

But she walks with them anyway, still hoping, off into the frosty night, the moon guiding them away from the Ohura, across the cleared fields of their own farm, behind the marae and then into the dark bush, this track heading for the quiet reaches of the Whanganui, below the Houseboat, and opposite the settlement of Tawhata. Here Danny's three great totara logs are waiting, hidden under a fringe of branches, prepared for their journey.

Stella's father, Bert Morrow, spoke with the hapu months earlier when most of Danny's flock was swept away in floods and they couldn't afford to buy replacements — not even a ram to put to their remaining ewes. In a ceremony that all the family attended, the tohunga of the family blessed these three logs and allowed them to be cut. The agreement was that in return Danny would supply, each year, a mutton carcass for every log that came off the family land. Danny knows the deal is generous to him. He will find some way to repay Stella's family. When their fortunes change.

The logs are magnificent, each close to five feet across and longer than a great canoe. Stella's uncles have trimmed them so they will ride the rapids sleekly, and then lashed them with flax hemp ropes to make a slim raft, about the same width as the riverboats themselves, and so designed to negotiate the rapids safely. On the two outer logs Danny has fitted rowlocks so that they might row the raft through the slow reaches.

'Oars will have more pull,' he argued with Pita, who favours paddles, 'and we will certainly need an oar at the stern to steer through the rapids.'

Pita nodded at that, grinning in anticipation. 'I will do the steering. You may be stronger but I know the rapids.'

There is no arguing on that matter. Pita has grown up on the river — boasts that he can guide a canoe through a hundred rapids with his eyes shut, which may be true. He has worked with the River Trust gangs and before that paddled up and down the river with his father, setting eel-traps or delivering food from one kainga to another. Pita likes to boast he could paddle before he walked, though no one believes this. Swim, perhaps, says his mother, batting her boastful son over the head. Up and down the river, people shake their heads over Pita — his wild behaviour, his bouts of drinking, his inability to stick with one task for more than a few days. His parents love him, naturally, but worry about his future. So far he has shown not the slightest sign of settling down. This adventure — bringing three valuable logs downriver — is much more to his taste. McPhee has promised good money for them down in the town, and Pita plans to spend his share of the payment on grog.

Now the three of them sit on the bank, waiting for first light. The dark water runs past swiftly; the tethered logs shift a little in the current as if anxious to start their journey.

Danny climbs onto the raft with a sack of food and a bundle of blankets wrapped in tarpaulin. He lashes these firmly to a post he has set on the central log. While he is about this, and hidden by a screen of branches, Pita produces from under a bush a fresh jar of liquor. He swallows deeply and winks at Stella.

'Warm the blood. Take a swallow.'

Stella shakes her head.

'Hey, girl, leave the sour lemons to your husband. A mouthful won't hurt.'

He stands over her and tips the jar against her mouth. Stella slaps away his arm and some of the liquid spills down her dress. She jumps away from him, spitting like a cat.

'Pita Morrow, you idiot! Dannyboy will kill you. Put that jar away!'

Pita, angry now, shoves his face close to hers. She feels the heat of him and doesn't like it.

'I will be captain on this little journey, and what the captain says is law. Understand?'

'Who's talking captain?' Danny laughs as he climbs back up the bank. He stops, though, when he sees the jar. 'We won't have that,' he says, calmly enough, but the anger is clear. In one quick movement he picks up the jar and tosses it far into the river.

'Hey!' shouts Pita. 'That's mine!'

'We must be sharp, man, you know that. No liquor.'

'I say we will,' says Pita. 'There is more and I will bring it.'

'No.'

'Two, maybe three nights on the river, brother. We will need the warmth.'

'Fire and food will do that without fuddling our minds.'

'Then take the logs down yourself. I cannot manage three nights without a drink.'

There is some shame in Pita's admission, but also he is adamant. The other two can see this.

Danny shifts his feet and dances a little as if preparing for a fight, then turns away, watching the river. 'Jesus, Pita.'

The three of them stand in the half light, mist rising around them. Stella breaks the stubborn silence. 'Let him take the liquor, Danny, but not for drinking till the day's work is done. A little at night. On dry land.'

Danny nods, reluctant, but anxious to be away. 'Pita?' Danny won't budge until he has an answer. Stella has rarely seen him so staunch.

'Ae . . . Ae.' Pita mumbles, still unable to look at them. 'Though I can ride the rapids with liquor just as easy . . .'

'No.'

A quick, shamed nod from Pita. He pulls a fresh jar from the undergrowth and climbs aboard without another word.

'Sweetheart,' says Danny, and Stella knows what he is going to say. 'Sweetheart, I will have my hands full with this man, your brother. It is better you go home now. Another time I will find a safer pilot and you will come too.' He kisses her and she smiles back. No point in arguing. Dannyboy is on fire now to be on the river. She unties the tethering ropes and holds them taut as Danny climbs onto the rocking raft. The two men shove against the bank with their long oars and slowly the heavy mass moves into open water. For a moment it seems to want to ride broadside to the flow, which would soon bring disaster — if these heavy logs beach, re-floating will be a nightmare — but the two men, using the oars as poles, turn their raft so it travels in line.

Stella stays on the bank watching. A milky mist has risen off the river to drift in and out of the dark trees. She can barely see the raft as it moves steadily, majestic, in the centre of the current. The men seem to have it under control. The shadowy figure of Pita waves to her and she waves back. He will be happier now he is on his beloved river. Then they are out of sight, swallowed by the mist.

Stella runs along the bank. She wants to see them take the

first rapid, Te Hue, but soon the track turns inland and the riverbank is blocked by dense bush. She stands shivering for a few minutes, listening. She can hear the tumble of water and knows Te Hue must be close. Not a difficult rapid really, but how will they control such a cumbersome craft? She hears a muffled whoop of triumph. That's Pita. An answering high shout of pure joy: Dannyboy. They are away downriver. No stopping now.

The birds are singing as Stella walks back. At first the song is muffled by the mist, then from the other side of the river, near the encampment, a shaft of sunlight breaks through and the birds shout in response. Stella recognises them all: the virtuoso tui, the pure dropping notes of the bellbird, the quick cheeps of piwakawaka, the fantail. Somewhere close by bossy magpies out-warble even the tuis. It will be a perfect day. Stella traces in her mind the twists of the river, the many rapids that the logs must travel. Perhaps they will reach Pipiriki tonight, but Stella doubts this. The long, slow stretches of calm water between high, sheer banks of the gorge will slow them down. And will Pita stay sober enough to pull his weight at those times?

NEW ZEALAND'S RHINE!

120 MILES OF *GORGEOUS* WATERWAYS
Wanganui up-River Steam Packet
and Tourist Steamer Line

✤ APPLY A. HATRICK & CO, ✤
WANGANUI

Promotional poster, c.1900

AT FIRST THE log raft travels straight and clean in the muddy river; the treacherous shingle banks that otherwise might beach the logs are well underwater. In these conditions, as both men know, the rapids are less dangerous, their channels wider and deeper. The two reach Retaruke as the mist burns away and the world of the river opens to them. Pita waves to a girl standing in sunlight on the bank high above, and she waves back. The settlement is beyond her, out of sight, on the rough track that leads inland to where the railway is being built. After Retaruke there is not even a bridle track; the river will be their only connection with the outside world.

Down on the riverbank, where the Retaruke River joins the Whanganui, a River Trust punt is moored. Three trust workers are squatting by a fire, waiting for their billy to boil. They stand and shout as the lograft drifts past. The water is slow here, made sluggish by the volume of tributary water entering it. Danny uses his oar to edge the craft into a swifter channel. He is nervous of the burly trust men, but Pita shouts to them in Maori, making a joke of their journey, dancing on the logs and taunting the men ashore. They call back insults, suggesting that the raft will soon beach and the loggers be begging for assistance, which will not be forthcoming. They shake their snagging poles but are laughing too, it seems. Clearly they know Pita, though Danny has not worked with this gang. Then the raft is sucked into the next rapid and they race down — nothing to do but let the logs follow the current — and into the gorge.

Soon the men develop an easy rhythm. Through the rapids Pita mans the stern oar, trying to keep the raft headed into the swiftest water, while Danny stands with his pole, ready to push away from the bank if they crowd too close. At first, in the quiet water between rapids they row a little, but the current is steady and the wind, which so often will blow up the river to slow progress, is absent today, so the men leave the raft to the current and enjoy the peace and beauty of the gorge.

It is cold still. The sun has not risen high enough to enter the river. Steep banks, dripping with ferns and small trees, tower above them. The birds are silent now, and the river too. Pita walks up and down the logs slapping his cold arms against his body. Dannyboy whistles the new tune Stella taught them the night before. Things are going well. Pita grins and whistles a different tune. He opens his mouth and lets out a truly tremendous shout, which ends in the falling notes of his song.

'Wha—nga—nui—e!'

The sheer walls and quiet water send the echo back, every note clear. Both men laugh. Pita tries again, embellishing his song, competing with and complementing the echo. Danny takes from his pocket a bone flute and adds his high piping notes to the piece. In the still gorge the sound is miraculous, echo building on echo. They don't want to stop, but Pita breaks off.

'Hey, man, here is rough water coming. And after that the devil Tarepokiore. We better watch our step.'

Danny nods agreement. Tarepokiore will be fearsome today — possibly their only real challenge of the whole trip. While the other rapids are tamer in flood times, the whirlpool Tarepokiore becomes more deadly. They say a taniwha is waiting on the riverbed, hungry to swallow anything, living or dead, that strays into its great rotating maw. Once Pita saw a huge totara log, at least forty feet long, slowly, relentlessly disappearing downwards. The hairs stood up on his neck at the sight. You could feel that taniwha licking his lips as he sucked.

Long ago, the Maori of these parts say, a giant slip blocked the entire river at this place. The river built up behind it, then ate its way through the debris, initially as a waterfall. The power of the falling water, they believe, formed a deep hole, now a whirlpool with resident taniwha.

The raft is into the dog-leg race and around the jutting prow of the cliff-face before the men are quite ready. The logs buck like a wild horse in the high waves and twist side-on to the current. Danny loses his balance and falls awkwardly, scrabbling for a handhold on the slippery logs. Pita abandons any hope of steering and crouches, clinging to the post of the rear rowlock as the waves crash over him. Both men look fearfully to the side, where the whirlpool, larger and deadlier than either has seen it before, churns, slow and oily, in the lee of their bucking water.

55

They are nearly through, coming level with the whirlpool, when Danny loses his grip and the tilting logs throw him into the water. He feels the pull of the current dragging him towards Tarepokiore's mouth. He is a strong swimmer and strikes out wildly but can make no progress against the drag.

'Danny! Dannyboy! Here!' Pita, spreadeagled on the logs, clinging to the centre pole now, thrusts his oar out as far as he can reach. Danny feels it, grips for dear life.

That is the way they descend the last of the rapid: Pita flat on the raft, Danny clinging to an oar, sliding under the water's surface like a hooked fish, the raft pitching and yawing, perilously close to the lip of the whirlpool but easing past. And as suddenly as they entered the rapid they are out again, riding smooth water, the raft somehow turning itself in line with the current, the roar of the torrent giving way to the silence and peace of the gorge.

Danny, coughing and spitting, heaves himself aboard. Both men are shaking.

'Thanks,' says Danny. 'She was pulling me in. She wanted me.'

Pita nods. 'I need a drink after that, brother.' He unties the jar and takes a deep swallow. 'Come on, man, you need it too.'

Danny gives in and accepts the offer, though his hands can scarcely hold the jar as he swallows. The liquor burns like fire and tastes foul. Pita smiles at his face and takes another deep swallow. He sighs.

'Oh, that is good. You can't deny it.'

Danny feels the warmth. 'Yes . . . Yes!' And, at Pita's urging, drinks more.

They remove their shirts, wring them and spread the rough cloth on the wood to dry. The sun has come over the tops of the cliffs now and the going will be smooth for a stretch.

Pita corks the jar and ties it back firmly. He is reluctant to share more with Dannyboy. They sit in the sun, letting the river take the raft at its own pace, using the oars only when they stray out of the strongest current.

'Why do you not drink?' asks Pita. 'You don't have to follow my sister's beliefs.'

Danny smiles. He feels his tongue loosened by the liquor, feels happier than he has for a long time.

'It is not only Stella,' he says. 'My da, back in Ireland, hated the stuff. Said the devil himself dwelt in every drop of strong liquor. He scared the daylights out of me and my brothers with his tales of the terrors awaiting us if ever a drop passed our lips.' Danny shrugs. 'I suppose we never formed the habit of drinking.'

Pita looks over at Danny, ready to argue, perhaps, but thinks better of it. 'Your brothers — did they leave home too?'

Danny laughs. 'Don't know. I was the first to go. Have spoken to not one of them since. My guess is they are nose to the grindstone in that dirty old shipyard, following after Da like good sons. I was the wild one.'

Pita slaps Danny's bare shoulder. 'E! A little wildness . . . nothing wrong with that. Look around you, man. Everything here is wild. How the world should be!'

Danny, his shoulders warm now in the sun, and the liquor still singing somewhere inside, thinks of his precious Stella, of their life spent trying to tame the wilderness. His hard-won acres of pasture and the relentless bush beyond.

'Someone must provide food. Make some use of this land,' he says. But his mood dips as he speaks. The easy freedom of his brother-in-law is unsettling. Pita has no wife, no home to call his own, no children. Danny has always considered him a wastrel. On the few occasions he has visited the farm he has drunk and slept too much and avoided any work about the place. Yet here he is, on the river, easy and happy. A good companion.

'Don't you want to have a family? A wife, children?' he asks.

Pita grins. His hands gesture rudely about his groin. 'E! A bit of this now and then will do me. Who knows — perhaps there is a son of my making growing up in the world. Better off without this wandering man for a father.'

Danny shakes his head but holds his peace. Pita has just saved his life, and the good Lord knows when assistance might be needed again. The river's moods change so quickly. But he would like to argue. Life on the land might be difficult and sometimes heartbreaking, but Danny has stuck with the farm for five long years. He is not ready to hear his hard work belittled.

AS NIGHT COMES the raft has made good progress but is still well short of Pipiriki. Pita has guided them through several rapids in the dusk, but neither he nor Danny will risk Ngaporo in the half-light. That rapid — one of the last big ones before Pipiriki — is wild and tricky: in fact it is three rapids in quick succession, with wide shingle beds on one side and a curving cliff on the other. The danger will be the shingle: they will need good light to avoid beaching.

The two men guide their craft into the bank well above Ngaporo. Here the land slopes gently but the river at the water's edge is deep enough to keep the logs afloat. Ponga ferns and kowhai lean over the water. They tie the logs fore and aft to trees and step ashore. Danny lights a small fire and they sit beside it, eating the damp bread and mutton Stella has provided. At least the blankets, wrapped in tarpaulin, are reasonably dry. Danny rolls up and lies close to the embers, happy to listen to the night sounds of the bush — the double notes of ruru the owl and the haunting cry of fossicking kiwi.

Pita sits on in the dark, drinking.

Ruvey Morrow, Pipiriki House

STAY AT
BEAUTIFUL
→ ◆ PIPIRIKI

PIPIRIKI HOUSE

This palatial new house, capable of accommodating 100 people, is appointed with every modern convenience, with electric light, hot and cold baths and up-to-date sanitary arrangements. The main dining hall seats 120 guests, and the upper promenade balcony (130 feet long) commands a magnificent view of the river and surrounding scenery, which is very fine, Pipiriki being situated in an amphitheatre of beautiful hills.

Early advertisement by A. Hatrick

THE NIGHT THOSE McPhees arrived at Pipiriki House I would gladly have given up my position and taken the vow with the nuns for a bit of peace. Bert came up from the riverboat with a face like a thundercloud, which is unusual for him. We've got trouble here, I thought — and was right. The manager was away for a few days, it being winter and the tourist parties smaller, so I was in charge at the House, which would normally be no problem. I was enjoying myself till the McPhees came up the steps, arguing and noisy as a gaggle of geese. It's not what we expect at Pipiriki. 'Enjoy the tranquillity of New Zealand's

Rhine. Take your ease in the splendour of Pipiriki House!' is how Mr Hatrick's poster puts it. Well, tranquillity was well short of the mark that night. One of the guests complained and I was at my wits' end how to calm down those McPhees.

Bert was at fault over the state of the road up to Raetihi, mind, though I never told the constable that. The blocked road should have been noted in the pigeon post. Mr Hatrick likes to know those things. Trouble is, Bert is not so neat with his writing and he cannot always fit all the words on those tiny messages. I would help, as my hand is quite as fine as a lady's, but Bert is so proud of his beloved pigeons and their postal notes down to Mr Hatrick and up to the Houseboat that I don't have the heart to interfere. So the McPhees all arrived and were stuck here, Mr McPhee carrying on as if he were lost in some blasted heath in the wilds of his native Scotland rather than safe and comfortable in the finest hotel in all the Dominion. I felt like giving him a piece of my mind but Mr Hatrick does not like the staff to be uppity. The guests are always right.

The little ones were no trouble, mind. Off to bed after their early tea, without a peep. Worn out by the long day and the sights, most like. I sent Mere up with the warming pan but they were already out to it, she said, pretty as little angels, all three fair-haired and milky-skinned like little lords and ladies. Life in Raetihi would soon change that.

But Mr McPhee had to let the whole world know his rage. I was in no mood to admit that my husband might be at fault. Not to this rude man with his bristling red beard, his voice needle-sharp, his finger stabbing. On and on he bleated — he should have been notified, how could he run a business with line of supply cut, where was the manager, till my Albert laid into him with a few rough words of his own about disturbing the other guests. Mr McPhee shut up like a lamb for a good ten minutes at that. Bert laughed afterwards and said it was his brown skin did the trick. He said men like McPhee don't know how to take it when the natives speak back. He would be right there, looking at how matters panned out later.

Then there was the endless fussing about who might sleep where. The plain one, Gertie, who was old enough to know better — I'd judge her eighteen or nineteen — went into a sulk that would shame someone half her age. Gertie wanted a room of her own: she didn't want to sleep with her sister; didn't like being in a room next to the little ones because they woke early. When I explained to her that families were put this end of the balcony to leave the adults in peace, she shouted that she was an adult too and clumped away on her ungainly plump legs before I had taken breath to answer. Down the verandah she stamped, banging her hand against the railing, kicking at the deckchairs, to finally plop herself down in one at the far end, right next to a nice quiet pair of travelling ladies on tour with their husbands from Scotland. They looked most disapproving at the display; I feared there would be a complaint.

I told the mother — stepmother it would have to be, looking at the age of her — that we could accommodate Miss McPhee in a room of her own but that there would be an extra charge, and *that* brought on another storm when Mrs McPhee took the news to her husband. All the while the other two McPhees, pretty Bridget and her brother, were pretending to be tourists from the home country, promenading the verandah arm in arm, putting on fancy language — 'Oh I say, what a splendid view!' 'Did you see that native in his canoe?' and so on, the cheeky devils, and giggling at themselves. They had the voices down to a T; I had to hide my own smile. Their sulky sister shooting them dark looks, then calling on them to run outside if they wanted to behave like children. As if she were the mother.

Those three older McPhees. A family look, but then again so different. My Stella, poor soul, wanted to know about them — what they were like that first day, before the accident. They had all inherited their father's red hair, I told her, but in different shades that made all the difference. Bridget's long curling hair had a dark gleam to it; you wanted to touch the rich silkiness of it. She knew she was pretty, that one; knew how to use it to good effect. Several of the gentlemen tourists had their eyes on her and she would give them a sweet smile and half a curtsey. Then she'd be off pell-mell with her brother, laughing and shrieking. Halfway between a lady and a child and not playing either role properly, to my mind.

They were a lovely pair to look at, though, she and her brother. The boy's hair shone brighter than hers — like well-polished copper — and where it flopped around his ears lighter again. A good-looking lad, but quiet. I don't believe he met my eyes once in the first year that I knew him. A quick glance, then away, those pale eyes sliding to the floor or out to the bush, and the flicker of a smile — gone before you could notice. Unhappy, I guessed, but not in a way that made you want to know. Not that night anyway. I was right fed up with the lot of them.

Gertie, now — you'd have to be sorry for Gertie if she weren't so difficult. She had the raw end of the stick every which way. The colour in her hair lacked all the fire of the other two. A dull yellowy orange, and so fine and dry it fell lifeless around her plump cheeks. I would have grown it and pulled it back in a bun if I owned such sorry locks. But then the plain face would have been on show, poor girl.

Well, that first night it was the sulks that were on show, and in the end it got her nowhere. The father was as tight with his money as he was free with his opinions.

'If you don't like your sister, sleep outside on the verandah,' he said. 'I will not spend good money on your moods.' And walked away back to his dinner, all her pouting and snorting completely ignored. I had to agree with the man at the time, but not with his manner. There was raw dislike in the way he spoke to her. He would not look directly at her but glanced quickly and away again, as if he couldn't bear to rest his eyes on his own daughter. I saw tears well up in the poor girl's eyes at that look. Perhaps she loved her father — there must have been some softness in the girl — but clearly any affection was not reciprocated. Mr Angus McPhee, in my book, was the sort who liked all his possessions, including wife and children, to be admirable.

I never saw how they sorted out the sleeping arrangements, for I was needed down in the dining room. All calm and pleasant there, with the nice roast of mutton and my good cherry tart for dessert. One of the ladies remarked how fine the cutlery was, stamped with Pipiriki House, and the china special too. She hadn't expected such refinement up here in the wild, she said — so many fine parlours, and a special ladies' drawing room, not to mention the billiard room for the men. If it was proper to talk back to the guests I could have told her that our Mr Hatrick knew how to run a good business. When he took over Huddle's Temperance Hotel, as it was then, it took him no time at all to build on our fine new rooms, better in every way and the most modern, Mr Hatrick says, in the whole Dominion. Huddle's was smart enough, mind you; I worked there myself, learning the ropes. But Mr Hatrick is a great man of the world and we are fortunate to work for him.

I'll admit that when my Albert first brought me upriver I held a dim view of how it might all pan out. So far away from a nice town, from shops and neighbours who spoke proper English. Bert was born to it, of course — grew up in these parts, loving the river and always working on it, but it scared me, all that wilderness. I settled to it, though, what with the work at Huddle's and then the babies born. Back when he was alive, Bert's father was one of the few Englishmen living up this way. He ran a flourmill. Both his workers were Maori and he married one of their sisters. As soon as he was old enough my Bert worked for the River Trust until he crushed his hand. Now he works at the house with me. That's how Mr Hatrick is — looks after his workers properly. Mind you, they are lucky to have Bert, with his river skills and his understanding of the flourmill, which is now our electric generator, run by the same water-wheel that used to turn the grindstone. And his knowledge of Maori ways. Mr Hatrick understands that. All his best riverboat captains have river Maori blood in their veins.

Well, that night. Most of the guests were travelling up to the Houseboat next day and were full of all the sights they had been promised. Captain Jamie Jamieson came across from crews' quarters as the gents were having their cigars and the ladies their tea. He kept them all agog with his stories of dangers and wonders upriver, and his advice to wear warm clothing. When he heard about the McPhees being stranded, he had the solution straight out. Captain Jamieson is a great one for calming troubled waters — it's probably all his experience with the rapids.

'Mr McPhee,' he said, smiling in his easy way, 'how about we hire you one of our draughthorses? If you are game to ride such a broad back, I'll wager old Snowball will plod up through the mud for you. Then we can send Mrs McPhee and the children up on your cart once the slip is clear and your own horses have arrived.'

Mrs McPhee was well pleased with that idea. The pink was back in her cheeks from a good meal and the warm fire in the grate. Clearly Pipiriki House was very much to her taste. You could see that her smile helped melt that frosty husband of hers.

She had a way with him all right.

'And I tell you what,' the captain went on with a wink to the younger McPhees. (Gertie had finally come to table and was wolfing down her mutton, which good-natured Mere had kept hot.) 'Why don't the two young ladies and the young gentleman here come upriver with me tomorrow? Give Mrs McPhee a quiet day with the young ones?'

He must have noticed the argument earlier, or maybe the exhausted way Mrs McPhee dragged herself around. Nothing much escapes Jamie Jamieson. He turned his attention to McPhee, who was all smiles now at the thought of getting on the move again.

'I have near an empty boat going up tomorrow and space for three coming down next day. What say we give them a free ride and you pay only for their night on the Houseboat? The trip is a great marvel, which any newcomer to these parts should experience.'

Captain Jamieson has his head screwed the right way. Mr Hatrick himself couldn't have done better. During winter, three more paying guests at the Houseboat is good business.

McPhee drew his brows together at the price, but you could see the mention of a bargain opening his purse-strings somewhat. And his wife's pleading look. But still he had to bargain for a cheaper deal, them all being children.

Captain Jamieson wasn't having any of that. Mr Hatrick's river captains are proud men — not the sort you mess about with. 'It's a good rate as is, sir,' he said, his smile just that bit stony now. 'Take it or leave it.'

Then while Mr McPhee was chewing his beard over that, my Bert put his head around the door with a problem from the kitchen. He was not dressed for serving the tables so would not enter the dining room, I was pleased to see. Times he forgets.

'I've got that new constable in the kitchen,' he said, 'having a bite with the staff.'

'Mercy,' I said, 'how did he get down here?'

'Horseback. The poor beast is knackered. Mud up to his barrel, head lower than his knees.'

Plain to see that Bert did not approve of driving a beast like that. But you have to admire man and horse who could find a way past that slip without falling into the gorge.

'Well, is there some problem?' I asked, for I was needed back in the parlour to pour tea.

'He wants to come into the parlour and introduce himself to all.'

I wasn't sure about *that*. Not sure what the rules were for constables, for we had not had one down to the House yet. And with the trouble over selling liquor, Mr Hatrick might not want us too cosy with the constabulary.

'He is a good enough lad,' said Bert, 'and has brought his good uniform down in a sack so he can come in clean.'

I popped into the kitchen to see for myself. There he was, very smart in his tunic and trousers and standing politely to see me come in. A tall man, a good head above Bert, who is no minnow. I took to him right away, with his manners and his eyes brown as raisins.

'Second Constable Tim Naylor,' he said. 'New appointed to the Raetihi Station.' His nod and his smile pleasant — not putting on side, nor yet servile.

'Mrs Ruvey Morrow,' I replied. 'Cook, and for the moment housekeeper. Pleased to meet you.' Which I was. After those McPhees it was a relief to find someone you could take to moving into the district.

It turned out he was not here for the sly-grogging at all, or not that he said. We have had a little trouble with the law over the drink. We are a dry area, praise the Lord, but Mr Hatrick has somehow obtained a packet licence for the boats. He is a crafty man who can argue a case with the best legal men. But word got out that the stewards on the boats would sell the odd drop when they were tied up at the landing. Bert said it was harmless, but I saw the queue of men from the kainga hopping aboard and off again with their brown paper parcels. It was not right. On that matter I would side with the law. I do not believe for a moment that Mr Hatrick would have known, though Bert said he did. Anyway, all that was put a stop to. Threats were made by some authority down in Wanganui and Mr Hatrick gave the order.

So we naturally thought the constable was here to check up. But no, the good man wanted to set eyes on the whole area covered by his station, which was a tall order, as it spread between Raetihi and Pipiriki and much of the river too. The last constable never came down once that I noticed. Constable Naylor had last served at the Foxton Station, so he said, and Patea before that, though he looked too young to have so much experience under his belt.

In the parlour he made his rounds, very sure of himself, a little bow to the ladies and a good firm handshake with the men. I noticed the constable was quick to sort out the visitors from locals. Captain Jamieson received special attention, and the two ladies from the River Trust farm upriver, both Mrs Feathers — married to brothers and down for a decent hot bath, they said, and a dose of civilised life. They were both fond of croquet and would come down to take advantage of our green and of Mr Hatrick's 'four-day-stay special'. Mr and Mrs McPhee received the constable's same careful treatment: a greeting, a smile, a few questions. You could imagine Constable Naylor noting it all down later for future reference or reports.

Through all this, Gertie McPhee changed her mood from

winter to full sun. Suddenly that young madam was all smiles and flushes, which did her complexion no good, poor thing. When her father failed to introduce her, young Gertie took it into her own hands — seized his arm awkwardly and gave her name.

'We are all coming up to Raetihi,' she gushed. 'I am *so* glad there will be someone pleasant to pass the time of day with.'

A very forward statement for a young lady to make, in my opinion, and also rude. There are several good souls up in Raetihi when you get to know them.

The constable smiled and took her hand. 'I hear we are to share a river trip tomorrow. I look forward to it.'

Clearly Gertie McPhee understood him to mean that she, rather than the river trip, was the event looked forward to. She beamed and bobbed and cast glances left and right to make sure we had all noticed. You had to feel sorry for her. In fact Bridget, her sister, smiling prettily at the prospect of the river trip, drew the constable's eye far more often, a blind man could see that.

Then, on top of all this, when the guests were settled and I had my poor feet up against the stove in the kitchen and a good cup of tea in my hand, Bert came in with the news that Dannyboy and our Pita were on the river with the logs.

Pipiriki to Houseboat: 59 miles, 107 rapids

The cruise up these fairy waterways with the cool fragrant forests all around, the gorgeous shadow, pictures in the water, the wonderful wild gardens of ferns on the bank, the murmur of the waterfalls and the rush of the river in one's ears is one of the most truly delightful in this land of a thousand fine tourist pilgrimages.

Lady tourist's journal, 1904, Wanganui Regional Museum

THE DARKNESS IS almost complete this time of a winter morning. Long ago the new moon has set. It must be the stars that give the river that faint glow, as if it is lit from beneath, not above. Stewie Biggs, fireman, stumbles down to the jetty, shaky-legged and sorry-headed after a convivial night in the crew's hut (liquor from the steamer's packet licence having mysteriously found its way ashore), stumbles twice on the rutted track before he pitches headlong into the mud. He curses and staggers to his feet again. Below he can just make out the black bulk of the *Waimarie* against the water. His smaller upriver *Wairua* will be alongside. The water is dead calm, not the slightest breeze to ruffle its strange luminous surface. A morepork calls twice; otherwise there is silence. Down here the early morning bustle up at the House — staff preparing an early breakfast for the departing guests — is unseen and unheard.

Moving by instinct rather than design, Stewie climbs aboard. Almost immediately he feels better. The slight uncertainty under his feet — the gentle pull of the current flowing under the boat — stabilises him in some way that he recognises but would never bother to express. He opens the small hatch to the engine-room and clambers down. Here he is sure-footed. He lights the hurricane lamp and hangs it on a nail. Late the previous night he emptied the fire-box, throwing the ashes overboard. Now he has to get a good fire going before Dusty Miller, the engineer, comes down. Stewie would like to be solitary, to enjoy being alone aboard the tough little *Wairua*, his favourite of all the riverboats. But here is a pale face at the hatchway, an uncertain smile on the lad's face.

'Hello,' says the fireman, busy with his shovel.

'Hello,' says Douglas. 'Can I watch?'

Stewie sighs. You get this: star-struck visitors wanting to help, only getting in the way. But he likes the gentleness of the boy, the sharp interest in his eyes. He picks up an oily rag.

'Come on, then. Wipe down the brassy bits. Engineer likes it to be winking clean.'

Douglas squeezes in beside the wiry little stoker and rubs away at the knobs and gauges and the round belly of the boiler itself. The little space soon heats up.

Stewie eyes the two water gauges and adds water to the boiler. When the level shows exactly half full he closes the tap. 'At least we have a plentiful supply of water on hand,' he jokes. 'Coming upriver, then?' He has heard about the McPhee business last night and suspects this is one of the brood.

'Yes.'

Not a talkative lad. The fireman approves. He slaps the boiler, sitting like a great sausage on top of the much bigger fire-box. 'This feller will have a heavy day of it. The flow will be swift. You watch for the triple rapid: Ngaporo and the one each side of him. My bet is we will have trouble.'

'Why?'

'Think about it, lad. Three rapids so close. We can't let pressure drop for even a minute. No time for the poor old boiler to gather strength before we are on to the next. Ngaporo, the middle rapid, is an unpredictable brute at the best of times. We'll have to winch up all three, no doubt.'

Douglas would like to ask about winching, but here comes Dusty Miller, the engineer, rubbing his chilly hands and climbing aboard, no nonsense. He gestures with his pipe for Douglas to move out, inspects the pressure gauge and nods to his stoker.

'Not quite one fifty yet. See if you can raise her a bit. We'll need it.'

Douglas climbs up away from the noise and warmth of the engine-room. Now he can hear the dawn chorus in full cry. He loves it all; can't remember when he felt so awake. All of it is good: the thrum of the boiler coming up through his feet, the gentle rocking of the boat as the deckhands come aboard with cargo. Douglas breathes in the dark smell of wet bush and muddy water.

His dreaming is broken by the shrieking of Bridget, running down the track from the House. 'Douglas, Douglas!'

He dodges behind the cabin structure, not wanting to share this moment, but the deckhands point out where he is. Bridget barrels on board, hair unbrushed, ribbons flying.

'Douglas! We didn't know where you were! Father is in a rage.

He wants you to go up with him to Raetihi. He says there is room on that great horse for two and you will be useful.'

Douglas's mouth drops wide open. He can say nothing for fear he might cry.

Bridget rushes on, perhaps not noticing his distress. Perhaps not caring. 'Father is ready and waiting with supplies loaded atop the nag. He is all a-boil to get going. You better skip to.'

Douglas pushes past her without a word. Head down, he steps ashore and walks up towards the House.

'Sorry, Douggie,' calls Bridget. Douglas turns to wave but already she is exclaiming over something else, her high voice carrying her views to the whole world.

Douglas has never rebelled before. But here he is, halfway up the bank on his usual route of obedience when the moment presents itself. Bert Morrow is bringing the horse and cart down with the passenger valises and other supplies for upriver. Without thinking, Douglas simply turns and walks down again, hidden by the cart, takes a large sack of something on his shoulder and walks aboard with it. He dumps it on the foredeck and then sits behind a screen of sacks and boxes. He hears his father shouting; hears Bridget shout back that Douglas is on his way. Then he closes his mind to the outside world and imagines a new adventure involving riverboats, powerful engines and dangerous rapids.

ABOVE THE TRIPLE rapid, only a few miles north of Pipiriki, Danny and Pita wait for the light. They have spent a cold night under a makeshift roof of fern leaves. Pita has drunk most of his liquor and is alternately talkative and argumentative.

'See then,' he says, prodding his brother-in-law in the shoulder, 'isn't it a better life on the river here — easy days and a full purse at the end?'

'Well, so you say. I have chosen farming.'

'Why not change? Farming is hard work. Logging is the way.'

Danny sighs. He has heard the argument too often; it cuts too close to the bone. 'You are free to change your life. I have land and a house to care for. A wife.'

'And your wife works cleaning rooms so you can care for your useless land.'

Danny stands suddenly, scattering their fern roof. He crashes into the bush, where Pita can hear him noisily relieving himself. When he returns his face is rigid with dislike.

'You have drunk too much so you say such things. Keep your ideas to yourself or we will have blows on this trip. I tell you this: I will take a different pilot next time.'

Pita laughs. 'Next time the logs will be mine, Dannyboy, and you will be at home scratching your poor soil. You forget who gave the timber.'

Danny tears at a piece of bread, chews hard to stem his words. He swallows cold sweet tea and watches his precious logs. He needs Pita and must control his anger. This adventure, so anticipated, is turning sour. Danny, easy with his friends, sunny-natured, had not considered for a moment that he and Pita would rub each other raw. Danny curses himself for not thinking of the liquor. Or of Pita's arrogant ways. He slaps at a mosquito, throws a crust to a pair of paddling ducks. 'Where's that damn *Wairua?*' His grating voice startles the ducks; they clatter away over the water and heave themselves into the morning mist.

'Let's go now,' says Pita, stretching. His voice is still slurred from the liquor. 'We're wasting time here.'

'She'll be on her way by now,' says Danny as calmly as he is able. 'Another hour and she will be up through Ngaporo. And you might be sober. Then we'll be clear to set out.'

He is wrong about that, though. On both counts.

Reports of the Accident

189 Upper Ngaporo rapid

Hauled over shadow at bottom of rapid. An extension of the wall from the R.B. would improve. The top of the rapid requires dredging and a snag and boulders require to be removed. Found bottom badly, also in a shadow above the rapid. A wall from the R.B. would assist this.

extract from a Wanganui River Trust report, Tour of Inspection, February 1908, by chairman T.D. Cummings

Captain's report

Wairua delayed two hours at Paparoa rapid w. stone in screw-shaft. Nosed into shingle while deckhands made clear. Delayed further below Ngaporo. Wire not found. Deckhands secured spare wire to tree and commenced to winch up.

Loggers (D. O'Dowd and P. Morrow) coming down through Ngaporo hit *Wairua* port bow 10.30 am. Two plates bent but not broached. Five rivets lost. All plugged w. wood pegs above rapid.

11.15 am — 1 passenger reported lost overboard. Miss B. McPhee. Brother and sister not sure when. Passengers difficult to control. Dispatched 1 pigeon to Pip House to warn them. Put Constable Naylor ashore at Ramanui Ldg to organise search.

3.30 pm — At Te Maire dispatched pigeons to Houseboat w. delay time and passenger numbers — 5 tourists 3 waysiders.

Arr. Houseboat 8.30 pm. Replaced wood plugs w. gutter-bolts and pumped out. Inspected damage. Prow bent off plumb to starboard. Will test how she goes downriver if urgent repair needed. Brother and sister still difficult.

A letter from Mrs Lily Feathers of Ramanui to her sister in Wanganui

Dear Fanny,

Holy Mother Mary bless you.

I am back at Ramanui after a treasured stay at Pipiriki House. What a pleasure it was to turn on a tap and out flows Hot Water! And a good roast meal every night, cooked by a hand not mine. Betty has become a dab at the croquet and beat me twice but it is all in the family, after all, so I didn't mind too much. After the four days Betty and I felt quite back in order again and ready to take up the reins on the farm. Were Rob and Mack pleased to see us? Who can tell? Our men are Good Sorts and Hard Workers but neither has much of a way with words. It is lucky we are two women together or our tongues would dry up and shrivel from lack of use!

While at Pipiriki we were blessed to be able to take the Morrows' small motor-canoe down to Jerusalem for Sunday Mass with Father Soulas. He is a great and tireless worker for the faith. We felt so proud to see that beautiful church on the hill, which the hands of our own men had helped build. All the Sisters' little convent children were lined up in the front pews. Clean Sunday smocks, brushed hair tied back, clean white ribbons in their dark locks. They are blessed to have such a start in life.

Coming home upriver on the steamboat there was a bit of excitement. Three of Angus McPhee's older children were up for the ride. You would remember him from last year, down your way, Fanny, the mill-owner with the ginger beard who made such a fuss in the paper about the Chinese, calling meetings and berating the Catholics in public because they would not take a stand. I do not take to the Chows, as you know, but the Presbyterians are worse in my book.

Well, these three McPhees were Trouble from the first minute. The older girl had some bone to pick with her younger sister. Some rivalry over the new Constable, I fancy. Would not let her be, and then started in on the boy for not taking her side. My head was ringing with her shrill accusations. I suggested they take their argument outside the cabin, which they thankfully did. God's beautiful scenery to marvel at, and all they could do was bicker. I think the boy went and pestered the engineer after that, while the two girls kept on.

Oh dear, what a screed, Fanny, but I am coming to the strange part. Captain ran into trouble at Paparoa rapid — a stone in the propeller screw, I believe — and back we drifted to the foot of the rapid. Nothing to be done but clear the obstruction. It is common enough. The deckhands into the water and diving underneath. For some reason the younger girl, Bridget, got it into her head that we were in danger. Scream! You would not believe the noise that girl could make. She screamed to see the Maori diving under, to feel the boat shifting and rocking, though we were secured to the bank — any fool could see that. She screamed again when the stone finally came loose and we began winching up Paparoa. By this time the older girl had latched on to the new Constable — did I tell you we now have one stationed at Raetihi, and zealous in his work, by all accounts? This older sister was clearly embarrassed by her sister's antics and would break off her attentions with the Constable to shout at young Bridget. I was quite out of sorts with it all. The delay and then this bad behaviour. The Protestants do not know how to bring up their children, I have said it before. Those little mites at Jerusalem could show them how to behave, Natives though they be.

But worse was to come. At Ngaporo — you know the rapid I mean, Fanny — we had trouble again, and more delays. The deckhands could not find the winching wire. Rangi must have spent half an hour fishing with his hook to find where it lay on the riverbed, but in the end the Captain sent him and Eru ashore to climb up with a spare wire, which they tied to a tree above the rapid and we winched up on that. Bridget was screaming her head off all over again. Then, just as we were mid-rapid, would you believe it! Loggers came tearing downstream! Three giant logs lashed together, and two men aboard. I knew them and told the Captain smartly, for loggers are not allowed on the river. Well! They hit us with a bang that shook my teeth near out of my head. We heeled to one side, Captain swearing and fighting to keep us afloat and two passengers rushing to take the poles and fending off the bank, as we were close to beaching. Dear oh dear; accustomed as I am to river travel this was a journey well forgotten. Be sure those men will be reported and prosecuted.

The next half hour was blessedly peaceful. We entered the gorge and steamed up, while one of the deckhands squeezed down below to hammer plugs into holes, as we were taking water. Five rivets had gone, Captain said. But Fanny, you would never guess why all was suddenly peaceful. The young McPhee girl was lost overboard! The boy, Douglas, finally took his head out of the engine-room and came into the cabin.

'Have you seen my young sister?' he asked, quite polite, I'll give him that. His older sister was still clinging to the Constable's arm, feigning fear, I don't doubt, no thought for poor Bridget. I blame her. She is the oldest and should have kept an eye.

When it was finally established that the girl was not aboard, the peace was shattered once more with shouts and recriminations from Miss McPhee to all and sundry. Her face so red and ugly I thought it would burst, and the boy quite the opposite — silent and pale, shaking like a leaf, as well he might.

We all thought she must have gone over when the logs struck, but it is beyond my comprehension how those two could have ignored their sister's absence for so long. Well, Captain took charge. We were close to our landing by now and Constable Naylor was put ashore to organise a search party downriver. Mack gave him a spare horse and went with him. As the *Wairua* pulled away I could still hear Miss McPhee going on at her brother. I would have stopped her mouth with soap if I were her mother, the things she said.

I can tell you I was glad to be back in my quiet house. Mack and the Constable didn't find Bridget McPhee, but returned with the news that she was safe back at Pipiriki House.

Well, Fanny, now you know about it from the horse's mouth. No doubt there will be something in the paper. Mr Hatrick is not one to let loggers get away with such behaviour.

Give dear Bernadette and Mary a kiss from their auntie, and save one for yourself.

Your loving sister,
Lil

Constable Tim Naylor

July 14th 1904

I travelled upriver on the steamboat *Wairua* between Pipiriki and the Houseboat at Maraekowhai. While the crew were winching up Ngaporo rapid, loggers struck the vessel. A passenger identified them as Danny O'Dowd and Pita Morrow. Forty-five minutes after leaving the rapid a lady passenger, Miss Bridget McPhee, was reported lost overboard. Captain James Jamieson pulled in to Ramanui landing and I disembarked along with two waysiders, both named Mrs Feathers. At 10 minutes to midday a farmer, Mack Feathers, and I proceeded by horseback downriver, stopping to search where we could, though the banks were high for the first half hour. No sign was seen of either clothing or the lady.

At 3.15 pm we reached Ngaporo rapid. Mr Feathers swam his horse across to take the true right bank and I remained to search the left. We searched thoroughly below the point of collision with the loggers. No sign. We then proceeded slowly downstream. Mr Feathers had difficulty due to the terrain and lack of bridle track. I passed through the vegetable gardens of the Chinese man but there was no person at home. At 4.30 pm I reached the hut of the recluse Samuel Blencoe. He informed me that the girl had been found and taken to Pipiriki. Further questioning proved fruitless. I formed the opinion that the old man is not inclined to speak freely to men of uniform.

Mr Feathers then swam his horse back across to join me and we proceeded to Pipiriki House. Miss McPhee was being cared for by her mother and hotel staff. The housekeeper, Mrs Morrow (mother of one of the loggers), was of the opinion that the victim's mind had been damaged, though she said it was too early to be sure, as shock might have been the cause, and a good night's sleep the cure.

Paid Mr Feathers 1/6d for the use of his horse.

Constable Tim Naylor,
RAETIHI STATION

Samuel Blencoe

I seen something move down by the river. Through the leaves I seen it all and it were ugly. Constable asked but I would never send no man to jail. Not even for that ugly thing.

On a fine morning I might walk up the river track to feel the warm mud under my toes and the sun on my poor scarred back. So it was that day. Just below the rapid they call Oakura, it were, the lowest of the triple. The birds shouting their news to all and sundry. I don't go no further upriver than this place. So I turned and that's when I saw. The river makes a little beach there, sandy and quiet, with the willows drooping close. It is an eddy, you might say, which pulls in any broken thing the rapids have spat out: branches, a sheep, fenceposts.

This time a man and a woman.

The man come up out of the river, dripping water and blood and dragging the dead weight of the woman. Pulling her by her torn skirts through the shallows. The man were Dannyboy O'Dowd. I didn't know him then but heard later that's who he were. He looked dead beat and she looked plain dead, lying still and white where he laid her. Down he knelt beside her, the blood from a head wound colouring the poor drowned skin of her face. A wet, white, still thing.

I watched from above.

Danny touched her face, so gentle. I heard his moan like a sick animal. He turned her to her side maybe to see if any wound might be there. She rolled like a dead weight. He held her there, waiting, kneeling over her, but no movement from that poor white body. The man stood. Even from above I could see him shake.

A second man come up from the river. Pita Morrow. That little eddy do catch them all. Their log raft came after. I heard they were going to try floating logs down, the daft buggers. Pita Morrow would sail a craft to hell and back for a bit of a lark. Those great tree trunks were turning lazy in the current; they would slip away soon enough if those men paid no heed.

I don't know what Pita said to Dannyboy. Some words passed, I seen that. Whatever it was might as well been bullets shot from a gun the way Danny bucked. In a trice he were roaring angry. He whipped around to face Pita, shouting into his face about it all being his fault and look what he done — that sort of blaming words. It happened so quick I hardly seen it. That sunny-faced man suddenly a living torrent of fury, fists flying and words shouted unto the heavens. Even the birds stopped their song. When I think back on that sight I see a man angry at more than a ruined girl. All manner of rage and despair rode on his back, gave strength to his arm.

I heard the smack of fist on head; I heard the crack of bone. I seen the dark man flung clean away off his feet and into the river. I seen the current take him, floating and still, away downriver. The logs moving, too, pushed out by his splash maybe — away they went, silent and still as poor Pita. A terrible sad sight.

When I looked back to see if Danny would run after the raft and the floating man he were on his knees again by the woman. Now she were bucking like a horse, a spout of water shooting from her mouth. She come back. Our Bridie come back from the dead. The poor soul coughing and retching and bringing up buckets full of river. Dannyboy holding her in his arms, wiping away the spew, no thought for the other man or his raft of trees.

I come down then. I seen the look on his face, so proud and loving. Who would think his rage had just sent Pita Morrow to his grave? You might think the man born again into a new life, so mild and sweet in all his ways towards the girl. That Dannyboy were crying like a baby, smiling to see her quieten in his arms and breathe more easy. Her eyes steady on his face. She were a beauty all right, with her copper hair wet and shining and her features neat and all in their right place, but the eyes dark and empty like, as if she were still in the river with the water running through her. A queer old sight the two of them.

He brung the girl down to my hut, holding her close like a newborn lamb.

'I saved her. I saved her.' He said it over and over, eyes shining at his own good deeds. What about the man he just ruined? But I never said no word. He sat on my log while I brung the fire back alive and put on a kettle. But she would drink no warm tea nor do nothing for herself. Dannyboy moaned to see her so limp and helpless. He would not lay her down by the fire but wrapped her in my blanket and rocked her, but still she shivered. He kissed her sweet face but ever it remained white as marble.

I spoke then. Danny would do nothing but rock her. 'She must go to Pipiriki,' I said. 'She needs a doctor or the Sisters. Take her to Mrs Morrow.'

That brought us both to our senses. The word Morrow. You could see the thoughts chasing around in the man's head.

'I cannot go there,' he said. First true words he had uttered since she come back.

Dear God, the man were useless. Clinging to the girl as if he were the drowning one and she the raft. So I walk upriver to

Charlie's. If God and me were not parted company long ago I would likely say a prayer that the girl be safe, be forgetful of her time in the river. Anyroad I said the hope out loud as I walked, with no one but the bush and the river to hear.

Charlie were in his garden hoeing away as ever. I asked him to come with his barrow and take the girl to Mrs Morrow. Charlie frowned a bit but he come ready enough. Dannyboy and the girl were in my hut then, I was glad to see, he keeping her warm on my bunk, but still the white cheeks and no life to her, arms and legs as loose as the water that ruined her. We put the blanket in the barrow and then our Bridie. Charlie Chee set off the five mile to Pipiriki. I seen him go, his bare feet slap slap and his pigtail flying. Five mile through the bush he ran with our Bridie. He is a tough bugger, Charlie Chee.

Seemed Danny couldn't let her go. I seen him dancing alongside, holding her lolling head still and banging his own head on branches the while. The track is narrow up our way. How far he went with Charlie I couldn't say. To my mind he should have been searching the river's edge for his brother's body.

I blew up the fire and drank my mug of tea, and prayed to the river to hold its peace for a day or two till I got my breath back.

Which it did not, for the great flood were on the way.

Ruvey Morrow

We heard it first from the pigeon post. Bert brought the tiny paper in to me in the kitchen.

'What can we make of this?' he said, scratching his head. 'Do they want a search party?' It worries Bert if he cannot make out what is needed or what to do.

Captain Jamieson is a fine river man but his handwriting

is so large that he can scarce get two words on the messages. *1 overboard Ngaporo* it said. Just that. He should have written help or some such as well.

Bert was all for taking the motor-waka up right away, which would be no easy task with the river rising, but he would manage it.

'Wait a bit,' I said. 'Jamie Jamieson would not leave anyone, and they have the constable aboard. They will have put ashore and found her.'

'Well, why the pigeon if they have it in hand?' said Bert.

He had a point there. But my view was that they wanted a hot bath and warm towels ready. Perhaps Captain was going to proceed and the constable would bring back the poor soul to dry out, Ngaporo being closer to us than the Houseboat. So Bert got the waka ready but held off till further news.

I felt in my bones it would be one of those McPhees. They were bad enough with the parents in sight. Let loose, who knows what they would be up to? But I should have guessed our Pita and Danny would be involved, knowing they were on the river with those logs. A black day.

Up till the luncheon it was peaceful at the House. Only two guests — Mrs McPhee, who sat quiet as a lamb in the winter-garden room, painting a pretty watercolour of the ferns, and a smart gentleman heading up to one of the new railway towns, he said; stuck till the slip was cleared but happy enough to wait, wise fellow, in the comfort of Pipiriki House. He knew which side his bread was buttered.

So I had my feet up against the stove and a cup of tea in my hand when Bert came running to say Charlie Chee had brought Miss McPhee in and to come quick.

Mercy, what a sight! Charlie Chee stood by his barrow, trying to get out a word or two. But his language is hard to make out at the best of times and now, with him puffing like a steamboat, his thin chest heaving in and out under his tunic, you could not make head nor tail. The poor silent girl sprawled in the wooden barrow, pale as her dress, arms and legs flopping like a rag doll. I must have been a sight myself, that first moment, for I was struck dumb by the girl's face. It was as if the river had washed all life out of her young features. We are so used to finding spirit of some sort in a face — anger or shyness or a smile — you read a person by their eyes and the stretch of the mouth or tilt of the head. Poor Bridget's face was fearsome in its blankness. I near cried out in my fright. It could have been the devil sitting behind those blank eye-sockets. Or God. Her gaze fixed on some distant thing away above my head. Not with any shred of recognition. She sighed then — a long slow breath as if weary of this world — and so did I, as her lids closed over those two black pits.

Bert gave me a good push, which shook me out of my trance, and we brought the girl inside. Mere was sent to fetch Mrs McPhee, and Charlie was sat down in the kitchen with a mug of hot tea and a scone. He is not fond of the mutton. Charlie is a good man; I will not have bad words said against the Chows when Charlie is about. He understands more than you think. Fancy running all that way with Bridget McPhee, who he did not know from Adam, to bring her to safety. A hero, I said. And said it again a few days later to Mr McPhee's very face I was that angry.

She could not walk, fell in a heap when we propped her up. Mere ran a hot bath and she and I carried her upstairs. Mrs McPhee wringing her hands but not inclined to put them to good use, I noticed. A grown girl in that state is more awkward than a sack of potatoes, but we two got her to the bathroom. We had to lay her on the floor to unbutton her clothes and pull off her pretty boots. All down her back were purple bruises coming up in the white flesh. You could see where her poor body had been rolled from rock to rock down the rapid. I looked over to the door to see if Mrs McPhee noticed, but that fine lady had disappeared, leaving us to care for the sad lost thing who had been Bridget McPhee.

Later Tim Naylor rode in with Mack Feathers. The constable had his notebook out, asking questions. When this, who that. I told him readily enough and so did Bert. Charlie Chee had gone back home by then; he is never one to waste time that could be spent earning a penny. But we both put in a good word for Charlie and the constable wrote it down.

'Have you seen a log raft come by?' he asked then.

'No,' I said, but I noticed Bert kept his mouth shut. Constable Naylor noticed too — there are no flies on that young man. He worried at my Bert with his questions like a dog after a buried bone.

'But you did see something?' And when Bert turned away: 'It could have been a log raft, then, Bert?'

Now my Bert took umbrage at that, as well he might. The constable addressed me as Mrs Morrow so why not afford my husband the same dignity? I have noticed it before with some of the newer Pakeha, who think a brown skin carries some sort of message.

Bert straightened his back and I knew we were in for one of his tirades.

'Yes, Constable Naylor, I saw three logs, cut by my whanau from what is left of their own Maori land, and blessed and given to my son-in-law. I saw the raft float past some time back. Mr Hatrick may shout all he wants about river traffic, but the law he laid down is only his law. Where is the law says no logs on our river, Constable? You show me. When I was a tama here on this river, how many times did I see Pakeha floating their logs down? Or cut and leave them to wash down in floods? Many, many times.'

Bert drew breath to continue but I laid my hand on his arm. 'Constable Naylor will want to be on his way,' I said, hoping to pour oil, or at least get him out of the kitchen. Once Bert is truly away he will break into his own language and then we will be stuck till suppertime.

But the constable was clearly not to be brow-beaten by native oratory. He looked at us sharpish. 'It was your boy Pita on that raft, and your daughter's man, Danny O'Dowd. They hit the *Wairua*, damaged her plates. We believe that is when the girl was tossed overboard.'

That was a blow. More than a blow, when it all sank in. I felt a dark cloud drifting slowly over our comfortable life at Pipiriki and said a quick Hail Mary to push it away. Mr Hatrick is not a man to forgive and forget.

Later I had a quiet word with Bert.

'What you said about the law — is that true?'

Bert grunted, giving me the mischievous look I'm so fond of. 'How would I know? You can bet he will be back to his rule books in the morning.'

But there was trouble also in those old eyes.

'What is it, Bert? Spit it out,' I said. 'If there is bad news we will bear it together.'

Bert sat to his dinner and ate a while before he spoke, my insides churning the longer he took to tell.

'I saw the logs all right,' he said finally, 'but no one aboard. I went down to the landing, thinking to paddle out and tow them ashore, but they were far on the other side. Then I saw, I think I saw — you know my eyes, Ruvey — a head in the water with the raft. It ducked down, then it seemed to come up again. For air, I suppose. Seemed like someone was trying not to be seen.'

'Just the one?'

'The one.'

'Was it our boy?'

'The hair was dark.'

'Every head of hair that's wet is dark,' I said.

Bert leaned over to give my hand a pat. A sure sign he was worried too, for he is not one to touch in public, even in the kitchen. 'We will find out soon enough,' he said.

An empty hope, as it happened, for the very next day the skies opened and the river rose over the landing and up to the sheds and we had our hands full carting the goods to higher ground. The pigeon post got down to Mr Hatrick in time to keep the *Waimarie* safe at Taupo Quay, thank goodness, but the coal bunker got away from its moorings at Pipiriki — drifted on down halfway to Jerusalem — and for a while we thought all Mr Hatrick's great enterprise here might be washed away downriver.

THE
🐝 HOUSEBOAT 🐝

Erected for the accommodation of Steamer Patrons, is the largest, most complete, and unique of its kind in the world. Has a Social Hall, Piano, Dining Room, Smoking Room, and Berth Accommodation for Seventy Persons. The Sanitary Arrangements are perfect: **Good Baths, Electric Light**, etc.

EVERY TOURIST should see the Houseboat and the magnificent river scenery between it and Pipiriki, the loveliest in New Zealand, the land of beauty.

Good trout fishing at the Houseboat

Hatrick & Co. brochure

STELLA STANDS AT the polished sideboard in the ladies' social hall, watching the guests for signs of need. Her dark maid's uniform — a sailor suit — is spotless, her thick hair neatly secured behind the starched cap. She tries to keep her eyes cast down and her hands folded as she has been taught, but the conversation is too interesting, the ladies' fine appearance too demanding of scrutiny.

The meal is long over. The men linger over cigars in the smoking room, while the two ladies chat quietly over tea. The Houseboat shifts gently against the current, but in this backwater

89

no hint of the mid-stream turbulence is felt by the tourists. The Pipiriki boat, the *Wairua*, is well overdue, and as usual when that happens, the guests from upriver want to stay up for the excitement of its arrival. Stella listens to the ladies' talk. Most of the party are from Australia, on a tour of the country. They seem to be farmers, though obviously in a wealthier situation than Danny. The five men and two ladies who have raced down from Taumarunui aboard the tough little *Ongarue* — ninety hair-raising rapids in a short thirty miles — arrived in time for afternoon tea and a stroll. They have now dressed for dinner in clothes that are a wonder to Stella. Silky reds and greens glow in the lamplight. Both women wear jewelled necklaces and long sparkling earrings.

'I wish now,' says the taller of the two, 'that I had travelled with Emily to see the mountains.'

'Oh, but the river trip was so exciting!' says the other, flapping her hands in mock terror. 'Wait till we tell them.' Stella gathers that there are three other women in the party, and several children, who have decided to take the overland coach trip through the Tongariro National Park, in hope of seeing the great volcanoes under snow — or perhaps, Stella guesses, to avoid the fierce rapids of the upper two legs of the boat trip. They will come down the coach road from Raetihi and join these friends at Pipiriki House.

'I do hope Pipiriki House is as good as the poster boasts, Tilda,' the tall one continues. 'I cannot quite believe such a palace exists in all this wilderness. What will Emily think of it, I wonder? She is used to the very best.'

'She is.'

Both ladies ponder Emily's opinion.

'She approved of the Bath House,' says Tilda, 'even though it is not quite completed.'

'The Bath House is indeed magnificent,' the tall one grudgingly admits. 'And the geysers. Rotorua is bound to prosper. We will see about Pipiriki House.'

'And the famous views from its balcony. They will have to be fine to compete with Rotorua.'

'Or the Blue Mountains.'

'True.'

Stella smiles brightly at the two as she pours more tea. She knows they will be impressed. Even foreigners from the other side of the world are full of praise and wonder. She thinks of Danny and Pita, who must by now be nearing the sea in their log raft. In her imagination Wanganui, which she has never seen, is a vast and magical town, like the clothes tonight's guests wear. She imagines tall buildings and wide streets, great ships bringing goods from all parts of the world and shops full of those goods. It is a world that she would like to see. Not from dissatisfaction with her present life — she loves upriver life — but simply out of curiosity. Perhaps, if Danny makes good money on the logs, they will both ride the steamers down to the sea and he can show her the sights.

A short blast of the approaching *Wairua*'s steam whistle has all the guests stirring. Stella hurries with the ladies to their cabins on the lower deck and helps them into warm coats. The air outside is bitter. The men, rumbling and jolly after their men's talk, join them at the stern, where they peer into the darkness, searching for signs of the approaching steamer.

Above the river the sky is iced with stars; the slopes up from the river are pitch black, except for the glow from the windows of the crew's huts on the rise beyond the flood line. The guests cheer to see the lights of the *Wairua* slide around the bend and to hear the chuff chuff of her slowing engine. The journey must have been difficult to have been so delayed.

The men look forward to tales of excitement. Stella sees uncertainty on the ladies' faces. Perhaps they are dreading the next day's adventure. The *Ongarue*, the motor-vessel from Taumarunui, is tied alongside the Houseboat to allow space for the new arrival. And here comes the *Wairua*, engines shut down, steam sighing as the pressure drops and she noses gently as a feeding lamb into the landing. Rangi and Eru jump ashore to tie up as the guests and crew exchange greetings.

Stella hears a woman's voice shouting on board the *Wairua*. Captain Jamie Jamieson climbs smartly up the gangway of the Houseboat, leaving the deckhands to usher the guests. This is unusual. Stella sees him mutter something to the Houseboat captain and watches with interest as Mrs White is brought out from the galley.

'See if you can calm them, Mrs White,' says Captain Jamieson. 'We don't want them disturbing the guests.'

Captain White puts out an arm to lead Stella away from the ladies.

'There's been an accident,' he says quietly. 'A woman lost overboard. The brother and sister are in a state. Are cabins 19 and 20 made up?'

'No', says Stella. 'We weren't expecting . . .'

'Make them up now. Mrs White will bring them directly to their cabins and then you bring a good hot dinner down to them there.'

'But I am supposed to serve . . .'

'Mrs White will serve the others. There are only three. Off with you.'

He pats her behind briskly. Captain is very particular to keep his beloved Houseboat shipshape and orderly.

Stella runs upstairs to the linen locker and then down again to the two aft cabins. These are always the last to be filled, as they are next to the ladies' and the gentlemen's bathrooms and therefore likely to be disturbed with comings and goings in the night. While the other guests climb wearily up to the dining saloon, Stella lights lamps in the little cabins and runs a duster over the washstands. In winter these cabins are seldom used. She smiles to see the beautiful grain of the wood glow. But a woman lost overboard! Despite floods and damage to boats, no person has been lost in the two years Stella has been working here. She shakes out sheets and pillowcases and smoothes the snowy counterpane. When she opens the door to leave, someone is standing there.

'I'm sorry,' she says, bobbing a curtsey as she has been taught, and then steps back to allow him entry.

He makes no move. Stands silhouetted in the doorway as if turned to stone.

'Come in,' she says gently. 'It's all right. This is your cabin.'

He clears his throat — a rasping sound that ends in a great sobbing groan. He turns a little and Stella thinks he might be going to run away. She puts out a hand and draws him into the cabin.

'Sit down,' she says, keeping her movements slow. He is like a shy wild animal who might bolt at any moment.

His legs give way suddenly. He sits on the edge of the bunk and covers his face with his hands. He is shaking with sobs but makes no sound. Stella stands in the doorway, wondering whether it is safe to leave him while she fetches food. She can hear a shrill voice in the port cabin opposite, and Mrs White's soothing words. That will be the sister. Something bangs against the partition — a fist or a boot — and the boy flinches.

'Don't worry,' says Stella. 'Is that your sister? Mrs White will look after her. Will you be all right here while I get you something to eat?'

He nods without looking at her, his whole body still heaving with sobs. Stella pats his bony shoulder as she would a spooked horse, and runs upstairs to the galley. Through the servery hatch she can see all the guests gathered in the dining room. They are talking excitedly. Liquor is not allowed on the Houseboat, as it is technically ashore, but Stella notices that the steward is offering them all a 'medicinal' brandy. Mrs White comes in while Stella is spooning gravy over two plates of mutton and vegetables.

'No need for food in cabin 19,' says Mrs White. 'I have given her a sleeping draught.' She frowns as she speaks, gives Stella a sharp look. 'There will be trouble now,' she says darkly.

'What is it? Is the sister dead?' asks Stella.

'We haven't heard yet. There is a search party out. But none of the Houseboat pigeons are downriver today, so we will have no news till tomorrow.'

'What happened?' Stella begins to fear what Mrs White will say.

'It was logs hit the *Wairua*, Stella. At Ngaporo. The vessel is damaged. The girl must have gone overboard then, but no one noticed till much later.' Mrs White steadies herself against the bench with a plump hand. 'Logs, my dear. They say your Danny was on them. And your brother.'

'Oh!' Stella knows she should take the food down below, keep silent and obey the rules, but she cannot hold back. 'But what of the men? Oh, is Danny hurt?'

'Keep your voice down, please.' Mrs White's voice is stern, her eyes hard. 'You would do well to think of the harm your husband has done. The lost girl. The damage to Mr Hatrick's boat. What was he thinking of, to endanger the service?'

'But is there news of him?' Stella whispers. She must know.

'There is not. We must wait for all news. Now take this food below before it is stone cold.'

Stella wants to run ashore, to question the deckhands, beg

Captain Jamieson for news. Instead she carries the plate of hot food carefully below to the lost girl's brother. If Danny has caused a death it is best that she does what she can to be kind to the boy. Possibly she will lose her position here anyway. But if Danny and Pita are charged with murder — what of them all then? The plate of food trembles in her hands.

She knocks quietly before entering. The boy has his back to her. He is washing his face at the stand in the corner. He is not so young after all, standing taller than her, his coppery hair shining in the lamplight. When he turns she sees a blotched and swollen face and ears that stand almost straight out from his head. His attempt at a smile goes horribly wrong and tears well up again.

Stella can't think what to say, faced with such raw misery. 'Eat it while it's hot,' she says at last.

He nods and seats himself at one end of the bunk. After the first mouthful he can't stop but eats ravenously. Stella watches him devour the bread and then drink down the sweet tea. It's as if he hasn't eaten in a week.

'Would you like some more?'

He nods and this time the smile works. His eyes are a pale blue and his mouth small. It is a gentle face.

When she returns with a heaped plate he is waiting for her. She sees that he finds it difficult to look at her.

'Please wait,' he says, his voice very quiet but clear. 'Would you sit?'

Stella is not allowed to sit with the tourists, but is desperate to hear any word of the accident. She does as the boy asks, sitting as far away from him as she can on the bunk.

After he has eaten a little he manages to look directly at her. 'Is there any news?'

'Of your sister? Not yet. We won't hear till tomorrow afternoon.'

He puts down his knife and fork. 'Oh.'

'But there are people living near that rapid. Someone will have helped her.'

He looks at her quickly and then away. 'Do you think so?'

Stella is not at all sure that either old Sam Blencoe or Charlie Chee would notice. 'Yes,' she says, smiling. 'I think so.'

He eats some more.

'What is your name?' she asks. This is bold, but she can't think what other conversation to make.

'Douglas McPhee.'

McPhee! Stella stares at him. Is the name a coincidence or can he be related to the very sawmiller who ordered the logs? What a strange irony. But this wretched boy certainly doesn't look like the son of a successful businessman.

Douglas speaks in a low voice. 'It was the best day of my life, and now it's the worst.'

Stella is curious. 'Why the best?'

'I disobeyed my father.' A flush rises through his pale skin. 'He ordered me to stay behind but I came anyway. Then I helped in the engine-room.' There is something defiant and proud in the way he looks at her. 'He said I was good at it.'

Stella smiles. She begins to rise, but Douglas asks quickly, 'Where is Gertie?' The way his head moves from side to side reminds her of a trapped animal.

'Your other sister? In the cabin behind you. Mrs White gave her a sleeping draught. We have such things here for nervous tourists.'

'She's not nervous,' says Douglas, looking down again, 'just angry. She says it's my fault. I should have watched out for Bridget. I should have known she was gone.' His voice is barely audible.

'That doesn't make sense,' says Stella, more sharply than she had intended. She is tired of his low spirits. Also she is anxious that he might discover that it was her husband whose logs caused the accident. She stands with her hand on the brass latch of the door. 'Your sister is the older, isn't she? Why didn't she watch out? You were busy helping in the engine-room.'

'Gertie never helps or watches out for anyone. I should have known that.'

Stella thinks this is a poor answer but holds her tongue. She takes the tray.

'You should get some sleep now. In the morning there will be breakfast. The boat downriver leaves early. You will hear news of your sister before we do. Goodnight.'

'No, wait!'

Stella tries to smile at him but all she feels is an ache to hear news of Dannyboy. 'I have work to do,' she says.

'What is your name? Please?' He smiles back at her. A hopeful, friendly offer.

'Stella.'

'That's a nice name.'

But Stella has had enough of his need. She closes the door on his eager face. Goes back up to the galley.

Later, as she crosses to the bank and climbs up to question the crew, she sees Douglas standing on the lower deck. He is quite still, his head up, watching her. In the dark Stella can't tell whether he is weeping still. From the way he looks up, the set of his bony shoulders, she thinks not.

O'Dowd's Farm

Local & General
News

Last week's flood topped a record set in February 1891. The river rose four feet over Taupo Quay and many low-lying properties were inundated. The riverbank at Taylorsville is undermined, causing a house and shop to fall in to the river. A. Hatrick's river service was cancelled for three days, though business is back to normal from today.

Wanganui Herald, *May 1904*

TWO DAYS AFTER the accident a violent storm sweeps up from the south, bringing torrential rain. For once the riverboat service is cancelled. Stella cannot remember another time. Neither can she remember the flooded river reaching so high. She has been released from Houseboat duty to see to the farm.

'I can manage here,' says the old caretaker, stumping fore and aft to ease the creaking mooring ropes. 'Best go ashore while you may.' He sounds confident but Stella eyes the rising floodwaters with alarm. The great bulk of the Houseboat heaves against its ropes. If it breaks loose there will be nothing can save it — no engine, no rudder. Three years ago she came to her mooring place after brilliant Captain Marshall and his crew winched, poled, lowered her on ropes, fending off banks and shallows, for six slow weeks, all the way from Taumarunui, down the thirty miles and ninety rapids of the upper Whanganui River. Here she must stay to ride out the flood.

Stella wades over the submerged gangplank and sloshes her way home over sodden fields. The track is already underwater. Through the driving rain she can see the Ohura Falls, no longer a pretty sight for the tourists but a frightening maelstrom of foaming mud and logs. Sad sheep huddle on patches of high ground among stumps of felled trees. Some will drown and others find their way through broken fences into the bush. She can only hope most will survive and return. At the farm she finds that the river has crept up the lower paddock and is approaching the kitchen garden.

'Holy Mother Mary!' says Stella, aloud. 'Will it come into the house this time?' There have been floods before, but this one promises disaster.

She calls out for Hone, but Finn, Danny's border collie, is the only one to come running. Her cousin, who should have been taking care of the animals, has gone. The kainga where he lives, on a shelf above the river, may well be flooded by now. He will be needed there. 'And where are you, Dannyboy, when I need you?' Stella shouts into the rising wind, more in anger than fear.

She cannot believe him dead. Though there has been no news of Danny or the logs, Stella has heard that the girl is found and alive with no bones broken. Surely Danny's body would have been found by now, had he drowned. And if the girl survived, it stands to reason that Danny and Pita, both strong swimmers who know the river, would also be alive. She can only hope that the men have made it down to Wanganui before this storm. Otherwise, with the river so high and wild, the raft would likely be driven ashore and stranded in some lonely place. Or swept, pell-mell, out to sea.

Stella stands on the porch facing the furious weather. She breathes in the damp air deeply and is suddenly filled with an odd pleasure. The threat of the rising water is in some way thrilling to her. There are tasks she must do quickly, and for the moment at least she feels up to the challenge. When Dannyboy returns he will be impressed. She talks cheerfully to the horse and the house cow as she leads them to high ground and tethers them safely to a sheltering tree. Finn seems to understand. He drives the sheep up from the lower paddock, barking and bossy, enjoying Stella's praise. Stella sings as she stumps through the sheeting rain to rescue onions that are floating up out of the garden soil and threatening to find their way downriver. 'Oh no you don't,' she yells, running after a rolling clump of potatoes. 'I'll have you inside, if you please!' She dashes back to the porch, fetches a sack and is soon bundling the muddy vegetables into it. The rain drums on her back.

'You will see, Dannyboy,' she sings to a tune of her own making, 'how I can cope on my own and look after the farm.' Then she adds, on a sadder note, 'But come back soon, my darling man, for your sweet wife is lonely.'

She drips her way inside, tears off her sodden clothes, pulls a dry shirt of Danny's over her head, then wraps an old blanket around her waist. Her sodden dress and jersey lie where they fall. Outside she can hear the water lapping at the porch steps. Stella rubs at her hair, looking around the house, planning the next move. This is like war, she thinks: me against flood.

An hour later the first creeping finger of water runs under the door. Stella lifts the sack of flour and places it on the table. The precious bag of sugar and tin of tea follow. Soon the table is piled with food, the mattress, blankets, the rug and their pillow. Stella looks around for any other soft thing. The towel, her pile of clean sacks, waiting for any of many uses. She leaves her wet clothes; they are already floating.

There is a desperate scratching at the door. Stella is unwilling to open it but Danny would never forgive her if she let Finn be swept away.

'Quick , in with you!' she says. In the brief moment the door is open a gush of muddy water enters. Finn shakes himself vigorously, showering Stella's dry clothes. When she shouts at him he flattens himself to the floor, loads his hair afresh with water and goes through the whole drenching process again. Stella can only laugh. She guides him up onto the bare boards of their bed, where he is for the moment above the rising tide.

Water pours in under the door, spreading wide and dirty over the floorboards. Stella tries stuffing a sack against the flow but the water is too strong. Inch by inch it rises. There is a crack in the wall almost a foot up from the floor and already water is pouring through it in a steady stream. Stella lights a lamp and hangs it high from the rafters. With a sigh and a cloud of sooty steam the fire on the hearth is extinguished. Now the rising water is black with ash. Stella stands ankle deep in the icy mess, holding the precious sack of seed potatoes which cannot find space on the piled table. She climbs onto the bed with the dog. He whines and pushes his muzzle into her leg. The water continues to rise. Finn growls at it; his hackles rise. He lowers his head and eyes the water but it will not hold still like the sheep.

'Oh Finn,' says Stella, fearful now and glad of his bedraggled presence. 'Please God it won't rise any further.' But it does, gradually reaching the top of the bed-boards. Stella shifts to the bench, which is only a few inches higher.

An hour later the water stops rising. Stella is still on the bench, her feet propped on the stool and the seed potatoes still cradled in her arms. Finn shivers on the submerged bed-boards. Stella shakes too. The blanket is a blessing but her hands are not free to pull it up around her shoulders. She would give anything for a hot drink.

'Danny, Danny,' she moans. 'Come home, my Dannyboy.' Her head rests on the rough hemp of the sack but she dares not fall asleep. What if Danny is caught in this flood? It will be far worse downriver. Stella imagines the great volume of water from the Ohura River and all the other tributaries that drain into the Whanganui. Surely the farms below the gorge will be swept clean away.

As dawn breaks, the water level inside the house begins to fall. Stella stands stiffly, heaves the wretched sack of potatoes to her shoulder and wades to the door. One-handed, she drags it open. Finn splashes over and they both watch as the water drains away out of the house, down into the waterlogged paddock below. Here is a new heartbreak: to see the goodness in the soil, the new-sown grass and most of the vegetables, sucked into the roaring muddy Ohura and away downriver.

LATER THAT MORNING, as she is sweeping the last of the water over the doorstep, she sees Danny walking up over the paddocks.

'Dannyboy!' shouts Stella. 'Oh Danny!'

He looks up for a moment, shielding his eyes, lifts a tired hand in greeting and plods on. Something about the way he walks — hatless, coatless, empty-handed — frightens her. There is also the fear of what she might hear.

Finn streaks down the field, yapping his greeting. Danny

touches his nose but shows none of his usual exuberant affection for the dog. Finn's tail droops. He settles quickly and trots quietly at his master's heels, looking up, ready for instructions that do not come. Danny looks right and left at the devastation — mud where grass should be, fences lying flat, a dead sheep caught in the wire. On he comes, up onto the porch and into Stella's arms. He lays his head on her shoulder with a deep groan and stays there, wordless, while she rocks him. He begins to sob then — dry, hopeless sobs the like of which she has never heard from him. Finn whines in sympathy.

'Dannyboy, Danny love,' says Stella. 'You're home. It's all right, sweetheart.'

But he won't be comforted. His clothes are torn and sodden, his muddy hair plastered flat to his head, his face lined with exhaustion. All he can do is bow his head on his wife's shoulder and sob.

Stella strokes his back as if he were a baby. Seats him gently on the porch bench. 'It's not all lost, sweetheart. I saved all the food inside, and most of the kitchen garden. See?' She shows him the sack of potatoes on the porch. 'And I took Freda and Nick to high ground. They are safe. Also the chickens. Oh, I worked so hard all night, Danny. You would be proud of me how I managed.'

He looks up at her sadly then. 'You manage better without me, Stell, and that's the truth.'

She chatters on, still high-spirited from the dangers of the night. 'The water came right into the house, Danny — you should have seen it! I piled every stitch of clothing and blankets on the table . . .' She breaks off at his impatient shrug.

'Aye, girl, I've got the message. You needed no man to lend a hand. You did just fine while your husband was away ruining his life forever.'

'Oh Danny.' Stella could bite her proud tongue out. 'I missed you so much.'

'So you say now.'

'Sit here. I'll get a fire going.'

She takes the axe and picks her way through clinging mud to the lean-to at the back of the house. The wood at the top of the stack is still dry. She splits one of the logs into kindling. It is a task she enjoys — the rhythm of it and the accuracy; the thunk at the end of each stroke as the iron blade beds into the soft wood of the old stump. Back in the house she coaxes a fire into healthy life and sets the kettle to heat. The sobbing on the porch has stopped but now there is silence — no reassuring rumble of his voice, no kind word for the dog. Stella has to know.

'What is it, Danny? Tell me!' She stands in front of his drooping figure but he will not look up. She goes to touch him, but before she reaches him he is on his feet and off the porch, down into the sea of mud below. Dogged, silent, he makes his way to the far end of the paddock, hauls at a fallen fencepost, heaving it upright, then wades through mud to the next and the next. As he sets each one straight he whacks it hard with a loose post, driving it back into its waterlogged hole. The strength it must take to haul post and wire out of the clinging mud can only be guessed at, but Danny works on, raising the free post high above his head each time to bring it down with a thud that echoes off the watery field. She can see each shockwave run through his body.

'Come in! Come in and eat!' calls Stella, startled and a little frightened by what she sees. Danny does not even glance in her direction. He must be driven far inside himself to behave so. She goes to the kitchen garden, ostensibly to gather or replant uprooted vegetables but in truth to watch over him. Now he is striding up the hill towards the animals. Stella runs after him.

'I have taken straw up,' she shouts. 'I've seen to them.'

He stops. Turns to looks at her. 'That is my task,' he says. 'You could leave some small thing for your husband to do.' His blue eyes seem almost black as they stare at her. She can see his legs trembling through his torn trousers.

'Danny,' she whispers, 'Danny, it's all right. The girl was saved, she is not drowned.'

'I know that.' His voice grates, not quite in control.

Stella is a little frightened of him — the first time she has ever felt fear in his presence — but she continues.

'Danny, you're too tired. Not thinking right. Come in and eat something.'

He stands there, looking at her, breathing hard. She reaches out to take his hand. 'Danny? It's so good you're back. God knows I need you, with all this . . .' she indicates the ruined fields and tries a smile, '. . . this bloody mess.'

He comes then, walking silently beside her. She can feel his hand in hers shaking violently. At the back door he stops suddenly.

'Stella . . . Stell.'

She waits. At least he has spoken her name.

He groans. 'Oh dear God, Stell.' He is swaying, almost out on his feet.

Stella pulls him inside. 'If you have lost the logs we can still manage.'

'It's not that.'

Stella thinks he means the girl. That they might come for him and take him to prison.

'Come in and warm yourself,' she says, drawing him forward gently as she would a wounded animal. 'We'll manage the other things later.'

He lets her fuss over him, stands silent as she draws off his wet shirt, clucking at the cuts and scratches. He will not look at her but his expression softens at her chatter, her rough worker's hands towelling him dry.

'Holy Mother, look at this bruise! Blacker than Satan himself, God bless us. Oh Danny, I worried that you might be gone. I couldn't have borne that. And the rain last night! You should have seen the flood. But were you out in all that? What is it like down at the landing? Now, where are your good trousers in all this mess? If you are not made decent this minute I will be getting ideas, you bad man.' And then, seeing him sway, 'Danny, love, sit down in the name of Heaven before you keel over.'

Danny sits, meek as a lamb, by the fire. Drinks his sweet tea and chews on a wedge of raisin loaf. The colour begins to creep back into his face, but he shakes still, and will not look up.

Finally he speaks. 'I have lost the logs.' He glances quickly up at his wife and then down again.

Stella draws in a breath, remains silent for a moment. 'Well then,' she says at last, 'I had guessed that. Nor was I ever a great one for the logs, if you remember. A madcap scheme. At least we have you back in one piece.'

Danny looks into the fire. His voice is so low she can hardly hear. 'Was the steamer damaged?'

Stella is eager to reassure him. 'Damaged a little. Not too bad. Some plates bent. Rivets lost. She set off downriver next day.'

'And the girl?' Danny's voice is stronger when he mentions her.

'All we know is Charlie Chee took her to Pipiriki House and she is safe. Alive.'

Danny sighs. Nods. A little smile nudges the corners of his mouth. 'Good. The sweetest young lady. At least she survived.'

After a moment Stella adds, 'She is a McPhee, Danny.'

Danny looks up at that. 'Strange . . . struck by the log her father was on fire to buy . . . very strange . . .'

'But how did you come to hit? What happened?' Stella needs to hear the rest: why he would risk that rapid before the *Wairua* steamed up it.

Danny presents both hands to her, palms up, fingers spread. It is a gesture she knows well — one he uses when he has made a mistake and wishes to exonerate himself. As if to show her that his hands are clean. Like Pontius Pilate, she thinks disloyally. His voice rises higher as he speaks. Indignation is there, but also fear.

'We waited and waited. He wanted to go . . . Pita . . . He was pushing at me to take risks — you know how he is, Stell. I said wait longer. He laughed at me for a coward. Still no boat came . . . Pita was drunk — hard to hold back . . . then even I thought the *Wairua* wouldn't come . . . thought maybe they had cancelled because of the high river . . .'

Stella bristles. 'You should know better than that, Danny. They never cancel.'

He looks at her, frowning. She has the sudden impression that he had forgotten she is there. 'Well, maybe, yes, it's easy to say that now. You weren't there, Stell. Pita was . . . difficult. He untied one rope and was worrying away at the other. By the time I noticed, the raft was swinging out. I could have stopped, I suppose.' His eyes plead with her to understand. 'I was angry . . . desperate.'

He tells then of the approach to the rapid, the fierce pull of it. His fear at seeing two deckhands on the bank at the top of Ngaporo with a winching rope around a tree, that sighting coming at the very moment the rapid dragged them into the V of fast water. Then the helpless rush towards the labouring steamer. If the *Wairua* had been in the centre of the rapid, says Danny, the boat would surely have been destroyed, but the winching line pulled her a little to one side, away from the roughest water, so the collision was a glancing blow.

'Even so, the shock tipped us both into the river . . .' Danny hesitates, frowning. 'I can't remember . . . I heard screaming. The river took me close to the bank and I held to a branch there for a moment . . . could see the *Wairua* pitching . . . heard screaming again. The boat seemed to steady . . . the winch was holding . . . then Ngaporo ripped me away and down I went. At the bottom I saw the raft and tried to swim to it . . .' He hesitates again.

'Go on,' says Stella. She wants to keep him talking. Wants to get at whatever is really troubling him.

'I think the raft must have hit me then. The rear end was swinging out.' He looks up. 'That might account for the bruise, Stell. I don't remember how I came to the bottom of the other rapid.'

He remembers bumping over rocks and boulders in the shallows. Remembers the shock of seeing the girl floating face down there beside him. When he turned her over she lay in the water — drowned, he thought — staring up at the sky with empty eyes.

'I dragged her to shore, poor wet thing. Dear God, I was desperate, Stell, thinking we had caused her death with our mad scheme.' Danny's speech slows.

Stella prompts him. 'And Pita?'

Danny doesn't answer. Perhaps he didn't hear. After a while he clears his throat — a rasping bark that shocks her after his jumbled words. 'I don't care about the logs. After . . .' he coughs again as if clearing away the drowning water — or other worse memories. '. . . After that, I had no more stomach for logging. I walked home.'

'You walked all the way up?' Stella smiles at him, amazed. 'Holy Mary! But you had to come home to your wife, my sweetheart.

108

And now you need to sleep.'

Indeed, Danny's eyes are already closing. He sways forward towards the fire.

Stella takes his arm, guides him towards the bed. 'You saved the girl, Danny. That will surely count in your favour.'

'I saved her, yes,' mumbles Danny into her neck. He stands in a stupor as she spreads sacks on the wet bed-boards and then lays down the mattress and blankets. She is surprised to feel him stumble forward, wrapping his poor scratched arms around her, kissing her dreamily. 'I saved the girl, didn't I? At least I did that.'

'Some might even say you're a hero,' says Stella, humouring him.

'A hero!' He kisses the back of her neck again then pushes hard against her. 'Come to bed. Come with me, love.' He is suddenly urgent, fumbling at her clothes.

'Danny,' she laughs, 'I would have thought there was no strength left in you!' But she lies with him gladly, eager to feel him inside her. The house is a muddy chaos, the farm in ruins, but he is back and in need of her.

Later she asks him again after her brother. 'What about Pita? Is he all right?'

But Danny is already asleep.

ALL THAT DAY and night Danny sleeps, restless, muttering, sometimes whimpering like a child. In his dreams he relives endlessly the long trek home through the bush: the slapping of wet branches, his own plodding feet, the chilly nights with only ferns for cover. He dreams that the track has disappeared; that the dark bush leans in, mocking him. He hears the crunch of broken bone and high cries of pain.

The cries are his own. Stella shakes him awake. 'Danny, love, you would raise the dead with your moans.'

He tries to sit up. Every muscle aches. How long was he walking? Two days? Three? How did he cross the river? Then remembers the canoe he 'borrowed' and left tied up but on the wrong bank. It will surely have been torn away in the storm. Another nail in his coffin.

Stella hands him a mug of tea and a wedge of bread. 'I'll be off shortly,' she says. 'The river is down. The service will be up again.' She speaks lightly but they are both wondering if she will be welcome down at the Houseboat. If Danny's actions cost her the job, then they are truly in trouble. It will be months before the farm is back in order.

Danny says nothing. Sucks at his tea.

'The McPhee girl,' says Stella. She has his attention now. 'How did she get to Pipiriki?'

'I carried her up to the hermit's hut and he went for Charlie Chee. The Chinese fellow brought his barrow and took the girl to Pipiriki. Then I left.'

'Why did you leave it to them?'

'Can't you see?' Danny cries out. 'They might arrest me! I thought maybe the boat was destroyed. And then . . . Also I had to look for . . .' Danny's face has closed down again.

'For Pita?'

'. . . Yes.'

'And the logs?'

'. . . Yes.'

'But you didn't find them?'

'No, Stell, I didn't. I had to come home.'

Stella is puzzled by his manner. There is something here he is not telling her. 'But Pita might be drowned! The logs might be stolen!'

'I know that! I know it, Stell!' Danny is shouting now, tears rolling down his face. 'I did nothing right. I couldn't think of anything but to come back here. I ran away, Stell! Ran away from the whole bloody mess.'

'Ah, Danny.' Stella sits beside him, lays an arm across his shoulders. 'It is not so terrible. The *Wairua* is not badly damaged. Pita is a good swimmer. Better than you. He'll be alive somewhere.'

'He won't, he won't!' Danny buries his face in his hands.

'And the girl is saved. You saved her.'

Danny groans. 'And then ran away. I left her and ran away. Left it to a Chow. I should have gone with her.'

'You were worried about Pita,' says Stella, but she is losing patience with his mood.

Danny clings to her. 'Don't go today. Don't go down there.'

'I must.'

'They might come for me! They might take me away!'

'Oh Danny!' Stella tries to laugh at his extravagant fears. 'No one is going to come all this way upriver to find you. We will need my work at the Houseboat; I must go. And I might hear news of Pita.'

But Danny follows her out to the porch, still begging her to stay.

ALL DAY, AS he and Finn search for the straggling sheep, Dannyboy fears what news Stella might bring back. Several of his animals have strayed up into the bracken and are now willing to come back to the higher paddock, which has recovered from the storm and promises better feed than the spurned pig-fern. Danny is heartened by the sight of the animals trotting down out of the bush, their wool full of debris, but at least they are

111

alive. It seems they have lost only two of their small flock. The muddy paddocks steam in the sun. Perhaps the layer of silt will do them good. Danny fixes a gate, chops kindling for the fire, feeds the horse, but can settle to nothing. His hands as he pulls at Freda's udders are shaking and she will not let down her milk. Danny slaps her side in frustration, earning him a stinging flick from her tail.

The fears return. He imagines Pita's bloated body hooked out of the river and laid out at Pipiriki for the Morrows to mourn. The smashed nose and broken jaw will be noticed. Questions will be asked. The old hermit will tell what he saw and they will come for him. He imagines Stella's horror, the Morrows' disgust. Worst of all, he fears standing in the courthouse for all to hear every moment of his shameful acts. 'Why did you not alert rescuers to your brother-in-law's fate?' 'What poor kind of fellow are you to run away from responsibility?' 'You struck your brother-in-law so hard as to break his jaw?' The accusations hammer at him as if he is already arrested. He has no answer to any.

'Stell, Stell, come back,' he whimpers, but she will not be home until tomorrow. And what dreadful news will come with her?

The flood

HIS FIRST SENSATION is of churning. The world has gone dizzy, is turning wildly around him — or is he the one spinning? He has been caught by Tarepokiore. The taniwha in the whirlpool is sucking him down. He spews mightily. The agony in his face seems to slow the spinning and he realises he is indeed in the water, but not the whirlpool. He closes his eyes. The pain is too great.

A little later — how long? — he is aware again of water and of movement. His cheek is resting on something rough. The slight movement of raising his head causes a pain so sharp that he screams and then spews again. Let it lie, this throbbing ball of fire. Let it lie.

Later again — or is he still in the same moment? — he feels a soft tug near his armpit. His jacket is pulled up on that side and something scrapes at his side. Oh, sweet Jesus, let him be free of this pain!

Gradually his foggy brain pieces together what is happening. His jacket is caught on the rowlock of the log raft. *Dannyboy hit him!* How did he become entangled with the raft? Pita doesn't remember that bit. The jacket has saved him from drowning. He can feel it now. He is being dragged downriver, his feet trailing in the water and his head resting on the rough bark of a totara log. That is enough to know for now. As long as the jacket holds.

It is dark when Pita's feet touch the stony riverbed. Here the water is rough and the logs buck, sending stabs of pain through his nose and eyes. They are racing down a rapid. He feels the raft driving faster. It strikes something — a rock — turns agonisingly and then slews, drifting into slower, calmer water in among trees. He feels their drooping leaves touch his battered head, sharp as knives. And now a new danger. Pita shouts in fear as the great totara logs, which have saved him and carried him — how far? — now pin him against the bank, crushing his ribs against the tangle of roots and stones at the river's edge. He is trapped, air driven from his lungs, feet gripped by bottomless mud, still hooked on the rowlock by his blessed jacket.

Once, twice, Pita hauls breath into his aching body. This is too hard. He would like to sink beneath the water and let it all end. But even that is not possible. He is held — crushed — with his head and shoulders firmly in the air and no firm purchase for his waterlogged feet. A third time he draws breath. Perhaps it is easier this time? Yes, the log is swinging away in the current. But before Pita's dulled mind can take advantage of the reprieve the raft bumps back, pinning him cruelly all over again.

But that moment of release has given him hope. Surely there will be another; this time he will be ready. Pita feels with his free arm up into the leaves above. His fingers search in the dark for a thicker branch, find one and grip. The other arm is tangled in his sleeve. Pita tries to free it but the pain is too strong. It feels as if the skin is cut there, under his armpit, and the rowlock bites deeper with every movement. He will have to rely on the thin branch above. He waits, clearer in his thinking now, though each rasping breath is still agony.

When the moment comes it is all too easy. The totara relents, moves away, gently as a floating feather. Pita hauls on his branch, kicks free of the mud and rolls over onto the raft. There, blissfully on his back, he pats the timber — his saviour and tormentor.

'You are mine now,' he growls, 'so watch out!'

Two days later Pita remembers those words and snorts. He should have known his Whanganui better. Ownership can never be taken for granted where this river is concerned.

PITA IS STILL on the same isolated bend of the Whanganui when the water begins to rise. Two nights and one day he has lain on the bank. He has done his best to secure the raft, has pulled fern leaves down and made a cover for the cold nights, but he can manage little before his strength gives out. Racked with thirst, he has crawled to the water's edge to cup water and drink. The supplies are gone — washed away, no doubt, when they struck the steamer — likewise mooring ropes and oars. The knife at his belt and the warm jacket are his only valuables. Whenever he falls into a restless sleep, Pita is tormented by nightmares. Again and again he sees the pale figure of the dead girl. Her ghost whispers accusations into his ears. 'Murderer! I will ride on your back for all time. Never will you be free!' Her cold fingers tangle in his hair and feel their way into his open mouth like fat worms.

Pita screams and wakes. Even that small movement causes the bones in his cheek to grind and the pain to engulf him. He is desperate for the ease of liquor.

And then he feels water at his feet, opens his eyes and sees the creep of it, stealthy as a thief, up over the waterlogged tree roots and onto the bank. Pita has seen this before many times and knows he must move quickly. Perhaps a storm will soon hit this place; certainly it must have been raining upriver for the water to rise so quickly. Carefully he raises his head. Mid-stream the river is ugly: a bucking, muddy torrent. A dead sheep is swept past and then a live cow, head still above water, eyes rolling as she fights the current. This will be a bad flood. Pita looks at his pitiful flax ties that moor the raft; they pull taut, then slacken as the logs bump the bank again and again. Then, as he watches, the ties snap and the great totara raft moves away, turning once lazily in the calmer water — a nonchalant farewell before it is swept downriver, a lethal bullet to any in its way, off towards the sea.

Pita crawls to higher ground, grunting with the pain. His face is stiff, though not as sore as it was, but his ribs and the cut on his side slow his progress.

A few drops of rain fall, then a great wind drives in from the west, heralding the downpour. The trees on the riverbank begin to thrash, groaning like humans under the weight of the wind. Almost immediately the rain sheets down, in seconds soaking clothes that have taken two days to dry.

Pita finds a rocky overhang, protected by a clump of bush, crawls into its shelter and crouches there, shivering. The creeping river follows. When the water reaches his feet he stumbles higher, fearing that the land will plateau and he will be trapped.

He looks for a tall tree but can see nothing but low scrub. This place must have been burnt off sometime in the past. Pita knows where he is — not far downriver from the mission settlement of Hiruharama — but on the wrong side of the river to find help. There are no farms or Maori kainga here.

The river follows him, faster now that the land is flattening. Pita stumbles on. This is a judgement. He is being punished. He crosses himself, mutters a Hail Mary, and, just in case, tries a karakia to appease the taniwha. The river rises. Pita has never seen such flooding. The rain has eased now and he looks back at the great expanse of river, roaring between its new, wider banks and full of tumbling debris. Pita has lived all his life around the river but this is the first time he has been terrified by it.

'I'm sorry!' he yells at the muddy fury. Whanganui creeps on after him.

To one side there is a rocky outcrop, not very high, but at least above the surrounding river terrace. Pita finds a foothold and then another, hauls his aching body onto the flat top and lies there. If the river rises above this he's done for.

Hours pass — or perhaps only minutes. As he lies there on his back he sees the clouds above him thin, and then shred, as, astoundingly, the sun breaks through. His clothes steam, the broken skin on his face tightens as it dries, but despite the pain Pita opens to the warmth as if to the fire of whisky in his belly. Below, the water has reached the base of his rocks but its force is dissipated by the flat terrace. The river flows quickly through the scrubland, spreading wider and wider but at last no higher.

BY THE TIME shadows creep over his rocky island Pita is ravenously hungry, desperately in need of a strong drink, and feeling better. The waters are receding, leaving this little plateau littered with debris. Grass, scrub, rocks — all are covered in a blanket of sticky mud. His world has turned brown. He notices movement below him and sees one — no, several — eels wriggling through the mud, heading back towards the river. Pita is down off his rock, faster than he climbed up it, and falling onto the nearest. The pain in his ribs is terrible but the thrashing eel is trapped under him. His knife is out; he slices behind the head and the slippery, muddy thing is his! He struggles to haul the tough skin away from the flesh — women's work — but hunger drives his knife and his fumbling hands. At last the meat is exposed and he sinks his teeth into it, taking the food, bones and all, in great gulping bites. Standing there, ankle deep in mud, he grins. Not as tasty as his mother's cooking — not nearly as good as a roast of mutton — but sweet and juicy all the same. He spits out bones and mud and takes another bite; feels his belly welcome the food, his body begin to strengthen.

Unwilling to trust the river's retreat, Pita spends the night shivering on the outcrop. Two freshly killed eels keep him company. But food in his belly cannot stave off the awful nightmares. The girl's white face returns to haunt him. He and Danny have killed the girl, have damaged a river steamer. Pita whimpers to think of Mr Hatrick's wrath, his parents' disgust. Danny's blows have broken his nose; he cannot breathe through it. His mood slides between terror and self-pity. Mr Hatrick will bring the law down upon them, that is certain. They will go to jail. And what lies might Danny tell? That quick-thinking fellow might lay the whole blame on Pita. Perhaps even now the police are searching. Pita curls tightly on himself for warmth and longs for morning.

First light brings a breeze, and with it something new: the smell of wood-smoke. Pita knows this part of the river — the Maori kainga is long deserted, and no one else has settled here.

He remembers rumours of an illicit still. Sly-groggers are active in these parts, as everyone knows, but the source of the liquor is unknown, even to Pita. Perhaps he has stumbled on it! The hope brings on a desire even stronger than hunger. His despair of the night forgotten, Pita climbs stiffly down into the mud and, dragging his two eels, tramps off in the direction of the smoke.

※

Police Station and McPhee Sawmill, Raetihi

Wanted Known

Patterson's Sawmill, Raetihi, is looking for hardworking and skilled tree-fellers.

Rate: £2.5/- per felled acre standing bush on Raetihi–Ohakune road.

Wanted Known

'I can go wherever a bullock team can go.' Pipiriki – Raetihi – Ohakune.

Timber, general goods, railway supplies.
E.P. Chase, carrier.

Advertisements, Waimarino Argus, *1905*

CONSTABLE TIM NAYLOR can find nothing in his rulebooks to help him with this case. He sits at his desk in the tiny, one-room police station, turning pages that deal with sly-groggers, droppers, drunkards, games of chance, theft, violence. He is familiar with all of these; indeed, he has a man in the two-room lock-up behind the station — 'drunk in charge of a horse' — whom he arrested last night. The fellow claims he came by the liquor legally, which cannot be proved one way or the other. A straightforward case, nonetheless. The drunkard will remain locked up for six hours, which is considered punishment enough, and his horse grazed in the police paddock until the fellow's sober enough to ride it home.

But this river business? Tim Naylor can find no mention in his manuals of logging or riverboats. Could he charge the loggers for being a nuisance in a public place? Is the river a public place? He has been told to tread carefully when it comes to the river Maori. His superior officer in Wanganui told him they were a touchy lot, prone to knowing their rights and arguing them in court. The harangue from Bert Morrow down at Pipiriki has unsettled his confidence. Perhaps the Maori down there do have the right to take their logs downriver? Constable Naylor, who prides himself on being sensible in this distant outpost of the law, decides to wait to see whether there are further complaints.

On the matter of the near-drowned girl he has also decided to stay his hand. While at Pipiriki he came across new and interesting information. Naylor feels pleased that his careful questioning of all parties has borne such fruit. Exactly as his training suggested: *Never overlook the small details of a case. The interviewing of seemingly unconnected persons may prove of significant interest.* Accordingly, Tim Naylor had stayed on at Pipiriki for a day or two making inquiries — and enjoying the beauty and comfort of the peaceful little settlement.

At Pipiriki landing the constable had taken the trouble to have a word with the two deckhands who had been on the riverbank at the top of Ngaporo with the winching cable when the logging raft struck. Naylor found Rangi and Eru repairing the damaged rivets in the *Wairua*'s under-plates.

'Won't be long, boss,' said Rangi, grinning up from the boat's hatchway. 'Watch here. You can learn a new trick.'

He disappeared again into the cramped belly of the boat while Eru leaned over the side with a boat-hook. At Rangi's shout, Eru fished under the water with his hook and soon brought up a piece of string attached to a nail. Rangi had evidently removed the temporary wooden bung and sent the tethered nail through the rivet hole. Quickly, for the *Wairua* would now be taking water, Eru removed the nail and attached a gutter-bolt. At his shout, Rangi hauled in the line and the gutter-bolt disappeared into the water. Later the constable, who liked to understand the workings of things, climbed into the tiny hold and watched as Rangi used a spanner to tighten the nuts on the gutter-bolts.

'She'll be good maybe some weeks,' Rangi said. 'Later she'll be fixed at Mr Hatrick's foundry downriver.' Naylor could see several other worn gutter-bolts studding the steel plates. Obviously losing a rivet or two in a rapid was commonplace.

'Can we talk now?' he asked, grinning in what he hoped was an easy-going way. There had been much talk, back at the training barracks, of the fighting spirit of the upriver Maori.

Rangi and Eru were happy enough to sit on the landing, light up their pipes and discuss the accident. They considered the whole event a bit of a joke. 'That Pita Morrow,' said Rangi, giggling like a schoolboy. 'Big heart, small head! He should know better than to take on a river steamer. Danny, too.'

'Did you see the logs hit?'

'Ae! Winch cable nearly break. Boat waving like a flag. Lucky our tree hold up good.' Both men grinned. There was pride in the way Rangi spoke.

'And did you see the girl fall?'

'No. No.' Eru sounded angry that the constable would even suggest such a thing. 'Or we would save her.'

'That nearly drowned girl,' said Rangi, serious now, 'Danny and Pita, their crash did not fall her into the river. No, boss.'

Naylor thought maybe they were protecting the two loggers, but Rangi seemed so sure. 'I seen that girl just the top of Ngaporo. I hear her scream very loud and I seen the other girl — her sister, you know — fighting her for something.'

'Fighting?' Tim Naylor was intrigued by this new slant to the accident.

Rangi laughed. 'Not big fighting — push shove, you know how sisters can do?'

'At the top of the rapid?'

'Surely. Eh, Eru?'

Eru seemed less sure. 'No, boss, I was watching captain for a sign. I dint see no fight. But the girl was there sure. Then we was busy with the rope.' He turned to Rangi. 'E, Rangi, you think the sister push her in?'

Rangi shrugged. 'Maybe. Anyway she's right now, eh, boss?'

When the constable told them the girl was not right in the head — couldn't speak — the two men were reluctant to say any more. If this was going to be a serious police matter they would rather not remember further details. But both were sure that Bridget McPhee had been on board *after* the log raft had done its worst and the captain had regained control of the *Wairua*.

SO NOW, HAVING managed to coax his unwilling horse past the many washouts and muddy spots on the Pipiriki–Raetihi road, and having found no guidance in his police manuals, Constable Tim Naylor has the unpleasant duty of informing Mr Angus McPhee that he sees no benefit in prosecuting any party for the accident. Indeed, on the contrary, it is rumoured that Mr Alexander Hatrick is on the warpath and has the McPhee sawmills in his sights.

The McPhees' Raetihi sawmill is only a short distance out of town on the road to Ohakune, but even so Naylor saddles his horse. After the last few days' storm any progress on foot through the sea of mud that blankets Raetihi is an effort. Mrs

Punch at the Waimarino Hotel has declared that she will not cross the 'ridiculously wide' main road until summer is come. Only yesterday the Hoddle family's five-year-old daughter fell into the muddy drain just outside their butcher's shop and was stuck there, only her head above the mud, until her father came to dig her out. A delegation of landowners has petitioned anyone prepared to listen but the roads in and out of the district remain a disgrace.

Naylor edges his horse around a suspiciously smooth patch of mud. If his mount's leg is broken, policing will come to a standstill in this sodden part of the dominion. He thinks of Pipiriki — the gentle sloping fields and beautiful tree-ferns, a handful of pretty houses looking out over the calm bend of the river. Nothing could be more different from the raw town he now picks his way through. Ahead and to his right, ramparts of unfelled bush crowd darkly against roughly hewn fields. To his left the felled hillside looks even more threatening: ugly spears of half-burnt trunks stand among a mess of fallen timber and the muddy scars of the fellers' tracks. Clearly the landowner has despaired of finding a sawmiller willing to clear the logs, and has burned off the lot.

Even here in the township timber is left lying. There is simply too much of it. Further south and down in Wanganui they are crying out for timber, but here, the problem is transport: how to get it out? Naylor has seen one landowner walk away, unable to meet his bills. Investors have bought blocks, hoping to lease them to sawmills and thus clear the land for later farming, only to find that even the tough breed of frontier sawmillers cannot find a cheap enough way to get the timber out. Until the railroad is opened, only those serving the overnight needs of the tourists are making much of a living. The railway is the lifeline everyone is holding out for. Next year, surely, they will complete it. A dreadful setback that it will go through Ohakune, not Raetihi as originally hoped, but a branch line has been promised, and in the meantime the road to Ohakune is reasonably flat; the tortuous Pipiriki road is closed yet again with slips.

He passes the grounds of the new school — awash; the tiny Church of England cannot be approached on foot; fences are half finished; soft, sticky, clinging mud is everywhere. Raetihi in the winter of 1907 is a sorry town for most of the inhabitants.

But Tim Naylor is pleased enough. He asked for a frontier placing and the challenge of policing this vast, rough area excites him. His only worry is that if he does not find a wife soon his superiors will move him to a larger station. One-man stations must be staffed by a married policeman. That is the rule. Then the wife can keep the station open while the husband is away on patrol. To date the only unmarried woman he has met has been the frightening McPhee girl. He hopes to avoid her now. The conversation with her father will be awkward enough without the complication of her presence.

POOR ROADS WILL never slow down a McPhee enterprise. Angus McPhee, mud-spattered to his knees, pipe pluming between clenched teeth, stands under a makeshift lean-to that bears a roughly painted sign: *McPhee and Son Sawmills*. He is supervising the unloading of newly felled totara logs. The giant trunks have been hauled from the nearby bush, along wooden rails. Other mill-owners have laid iron rails but McPhee is in a hurry and the iron is expensive to transport up the river and then from Pipiriki. So his line of six draughthorses must struggle to pull the heavy truck. Naylor, watching the straining horses, hopes that the abundant groundwater will at least lubricate the rough wooden rails.

'Can you spare a minute?' he shouts over the racket of the mill.

McPhee looks over, registers the police uniform and nods, none too pleased, it seems, at the interruption. You would think he might be eager for news of his daughter at least. He shouts instructions to his mill-hands and leads the way to his office at the back of the lean-to. Close by, a newly finished house stands in a paddock barren of any blade of grass or shred of foliage. A fence of fresh totara posts encloses the empty field and house. Beyond the fence the great rampart of dark bush looms.

McPhee seems to expect congratulations. 'Clap your eyes on that!' he says, pointing with his pipe stem at the stark and lonely homestead. 'Finest house in town, and completed in two weeks. That is what good planning and hard work can accomplish on this earth. Take note, young man.'

Naylor is not sure whether the admonition is meant as warning or encouragement. He nods and follows McPhee into an icy-cold room, bare of any furniture except a desk and a chair that McPhee immediately inhabits.

'Well now,' he says to the standing constable. 'Well now.'

Tim Naylor is annoyed by the brusque treatment, the lack of even a rudimentary welcome. He clears his throat and comes to the point perhaps more abruptly than he had planned. As McPhee's red eyebrows lower and meet above his sharp blue eyes, the constable gives his reasons for prosecuting no one in the case of his daughter's accident.

'Indeed, sir,' he finishes, 'it is common knowledge on the river that it was your own offer that led to the loggers attempting to float down. It is said that Mr Hatrick is contemplating laying charges.'

'Common knowledge?' McPhee's voice rises in pitch to match his anger. 'It is said? Are these the terms a police constable is taught to use these days? Where is your evidence, young man? Where the sworn statements? Did my mills in Wanganui buy floated logs? Did they?'

'Ah . . . I am sure Mr Hatrick will ascertain —'

'Mr Hatrick has no leg to stand on. He will unearth no transaction concerning floated logs. He charges exorbitant amounts to bring our supplies upriver. He favours his precious tourist trade above us worthy settlers. And he would dare to press charges against me? I think not, Constable. Now, I at least am busy, even if you have nothing better to do than bring me tales of hearsay and tattle.' McPhee stands, terrier-like, his head thrust forward, red beard jutting.

Tim Naylor stands his ground. 'There is news of your daughter's accident and of her well-being, Mr McPhee.'

'I will gather my own news, if you don't mind. How can I trust someone who listens to rubbish?'

Angus McPhee strides out of the little room, shouts angry instructions at someone unlucky enough to be within earshot and returns to his noisy mill.

While Tim Naylor is still shaking his head over the fiery Scot, his son, Douglas, slips quickly into the room. Perhaps the boy has been listening. He is clearly embarrassed by his father's outburst. He looks at the floor. Clears his throat.

'Sorry,' is all he can manage. 'Sorry, sir.' And then 'Ah . . .'

Naylor waits.

'Ah . . . Did you . . . did you say there was news of Bridget?'

Naylor nods. 'There is news, son. I don't know if it is happy news. The Sisters at Jerusalem say she is well . . . and happy in a way. But her condition is unchanged. She seems not to understand more than a small child might. The Sisters are trying some of Mother Aubert's famous remedies. They suggest she stays with them for a little longer. Can you tell your stepmother this?'

127

Douglas nods. He stands there, shoulders drooping.

Naylor is not sure whether to offer his other news, but in the end speaks, perhaps out of a desire to see some reaction from this boy, who is as annoyingly spiritless as his father is fiery.

'The deckhands have reported,' he says, 'that your sister was still aboard some time after the collision. They both saw her with — Gertie — at the head of the rapid.'

If Naylor wished to provoke a response he certainly succeeded. Douglas's head shoots up. 'With Gertie? My sister?'

'Yes. They say there was an argument. Some pushing and shoving, they said. It is possible that she fell overboard at that time.'

'Oh,' says Douglas. He is breathing hard, his eyes bright. 'Oh.'

'I have told your father that I do not consider prosecution is in order.'

'Does Gertie know this?'

'Presumably she has always known it.'

'No but . . . have you told her?'

Tim Naylor watches as the boy's pale cheeks flush with what looks like a deep pleasure. What a strange family this is!

'No,' he says gently, suspecting that the sister has been persecuting this withdrawn fellow. 'Perhaps you would tell her from me?'

Douglas cannot keep his pleasure hidden. 'Yes. I will. Thank you.' He looks directly at the constable for the first time. 'Did you see Bridget?'

Tim Naylor smiles at the memory. 'I did, yes. She is walking now — in fact wandering more than the Sisters would like. And has a smile for everyone. But you must be prepared for a change in her. The Sisters think that since she has not improved in her speech or childish ways after two weeks, perhaps the damage is permanent.'

The constable had enjoyed his ride down to Jerusalem on a rare sunny day, the river sparkling and the banks lush after the recent storm. The Sisters had welcomed him with a splendid meal and taken him on a tour of their many enterprises. 'Our little Bridie', as they called Bridget, had walked with him, often holding his hand in a way that somehow disturbed him — the touch was so childish, but the hand so soft and adult. And to look in her face — which he did only once — also unnerved him. She was beautiful, calm, and yet beyond that beauty — nothing. No spark of give and take, no teasing pressure of fingers, no show of fear or anger. Simply a pleasant smile — and what did that signify?

Tim Naylor does not speak of this impression to the boy. 'You should visit her,' he says. The Sisters had been puzzled by the lack of interest the family seemed to take in their beautiful, simple Bridie. 'Perhaps you can help her to remember her old life.'

Douglas smiles — an odd, lost expression. 'Perhaps she doesn't want to remember,' he says. 'She might be happier.'

'Buck up, lad,' says Naylor, irritated by the lassitude that seems to blanket the lanky boy. 'Go down and see her. It will do you both good.'

'I won't be allowed,' says Douglas flatly. He has a thought. 'Could you take me down with you when you go next? Could you tell my father?'

'No,' says Naylor. 'I have other areas to visit next. You'll have to tell him yourself. Or just go. Hape is taking his bullock train down tomorrow. There's a load of supplies to be brought up to the railway camps. He might be glad of a hand with a shovel over the slips.'

The lad nods, but the constable has not much hope that he will act on the advice. He leaves Douglas to his thoughts and walks back to his horse. It is raining again.

Riding back to the station, the constable sees a notice pinned to the new Social Hall. He leans down to read it.

Anti Asiatic League
Local Branch meeting Saturday October 5th 6.30 pm
Come and hear Mr Angus McPhee speak on what we must do to contain the spread of the Yellow Peril within our frontier town.
Signed A. Nicol, Branch Secretary

Tim Naylor is intrigued. How does the worthy Angus McPhee deal with the fact that Charlie Chee, one of the dreaded 'Yellow Peril', possibly saved his daughter's life?

BACK AT THE mill Douglas, trembling but for once resolved, faces his father.

'I am not cut out for this life,' he says, the words tumbling out before his courage fails. 'Engineering is what I like, Father, and the river. I will do well there. I will only fail at sawmilling.'

'You young puppy! Don't you dare speak to me like that! You'll do what I say!' Angus McPhee's rage is prolonged and white hot. A day earlier Douglas might have submitted to the rant: the demand to follow family tradition, to feel some pride in his father's work and gratitude for the sustenance it has afforded him thus far. And so on. But this day Douglas simply walks out. Turns on his heel, marches away from his raging father and the mill, runs across the field and up to his room, where he gathers clothes into a sack. His stepmother watches from the doorway but makes no plea for him to stay.

The younger ones are at school. 'Say goodbye to them for me,' mutters Douglas to his silent stepmother. Then, breathing quickly, dizzy with excitement, he charges downstairs in search of Gertie. He finds her in the dining room, laying out a paper pattern on new cloth for a dress. He watches her for a moment. She's aware of him but doesn't bother to turn.

He shouts at her back. 'The accident. You knew it wasn't me. You knew all the time. You pushed her yourself!'

'What rubbish.' Gertie is never one to admit fault. 'Who told you such nonsense?'

'The constable. He said the deckhands saw it and reported to him.'

That stops her in her tracks. Gertie grows pale. The piece of cloth she's cutting falls to the floor. 'Tim Naylor? He said that?'

'He said for me to let you know. He said he would not be pressing charges unless someone laid a complaint.'

'Oh.' Gertie turns away from him. Douglas thinks she might be in tears for the first time that he can remember. Rages, tantrums and shouting matches, yes, but tears never. 'Oh,' she says again. And then, in a terrible cold rage, 'Go away.'

And he goes. Out of the house and down to the bullocky. 'I'm going to be a riverman,' he says proudly. 'Will you give me a lift to Pipiriki?'

'If you're handy with a spade and don't mind muddy shanks, you're welcome,' says Hape.

Douglas doesn't look back.

Summer 1908

Danny's Obsession

NO ONE TALKED much about Danny's obsession. At first, of
course, no one knew. He lived way upriver, off the beaten track.
He would come down to the landing at Maraekowhai with his
wool clip or to collect supplies, would laugh and chat with the
river men, would sometimes stay to sing with his wife for the
tourists; that was about it, as far as Danny's social life went. Once
a year his wife brought him to church at Jerusalem (if they were
lucky and no emergency at the farm presented itself). He would
sit in his pew, hair neatly trimmed, threadbare suit freshly pressed;
he would sing the hymns in a voice that rose above the rest, then

shake hands with Father Soulas and tease the Sisters until they blushed like children. Everyone on the river liked Danny — for his charm and for the fact that their own Stella loved him.

Behind his back, though, they were less admiring. Stella deserved better; why was the farm not prospering? Where were the children Stella so longed for? Stella's lack of new clothes was observed. It was whispered that she still cooked on an open hearth. That she wore cast-off shoes donated by the Houseboat captain's wife. Danny, who longed to shower gifts on his wife, who dreamed of showing off his wealth in extravagant ways, noticed the way their eyes slid sideways sometimes when he talked. He didn't fit, down at Jerusalem; he had been brought up Catholic, true, but *Irish* Catholic, a good few steps down the ladder from the sophisticated Europeans who led the river missions. At any rate Danny had left his religious ways back home in County Cork: he had not been to Mass in all the years he wandered. When he married into the Morrow family his appearance was expected at Mass for Easter and Christmas at the very least, naturally, but faith ran very shallow in Danny's veins, that was plain to see.

Down at Jerusalem Danny could not keep up his high-spirited blarney. He became uneasy when his wife chatted at length with the Sisters and exchanged news with friends she had grown up with. Most of these people had been to school, could read the newspapers and follow what was happening in the world. Danny, who could not read or write well, felt ill at ease in this literate company. He would smile, friendly enough, but the river folk noticed that he was always first back in Bert's motor-waka for the trip back to Pipiriki and Sunday dinner.

Poor men were not unusual in these parts: Danny was not alone in that respect. He was pitied sometimes for his poor farm and his bad luck, as were many others, but Danny was known to be a good husband at least, neither drunkard nor violent. More than a few farmers upriver went to the bad one way or another when hard times hit. Or killed themselves — the coward's way out, as Father Soulas would point out from the pulpit — abhorrent to God and earning damnation of the soul.

Danny would never take the coward's way out of his troubles, you could be reasonably sure of that. He soldiered on, cheerful enough. A naturally sunny nature, all agreed, and likeable. So when people began to notice his strange behaviour they kept it to themselves at first, thinking that they had been mistaken or that there was another explanation. When he was seen more often down at Jerusalem the river people thought maybe he had come to help with the building there. And his visits to Pipiriki were put down to family concerns — keeping an eye on his in-laws' well-being.

Even when it became clear that he was always searching for Bridie — wasn't it natural that he should show concern, since he was the one to save her from drowning? This was said at first but as the weeks and months went by, excuses could no longer be invented, and goodwill stretched to breaking. Danny should be back home with his wife. How could the farm survive with all this wandering? Bridie was in no danger. The river people kept an eye on her. What was Danny thinking?

When it became clear she was with child, Danny's behaviour, naturally enough, set tongues wagging even faster.

Samuel Blencoe

SHE WERE PRETTY, our Bridie, and sweet. Strangers found her fearsome — the way she would say nought or would stare at you in that empty way. Often a wide smile as if there were something odd about you. But those that knew her loved her, far as I could tell. Always you could tell when she had stopped with the Sisters a day or two; her smock would be fresh washed and her hair brushed shining. After the first while the good ladies maybe decided to accept her wandering. They cut the tangles and sticks and what-all from that glory of bright copper hair whenever they might lay hands on her and washed her clean and let her be.

Bridie walked barefoot like the Maori but not like them in any other way. Such thin white limbs, so quiet. Some of the river Maori — the children — were afeared of her. If she would stand, pale and smiling, to watch as they cleared their eel-traps or scrubbed potatoes in the sun, they might turn away in case she put a spook on them, or they might place a piece of mutton in her hand and push her along. But the elders knew her story and would chide the children and would let her stand there. In truth, there were no harmful bone in her body. Mayhap that were the strange and fearsome thing to some.

I never seen her at Jerusalem to know did she work for the Sisters. Maybe she picked their cherries in the season, for her lips were often red with them and once she brought me a pocketful. She would work for Charlie Chee, though. I seen that. Seen her bending over his neat lines of carrot tops, picking at the tiniest weeds, then walking slow to drop them in his bucket and then back to the patch. Myself, I could see no trace of any leaf save for carrot-top but she would bend again and find some imposter. Charlie would laugh and pat her shoulder and nod, and back she would go to her work. I liked to watch them.

Charlie had a patch of clear land on the roll of a hill where the bush stood back. He had it from a Maori hapu upriver of him and paid them in vegetables. It were a sweet place, views upriver and down and sun most hours of the day, even in winter. His hut were not much bigger than mine but a deal more neat, with a thatch roof like the Maori and a chimbley of tin, and stones round the doorway and a rose bush. Out back he kept his tools under a little shelter made of ponga fern, and next was his pile of stuff — leaves and vegetable scrapings and his chicken shit and whatall for digging back in. They say he put his own shit in too, and maybe he did. I never seen it.

Charlie wore Chow clothes — a tunic thing and loose

139

trousers and a long pigtail down his back, not like his brother.
Charlie's brother walked upriver to visit once some years back.
Come down from up north somewhere. Very smart he was in his
coat and jacket and tie, just like a white man, and a proper hat,
not like Charlie's pointy straw. Charlie's brother had a wife from
China and two boys and a vegetable garden just like Charlie, and
maybe a shop too up on the plateau, or maybe I heard wrong. You
don't think of Chows owning a shop. But then Charlie Chee had
plans too — he was saving his money. Maybe that was why he
didn't buy proper clothes. He wanted a Chow wife too, and that
cost plenty. After that one time the brother never come again.
Maybe he moved away.

With me Bridie did no weeding nor any other work. She
would sit quiet by the river. Watch whatever might float by. With
Charlie Chee it was weeding. Maybe she took the flavour of the
body she were with and echoed it, like. Did she pray to Mary
with the Sisters, I wonder?

It would be about Christmas that her belly swole for all to see.
Her being so thin. I said naught. Nor did Charlie Chee but likely
he noticed. I seen the same thing on Norfolk with the women
lags. Them that got to work in the soldiers' homes. Their bellies
would swell and they would be sent back to the women's prison.
I seen a screaming woman throw her newborn babby into the sea
over on that cursed island and then follow with her own self to
smash like a red flower on the rocks.

But this is Bridie, not that woman. All us knew the Sisters
would take the babe; they were most kindly that way.

I NEVER SEEN Pita Morrow since that day. He was always
a wandering man but a body would notice the fellow. And he
loved the river. Since he were a boy, I seen him up often, paddling

140

his canoe helter-skelter downriver, or standing tall to pole it up against the current. A shout and a wave if he saw me. I seen him work on the River Trust gangs, snagging logs that would try the strength of a elephant. A wild lad. I seen him fall out the canoe dead drunk but float down with it to come ashore and live to tell the tale. But I reckoned he maybe drowned when Danny clobbered him, or we'd have seen him on the water by now.

After the accident poor Danny come down more than once. First time would be two, maybe three week after our Bridie were washed up. Must have been to Pipiriki for something for he walked on foot to me from downriver. Never come up my way before except when he were washed up. A clear still morning: birds finished with their morning shout, the riverboat already chugged upriver, the tourists sitting on the deck in the sun taking in the sights. Dannyboy nodded to me and took his place on the log by my door. Where they all sit if they want to talk. That fellow sat by me, quiet, which is not his way, they say. I reckon he had no stomach to remember that time with Bridie, for he turned with his back to the river, looked up into the dark bush.

'Did you see what happened?' he said after a long silence.

'I did,' says I.

He asked no more for a long bit.

'Did he drown?' he asked then. I scarce heard, he were so quiet, but knew that would be his question.

'I can't say,' I says. 'I seen him fall in the water, I seen him and the logs caught in the current. Succour to the girl were more important.'

More than I said in many a day but the poor man deserved a fair reply. Clear to see he were racked.

Then I said, because I was tired of questions, 'I said naught to the law. Nor won't.'

He is a good man, Dannyboy, for all his short temper. He

knew I had enough questioning. Any talk of law or punishment knots my gut till I might puke. Even now.

'Thank you, Samuel Blencoe,' says he, formal like a speech. How he known my whole name I could not say. He stood, laid a packet of three good mutton chops on the log, and walked away back towards Pipiriki.

Two more times he come, looking for Bridie he said, his eyes bright and hopeful. To my knowledge he never come across her up our way. Searching for Bridie were no earthly use, as the Sisters knew well. Bridie were like the bush creatures. She might come if you stayed put. Or not. I reckon Danny never learned that. They said he were up and down river like a cur after a bone, poor sod. I seen men like that on Norfolk — naught but one thought in their head. A ruinous state. One old feller would take fifty lashes rather than spit out his wad of baccy. Would suffer any unnatural indignity from warder or lag to earn the taste and comfort of a wad under his tongue. He died of it in the end, his back shredded to ribbons, no skin left to heal. I seen that same yearning look in Danny's eyes and feared for him.

Then in the summer our Bridie's belly swole. No hiding that.

O'Dowds' Farm

The Rhine of Maoriland
New Overland Route

Connecting with **Central Railway, Auckland, Rotorua, Wellington (or vice-versa) via Wanganui**

TAUMARUNUI—PIPIRIKI Tuesdays Saturdays 6 a.m
PIPIRIKI—TAUMARUNUI Mondays Fridays 6 a.m

Fares: Single 35/- Return: £2 10/-
Through from **TAUMARUNUI—WANGANUI** 50/-

A. Hatrick & Co. timetable (extract), 1908

STELLA BRINGS A mug of tea out to the porch where Danny is banging nails as if they were vermin to be killed. He whistles through his teeth, but tunelessly. She can see already that this will be a bad day. She is sick to death of his swinging moods. Two days ago he set out for Pipiriki, cheerful as a cricket, adamant that a harness must be fixed and that he couldn't manage the task himself. He walked down to the Houseboat with her, laughing and chattering in a brittle way that unnerved and puzzled her. At the landing he wangled a free ride downriver in return for help with the rapids on the return trip, and waved

143

her goodbye, grinning like a naughty boy. Yesterday he returned, eyes glittering, exhausted, and the harness still broken.

'So what did you do down there that was so important?' she demanded.

Danny slumped into bed without a word. Slept like the dead.

Now she is determined to have it out with him. These past months since the accident and then the flood, the farm has staggered from one crisis to another. More than half the sheep didn't lamb — although the ram had been put to them and seemed to do his business. Then the house cow's calf died. The River Trust block downriver has begun to revive, as Mack Feathers had predicted, the silt deposited by the flood enriching the greening river terraces. But Danny's paddocks remain muddy and sullen, pig-fern and thistle invading the hard-won pasture. The sheep are losing condition. Stumps that Danny had not managed to uproot refuse to rot away. The whole place, as Danny says on his black days, is as ugly a farm as you could imagine. Yet this morning he has proposed another trip downriver: a break, he says, for both of them. They will take the riverboat down to Pipiriki next week, visit the Morrows and then go with them to Mass at Jerusalem.

'No,' said Stella. 'We can't afford another break. How can you suggest it?'

'The old folk will be pleased to see you,' he said, spooning his porridge, 'and we might visit the girl I saved.'

'Danny,' she said, frightened by the way he will not look at her, 'we cannot spare the time. You know this.'

It was as if she hadn't spoken. All he thinks about, it seems, is the wretched idiot girl, while the farm decays and she supports them both with Houseboat money.

'Sit down, Danny,' she says now. 'This can't go on.'

He stops his banging. Stands in the sunlight squinting up at her. Smiling, she holds the mug of tea towards him. 'Come and sit with me, love.' It's like enticing a child.

Danny reads her thoughts. 'When you use that voice I'm in for it, don't I know. I'm not your child, Stella.' But he drops the hammer, comes over and takes the tea.

They sit side by side on the porch, gulping at the warm tea. Beyond, the scruffy paddocks are drying in the morning sun, what grass there is wilting before their eyes.

'This can't go on,' she says again.

'The farm?' says Danny. 'We should leave it, you think?' An odd smile on his face. His eyes, when he glances at her, are hard, unreadable. She used to know all his moods.

'You know I don't mean that. Pa gave us this land. I love it.' She sighs, 'Or used to. What is it, Danny? Ever since the logs, nothing is right. Between us.'

Danny sits silent, his head hanging.

'The McPhee girl. It wasn't your fault . . .'

'I know that!' Danny shouts the words. The dog leaps to his feet, growling.

'Then why do you go on and on about her? She's lost her mind. What is she to you? To anyone?'

Danny turns on her. 'Someone has to watch over her. I saved her, didn't I? It's up to me, then.'

'Oh, Danny.' Stella feels sick. 'You're speaking nonsense. The Sisters watch over her. Ma keeps an eye.'

'They don't, they don't! They don't really care.'

'And you do? Oh, Danny, she wouldn't even recognise you.'

Danny puts down his mug, takes both her hands in his. Now it is Stella who wants to look away. He blazes at her, so earnest, so certain. 'Yes, she does, Stell. She does recognise me! I'm sure of it. I think perhaps she remembers a little. Some shadow in her mind remembers that I was the one pulled her out, breathed life into her. I think I might be able to bring her mind back. If I say my name she repeats it. Says "Danny" with such a sweet smile. It would bring tears to your eyes, Stell.'

Danny's hopeful smile infuriates her. 'Tears of laughter, perhaps,' she says sourly. 'You are turned to an idiot yourself — can't you see it?' She beats her fist on the rough planks of the bench. 'Those damn logs!'

Danny's smile fades. He gazes out on the ruined paddocks. Stella watches him. After a while she says, more gently, 'It's Pita, isn't it?'

He looks at her sharply, then slowly, sadly, he nods. Mumbles something she can't hear. 'It's not your fault, you know that,' she says. It has been said many times.

He goes to speak, but in the end only sighs, his head hanging. Stella waits. There is always something left unsaid.

'Pita saved my life on that trip,' mutters Danny. 'Pulled me from the whirlpool.'

'Yes, I know. He might still come back . . .'

'He was my friend. Your brother.'

'Danny . . . I know all that.'

Danny jumps to his feet and again the dog rises with him, ready to attack the unseen enemy. 'You don't know!' he howls. 'Stop saying that! How can you know?'

Stella rises too, her patience worn thin. 'Then in God's name tell me, Danny! How can I help if you won't say?'

Danny jumps down off the porch, the dog at his heels. 'I don't need help!' he shouts over his shoulder.

But Stella can hear the sobs catching the words.

AN HOUR LATER Danny is back in the house. Stella has her precious preserving pan boiling on the fire, the glass jars of

146

fruit sterilising before she seals the lids down. At least there'll be puddings all winter, thanks to the Sisters' cherry orchard. The sight of the deep red fruit suspended and gleaming in their syrup fills her with pleasure. Bottling always puts her in the best of moods. Such a solid and beautiful achievement.

Perhaps Danny knows this. He smiles at her, touches his finger to a drop of sweat on her chin. 'Almost finished?'

'Almost.' She pushes damp hair away from her face, smiles back at him. How can he change so quickly? He is so different from her steady parents — from anyone else she knows. She used to love him for this — the light and shade, the wonderful unpredictability of their life together. Now she is unsettled. The light moments are fewer and even they seem to carry their own shadow.

'Come outside when you are done.' His eyes are bright and full of love. 'Something to show you.'

Stella uses a rag to haul the jars from the steaming pan, clips the glass lids down while the syrup still bubbles inside the jars. They are perfect. Delicious jewels. She leaves them on the table in a row to cool.

Out on the porch Danny takes her in his arms, burying his nose in her neck. 'Mmm. My cherry syrup wife. I could lick you all to glory this very minute.'

He runs the tip of his tongue up to her ear and then drives inside it until she can't control her shivers and screams at him to stop. 'Danny, Danny! You wicked man!' She plants her sticky, syrupy hands on his face and he sets to licking them, growling and nuzzling like a dog. Finn senses the game and joins in jumping and wagging until the three of them fall to the boards, laughing and helpless.

It's from this position that she sees the rocking chair. Stella stops teasing and rolls onto her knees. 'Danny? What's this then?'

His hopeful look would break your heart. 'A present. You said you'd love one.'

'But it's so beautiful, sweetheart. You made it?' She walks over to the lovely thing.

He scrambles up, holding out a warning hand, 'Wait, wait — don't sit yet! The glue is not yet dry!'

Stella laughs out loud. It is so like Danny to show it before it is quite ready. He can never hold back his own excitement. 'Oh, Danny,' she says, 'it's so beautiful.' And it is: hewn out of pale kahikatea wood, with an arching leafy pattern carved into the timber of the back. She touches the arm and the chair rocks gently, promising peaceful evenings on the porch or in front of the fire.

Stella kisses him. 'I knew you were up to something in the shed these last days, but I thought you were just avoiding me. In a mood.'

'I'm sorry. I know.' He spreads his hands. 'I'm hopeless.' Then grins, banishing the penitent. 'It turned out all right, eh?'

'It's a beauty. When can I sit on it?'

'When you get back from the Houseboat. Tomorrow.'

Arm in arm, they go inside for their meal.

BUT IN THE afternoon, as Stella leaves for the Houseboat, Danny is back in his darkness. She looks for him, to say goodbye. These leave-takings were once a treasured ritual: kisses and hugs and then a walk hand in hand along the river to the bend by the ruined mill, where Danny would hug her again and demand a quick return. 'Goodbye, my little black crow,' he would say, laughing at the strange sight of her, standing so neat and starched in her black uniform with the white collar, amidst the messy chaos of their half-cleared fields. 'And no winking at the

gentlemen, mind, or they will have Danny's fist in their faces.'
She would laugh and flirt with her eyes as if he were a tourist, to
drive him mad. Then kiss her dear man and dance off down the
track singing, so he could hear her go. Now, often, he scarcely
notices when she leaves.

She sees him, up the hill, standing motionless, staring at
nothing, it would seem.

'Danny!' she calls. 'I'm away!'

He raises his hand a little without turning. No word, no smile.
Suddenly Stella is out of patience with him. She opens the gate
and sets off without looking back. As she walks her spirits rise
and she starts to sing: '. . . *will never meet again, on the bonnie
bonnie hills of Loch Lomond*' — a tune the new fireman on the
Wairua taught her. He is sweet on her, the silly puppy.

Ruvey Morrow

What to do at
❖ PIPIRIKI ❖

Drive through the beautiful scenic gorge to the top of
Waipuna Saddle, 2,400 feet high and **view** the beautiful
snowclad mountains Ruapehu 9,175, Tongariro 6,455 and the
active volcano Ngauruhoe 7,515 feet above sea level. **Walk** to
the old mill along the old mill race, **cross** the suspension
bridge. **Canoe** trip to the caves, **visit** the Native village.

A. Hatrick & Co. timetable brochure, 1908

THAT SUMMER, BEGINNING of a new year, seemed
golden at first. Day after day of clear sunny weather, a treat
after that black winter and the flood scouring the land till we
wondered would any be left for a soul to set foot on, or all wash
downriver and out to sea. All January the tourists were thick
as flies on the steamers, and the House full day after day. Mr
Hatrick offered an extra pound a week on our wages when we
were full so Bert and me were in good pocket. That was before
we started worrying about Pita. Our boy was often gone months
on end. He was wandering about, I thought, shamed by his

logging accident. Or worse, maybe, selling the logs and keeping the proceeds to himself, so I was not inclined to fret too much.

The great joy was that Stella was downriver more often. I thought it a sign that Danny was finally coming to his senses. That sulky farm wasn't worth tuppence, in my view, and the sooner they walked off like the other upriver farmers and got on with a different way of life the better. Bert had a different view. He admired Danny for his persistence and his love of that remote part of the river. Well, he would — his family comes from up that way — but these days a man has to think of supporting his family — and the older generation too, I'm not too proud to say it. Bert and I are beginning to feel the aches. I see it in the way he walks, and goodness knows I would happily chop my feet off at the ankles the way they give me gyp come the end of a long day. My dream is for Stella and Danny to take over from us here at the House. Then Bert and me could settle in a little cottage just above the river — I have my eye on a pretty one belongs to James Bertram — and have our family near by.

Well, so I thought — more fool me — when Danny started to come to church of a Sunday, not just the Christmas visit and Easter if we were lucky. The two of them arrived at the kitchen door, neat as pins in their Sunday clothes and smiling at our surprise. They are a handsome pair when they put their mind to it, Danny so slim and blue-eyed. He could charm the guests, no trouble, while he brought up the bags and cases from the boat. 'Are you free to take us down to Jerusalem in the motor-canoe?' asks Danny, more civil than I ever heard him since his wedding day.

'Indeed we are,' say I, a tear in my eye for the pleasure of seeing them, 'and you shall come back here for a good Sunday roast after. The mutton is already in the oven for the guests and there will be plenty for the staff.'

Then the four of us walked down to the river, as smart as the guests themselves, and took our places in the motor-waka along with the Mrs Feathers, who were down for Mass. Bert started the motor with a single pull — there is none to match Bert with the new motor. Stella had her eye on someone on the bank, I noticed, and gave him a wave and a shout that rocked the boat and earned her a stern look from Bert. That quiet fellow Douglas McPhee, I fancied; she must know him from upriver. He is turning into a good river man, despite his wretched father.

That first Sunday Danny sat behind me in the waka and leaned forward to shout over the racket of the motor, asking about the near-drowned girl Bridget McPhee, how she was doing, was her mind any clearer, were the Sisters taking good care and so on. I thought it civil of him to ask and showed a proper conscience, since he contributed in some way to her fall. I have always considered Danny a flighty lad, not a patch on our Stell for cleverness. I suspect he cannot read or write from something he said once, though Stella keeps mum on that front. She is a loyal wife. Well, he kept the questions up the full six miles down to the landing at Jerusalem, his handsome face showing concern, and I thought the better of him for it at the time.

That was the first visit. Two weeks later another, and then once he came on his own in the middle of the week. Knock on the kitchen door, something about collecting a harness or a cart-wheel, which made no sense since the *Wairua* could deliver to Maraekowhai and save him the trip. Was Bridie around? he asked. Had I seen her? He must have gone down to the Sisters because he said she wasn't to be found at Jerusalem.

'Danny,' I said, 'she was here this morning but gone now. It is good of you to take an interest, but she is safe enough. We all keep an eye out for her.'

'And is she eating properly? Does she seem happy?'

'She is,' I said, that bit tart with him now, 'and she does, to the extent a mindless waif can be happy. To be frank, Danny, I have not heard you take such a care for your wife. Is she eating well and is she happy?'

That brought him up short. He gave me a sort of hangdog smile that some would find charming.

'You are right,' said he, 'but I can't stop worrying about the girl — she is so lost and alone.'

The silly chump. His mind still stuck in the same rut.

I only saw him and Bridie together the once. It was down at Jerusalem — early February it would have been. A beautiful still day, the new church standing in its fresh white paint on the hill, its bell calling out across the river, the windows of the convent shining in the sun. Father Soulas himself was there to take Mass, standing at the church door in his Sunday robes and the Sisters bringing the children across from their building, all in line — smallest in front and the older ones behind — neatly dressed and meek as little lambs. Bridie among them for once, walking hand in hand with Sister Agatha and smiling at all the world in general, no one in particular, as is her way, poor lamb.

Mass was a joy and a privilege as usual. We are lucky to have Father Soulas. The Mrs Feathers think he should be sainted, which might be going too far, but he is a great man. I would put Mother Aubert ahead as far as sainthood goes, but as Lily Feathers pointed out, she has gone to Wellington for one thing, and for another she is too worldly for a nun, selling her remedies to all and sundry and then taking that big company down there to court for watering her medicines. Well, I said to Lily, she may be a great one to stir things up, and we need a stirrer or two among the saints these days, with all the changes going on. Take the railways, I said. My Bert says the gangs working on the tracks up Ohakune and Raurimu way would curl your hair the things they get up to. Lily had no reply to *that*.

Well, we came out into the sunshine, all blessed from a good Mass. Danny walked straight out of the church, took Bridie's hand and away he went with her, up the hill towards the cherry orchard, not a word to Father at the door or the Sisters. Stella was busy chatting to friends but I noticed. Danny sat the girl on the grass under a tree, still holding her hand, and seemed to be talking to her. In full view he was, stroking her hair, and talking — gentle enough from where I stood, but not proper for a man. Not when the woman concerned is no relation at all. And him known for a cheeky way with the ladies — before he was married, I should say. He has been on his best behaviour since he married our Stell. And thankfully lives upriver, away from temptation.

Stella finally noticed that people were staring. She gathered some of the Sisters' homeless children and they all ran up the hill with baskets to collect cherries. Some of us followed, for the Jerusalem cherries are a treat and the Sisters will allow anyone to pick for a small donation to their work. I make a cherry pie for the guests at Pipiriki House, which is greatly praised. Those dear children up in the cherry trees like a flock of big white birds, shaking down the bunches of red cherries, is a sight to bring tears to your eyes. Up rode Sister Agatha, side-saddle on horseback, her habit draped down over the horse's flank and a big basket on each arm. Most of the Sisters can ride — I don't know how they manage in all that swelter of clothes. Stella, up a tree, too much ankle showing, called to Danny to join in but he might have been deaf the notice he took. He sat in the middle of all this activity, stroking poor Bridie's hair as if she were a stray animal, and feeding ripe cherries into her mouth, cupping his hand for her to spit the pips.

In the end he came down with the cherry pickers. But even with his own wife at his side he still held Bridie's hand, smiling like he was proud of her, ready to show her off. It was a strange thing to see; I didn't know how to take it. When I walked over to join him he was having a word to Sister Agatha, very earnest, questioning her.

'Surely,' he was saying, 'some of Mother Aubert's medicines can do some good?'

Sister Agatha was not having her care questioned. She is not one to be crossed. 'We have tried all cures,' she said firmly, 'long ago. We must accept God's will. She will remain a child in her mind, even though' (and here she looked most sternly at him) 'she has the body of a woman.'

All the while poor Bridie stood there, her copper hair shining, lips stained red with cherry juice and her smock clean for once, smiling and standing close to Danny. It is a worry how she will stand close. She has no idea. Stella fidgeting in her Sunday dress — you could see how she wanted to pull Danny away. In the end I took Bridie's hand and walked away smartly, giving Stell the nod to come too. When I turned to look back I thought I saw Danny give the Sister something. Money it looked like. I had a quiet word to him about that later, back at Pipiriki.

'Did I see you give money to the Sister?'

He nodded. Back to his old silent self now Bridie was not about.

'Danny,' I said, 'your own wife could do with a treat if you are looking to spend what little you have.' I was that angry to think of him wasting good money on Bridie, who needs nothing but a bite now and then and a kind word, while my Stella is still lacking a proper stove to cook on.

He nodded again. Walked away down to the river without a word. Likely nothing I said sank in. Goodness knows what has got into the man.

The **Wairua** *and the Houseboat*

Screw Steamer *Wairua*

Name meaning:	Spirit
Type:	Screw steamer (later motor vessel)
Built:	1904 Yarrow & Co. Poplar, England, assembled at Hatrick's Foundry, Wanganui
Propulsion:	1 screw in tunnel
Length:	65 feet; beam: 8 feet; depth: 3 feet 6 inches (as built)
Passengers:	87
Usual passage:	Pipiriki to Houseboat
Machinery:	1 Steam/Simpson, Strickland & Co. 66 IHP

Wanganui Riverboat Museum

DOUGLAS MCPHEE HEARS about his sister's condition from a stranger. He is shovelling coal into the *Wairua*'s temperamental fire-box when he overhears two women chatting as they lean over the side-rail.

'. . . a scandal,' he hears. 'Strutting about in her state for all the world to see. That poor, simple woman should be locked up.'

'So she should. I said as much to the housekeeper at Pipiriki and she nodded and said the matter was in hand.'

'In hand! I can't see what is in hand if a simpleton is permitted to wander alone in these parts, let alone get herself with child.

I feel we should report it to the authorities when we reach civilisation.'

The women move out of earshot. Douglas frowns and shovels on. The next rapid is approaching and with the river low it will be a tough haul up to the Houseboat.

Bridie with child! Douglas saw her just yesterday at Pipiriki. He had been pleased to see that she had put on a little fat. That she might be having a child did not occur to him. Who on earth would take advantage of a simple girl? Douglas is used, by now, to her wandering ways, and like most at Pipiriki does what he can to make her comfortable. Last night he took her by the hand and led her to his tiny room in the crew's quarters. He shared his meal with her and smiled — a little uncomfortably, to tell the truth — when she snuggled up close to him and kissed his cheek. Sometimes she acts like a lover with her stroking and clinging. But that is her simple way. She was happy enough to sleep on his bunk while he took the floor. By morning she was gone.

The Sisters do not approve. Sister Carmel in particular.

'Douglas,' she said last month, when he walked down to Jerusalem on his day off, 'she is not here. Not *anywhere*. She is a bad girl to run away from our love. Speak to your father, please.' When Sister Carmel is upset her French accent becomes more pronounced and her eyes blacker than usual. Her rolled 'r' growls like a dog. 'We cannot be r-r-responsible!'

Douglas had nodded and walked away, back towards Pipiriki. He doubted there would be any conversation with his father over Bridie or anything else. Angus McPhee had visited Jerusalem only once, as far as Douglas knew. He gave the Sisters a small donation and a free hand with his daughter. Somehow his Presbyterian hatred of the Catholics didn't prevent him from depositing poor lost Bridget at the Sisters' doorstep.

Surely, he thinks now, as he shovels coal, banging the door

157

closed after he hurls the black stuff in, surely no one would take advantage of her. Douglas has heard the term — *taking advantage* — has read of it with interest in the novels he borrows from the guests' library at Pipiriki House, but has no clear idea of what it entails. He is inclined to disbelieve the gossip he has overheard.

THE TRIP UP is uneventful, if arduous. When the river is low the difficult rapids are swift and troublesome but at least the wire rope lying on the riverbed is easily fished up and attached to the winch. Douglas loves the nuggety *Wairua* and feels a family pride when it manages to churn and haul its way up to the Houseboat on time; he takes it as a personal compliment when a farmer waiting on his landing expresses thanks for a sack of flour or a piece of equipment safely delivered. For three months he has been fireman and for a spell before that general hand at Hatrick's foundry down at the port. Mr Billy Coates, foreman at the foundry, had been short a hand and gave him work, but it was upriver that drew Douglas. As soon as the position of stoker came up he applied.

Mr Hatrick had looked him over. 'One of Angus McPhee's?'

Douglas had nodded briefly, hoping he seemed sufficiently off-hand.

'Were you on board when the accident . . . ?' Mr Hatrick had eyed him fiercely.

'Aye.' Douglas nodded again, 'But I am not with my father any more. I would like to train as riverboat engineer.'

'Would you indeed? And what does your father have to say to that?'

Douglas had dared to look the great man in the eye. 'My father is displeased, sir, but I am my own man now.'

Mr Hatrick had seemed amused at the chance to do something

that might augment Angus McPhee's displeasure. 'We'll try you in the foundry. Mr Coates will test whether you have aptitude for the engineering and then we will see.'

And Douglas has not regretted one grinding, dirty, blistering minute of the past three months. Especially the nights he spends at Maraekowhai.

STELLA IS THERE, leaning over the top deck-rail of the Houseboat as they drift in to the landing. To Douglas she stands out from the crowd of tourists, who point and clap as the *Wairua* comes alongside. Stella wears the Hatrick uniform — sailor dress and apron, black cap trimmed with white lace. The smile on her pretty dark face and the little wave could be for him, he's almost sure of it. He lifts a grimy hand in reply. Later, if he's lucky, he might see her up at the crew's quarters. But for now she will be busy. Douglas takes the long-handled rake and shoves the red-hot coals to the back of the fire-box, where they will burn themselves out. He tops up the two coal bunkers, raking the fuel to be ready at hand for the downriver trip in the morning. He rubs an oily rag over the handles and valves and checks the water level in the boiler. Then it's a good sluice with a bucket of river-water before he goes up into the galley for a blessed mug of hot sweet tea.

Through the servery hatch he can see Stella moving up and down the two long tables with dishes of meat and vegetables. He knows she's married but because he has never set eyes on the husband, Douglas finds it easy to ignore that fact. He dreams of a life with the pretty maid whose songs excite him in a way that is hard to bear. He would die for her, he's quite sure of that. He tries to catch her eye through the servery.

The dining saloon is full, which means there will be forty

tourists travelling downriver, along with the wool bales and extra waysiders picked up en route. Summer brings good business for Mr Hatrick. It is good for Douglas, too, as Stella will stay the night, until the tourists have had their breakfast and their rooms are cleaned. He smiles and waves when she glances his way. She winked! He's sure of it. He stumbles out onto the bank and up into the bushes to hide — and then relieve — the wonderful swelling in his crotch.

These summer evenings daylight lingers well into the evening. While some tourists prefer to talk in the smoking room or social hall, others go ashore and wander through the bush tracks or sit on the bank in the gardens the captain and his wife have planted. Douglas has brought his new banjo with him; he wants to impress Stella. He sits outside his hut trying to pick out a Highland song his mother used to sing before she died. He can get the first line but then is stuck. As he works away, repeating the few notes over and over, he is suddenly aware that a man is standing near, listening. Douglas judges him to be a local by his clothes, which are worn and stained with sweat. He nods to Douglas, who stops playing, shy to be overheard when he is just learning.

'Don't give up on me,' says the man, smiling. 'I was listening. Scottish, is it?'

'Aye,' says Douglas. 'All I know yet.' Even with encouragement he will not play on. The man sits beside him.

'I used to play one of those but have sold my instrument. All I have now is . . .' The man pulls from his pocket a beautifully carved pipe, made from the bone of some animal. He offers it. The light is fading now and the stars beginning to show. Douglas can just make out Maori designs mixed with other shapes he doesn't recognise. He hands the precious thing back.

'Did you make it?'

'No. My wife's . . . brother.'

Douglas smiles shyly at the man. He is not like the chattering tourists or the boisterous river men, but gentle in a way that puts Douglas at ease. 'Are you a farmer around here?' he asks.

The man smiles. 'You guessed well. I am down with my wool bales.' He frowns. 'I hope the steamer can fit them aboard, for I am dead in need of the money. That is a great crowd of travellers to fit aboard.'

'I expect there will be room for goods on the foredeck. You are lucky to be at the start of the trip. There are bales waiting at two other landings downriver.'

'You are a riverboat man then?'

'Fireman,' says Douglas proudly.

The farmer looks at him more closely then, leaning forward in the dark. His face is strained and tired. 'Ah,' he says. 'I used to work on the river. Snagging.'

Douglas whistles. 'That's a hard life, they say. You must be stronger than you look.'

The farmer laughs. 'Thanks for the compliment, lad. What do they call you?'

'Douglas. Douglas McPhee.' He offers his hand.

The man in the shadows stands suddenly without taking the offered hand. 'McPhee? Are you one of Angus McPhee's?'

Douglas stands too, taken aback by this sudden change of manner. 'Yes, sir,' he says, 'but . . . not . . .' He cannot think what to say. 'I am a river man, not a sawmiller,' he says at last.

The farmer sighs. 'Yes. Yes. Well.' He picks up his old coat, shakes it and drapes it over one broad shoulder. 'I must be on my way,' he says. 'Back to the farm.'

He walks away without another word, up the bank and into the black edge of the bush.

'What did I do wrong?' Douglas says aloud, dismayed to see

his new friend disappear so suddenly. He picks up his instrument again but has lost heart. His fingers slow, then lie still on the strings. He stares into the dark, waiting for Stella to finish her work. From the crew's hut above, laughter and argument break the peace of the night, but Douglas is not of a mind to join them.

There is a sudden movement beside him and Douglas jumps as the farmer sits easily, settles his back against a tree trunk as if nothing has happened.

'I'm back,' he says, offering his hand now. 'Danny. Most call me Dannyboy.'

Now it is Douglas's turn for shock. Stella's husband!

'I did poorly,' says Danny, smiling, 'to walk out on you so sudden.'

Douglas breathes more easily. 'Mr O'Dowd?' he says, feeling for the right words. 'I do no harm to your wife. We are friends is all.'

Danny frowns. His mind seems to be elsewhere. 'What harm would you do? You have met her, then?'

'Does she not mention me?'

'She sometimes tells about the doings down here.' Danny gestures down towards the Houseboat. 'But I never heard her mention a Douglas McPhee.'

Douglas is excited by this piece of news. She is hiding her feelings from her husband! He wants to ask about her — what she is like at home, at the farm — but can't find the words.

Finally it is Danny who speaks. 'Your name,' he says, 'shocked me. It came too sudden. It was rude to walk away.' He smiles and Douglas recognises the charm. He had imagined someone older, inarticulate and dull.

'Mr O'Dowd . . .'

'I'm Danny to my friends.'

162

'Mr . . . Danny. My sister. It was an accident. The blow of the raft did not cause her to fall.'

Danny smiles. 'I know that, lad. Stella told me. No doubt she had it from you. I was right glad to hear it.' After another silence he adds, 'You have a very pretty sister.'

Douglas wants to reply, 'And you have a pretty wife,' but all he says is, 'Bridget? Yes, she was pretty.'

'Still is, to my mind. What was she like before . . .'

To begin with, Douglas is happy to speak of his sister. 'She was so different from now. I suppose some would call her noisy. She was full of life, jumping here and there, shouting to look at this, look at that. Never still. Friends with everyone . . .' He stops speaking, remembering the overheard words on the boat.

'Go on.'

But Douglas finds he doesn't want to remember the old Bridget any more. Bridget is dead. Bridie is a different person — gossiped about, perhaps behaving shamefully. No longer really his sister. He shakes his head and lets the silence grow between them.

In the dark Danny stirs, goes to speak, and then coughs as if to silence the thought. He picks up Douglas's banjo and picks at it idly. The single notes sound sweetly — a tune familiar to Douglas but one he can't place. The discovery that Danny is a good musician grates. Danny stops mid-phrase with a strummed chord and lays the banjo down again. Douglas, lost in his own thoughts, stares out at the darkening river.

'There is another side to that day . . .' says Danny at last. 'The day your sister . . .' The words tail off and silence settles again between them. From the Houseboat comes a splash. Perhaps Stella is throwing scraps overboard. Lights flicker now in the rows of cabin windows on the lower deck. Well-shod feet clip along the decks as the tourists go back and forth from the bathrooms in the stern. A bright half moon rises above the bush on the opposite bank, sending a shimmering pathway across the water to link the busy Houseboat with the wilderness all around.

Danny's hands are clasped between his knees. Moonlight turns his narrow face into a landscape of bright planes and dark shadows. He speaks as if to himself, looking down at his hands, which twist and knot with a life of their own as he tells his story.

'Stella's brother Pita was with me that day. He was drunk and goading me. I should have kept my anger inside but all the terror of that crash, and then seeing the girl — your sister — dead, as I thought . . .' Danny growls like an angry dog. 'My head filled with rage . . . I hit him hard enough to hear bones crack and sent him into the river senseless. In my rage I left him there and went to the girl — your sister.' He groans. 'Ah, sweet Jesus, I killed Stella's brother — and my friend. I have killed a man I knew well. It turns like a knife in me every day since . . . It's the dead man's smashed face I see, and drowned Pita whispering in my ear that I must be punished for my sin.' Danny shifts restlessly. 'They all think him drowned. A simple drowned man, easy to mourn, no questions asked.'

Douglas clears his throat and Danny turns suddenly as if surprised so find him there.

'Does Stella blame you?' asks Douglas. He hopes to hear of a rift.

Danny hangs his head. 'I cannot tell her. The words dry in my throat.'

'But why would you tell me, then?'

Danny's voice is glum. 'Yes. Why? Sorry, lad — it just came out, like. Why would I put that burden on you and not on my own wife?' He looks down to the dark and shining water as if he would find an answer. 'It's a strange thing. Perhaps because you are her brother. Bridie's brother. I think of her too, every day. She brings a sweetness in all this sour mess. Why would that be, do you think? Your sister holds my heart in her soft hands. Sweet Bridie . . .'

Douglas is shocked to hear a grown man talk like this. He looks at the dark shape of him — a man he has only just met who has told him an uncomfortable secret. It is a puzzle what to do. 'Stella says you have been silent around the farm since the accident.'

'Stella told you this?' Danny is sharp now, his shadowy eyes boring at him.

Douglas feels himself blush and is glad of the darkness. In truth, her remark was made to Mrs White, a conversation that Douglas overheard.

He fiddles with his banjo. 'Perhaps she needed someone to talk to,' he says, defiant in the face of Danny's scrutiny, 'if you do not tell her truths she should hear.'

'Cheeky pup! What would you know?' Danny shoots out a hand suddenly and Douglas flinches. But Danny is only grabbing a branch, hauling himself to his feet. He picks up his coat and is gone, for the second time, into the night, not waiting for a word with his wife, who is stepping quietly up the bank, leaving the tourists on board to sleep.

Douglas smiles in the dark. Her husband is rude, and a liar. Also possibly a murderer. He suspected as much.

Ruvey Morrow

What to do at
❧ PIPIRIKI ❧

Walk or **boat** to the wonderful Mineral Hot Spring 'Wairoa' (living waters) two miles above Pipiriki, and **drink** from this health giving fountain. **See** Dr. Wolhmann, Government Balneologist's report on this water. **Visit** the Houseboat. Splendid Mineral **Bath** at Pipiriki. Thermal Springs. Also – **FISHING, SHOOTING, CANOEING**

A. Hatrick & Co. timetable brochure, 1908

WHEN BERT'S FATHER asked did we want a tangi for Pita up at his marae, neither of us had the stomach for it. I had no feeling he was dead; nor did Bert. He said if Pita were drowned and his body stuck under some rock or branches, surely the great flood three days later would have dislodged it. Drowned bodies have a way of appearing with the bloat anyway. Sooner or later, he said, the body would come past and someone would notice. Then there was the matter of the logs and what Bert thought he saw. His eyes are a touch milky these days and he must ask me to read the pigeon post — he hates that — but on the water he has a feeling for what is natural and what not, even if it is no more than blurry shapes. I would trust him to recognise a head from a branch. But was it a dead head, caught against the log, or someone stealing the logs and trying to sneak past Pipiriki unnoticed, or even Pita hiding? That boy could be up to no good as often as not.

They say a mother knows these things, but would I know about Pita? He goes away for months sometimes and I have no feeling is he happy or in trouble or hurt. I have to say that neither of my two children are as close as I would like. They have their troubles and their busy lives and I have mine and not much time for chit-chat in between. I see Stella from time to time. She will come down on the boat when the captain gives her a free passage and we two have a good gossip about life upriver and what everyone on the Houseboat is up to, how the farm is doing — usually poorly, though she is loyal to Danny, as is right and proper.

The strange thing is that the logs never came to light. Now a body might go missing, but three big totaras? Nothing could hide them. Even in the big flood surely they would fetch up above high-flood mark and we would hear. Bert says if they arrived on some farmer's paddock he would likely get them sawn for a shed or house or sell them himself and ask no questions. I still say we would hear. There are not many secrets don't come upriver or down with the deckhands or the captains. The post office here is not the only way news gets to Pipiriki.

So we said thanks but taihoa about the tangi and hoped for better news.

SIX MONTHS LATER we were beginning to wonder. Pita loved his river — if not his parents — and would not be away so long unless something bad had happened. I saw Bert throw a bunch of leaves on the water one day. He stood there, downriver of the landing where the big willow leans over. Perhaps he was hiding his fears from me or maybe just being private, but I usually knew where Bert was. From the kitchen door I could just see him standing with the pale new willow leaves weeping down around his shoulders, just a shadow behind that curtain. Very still, he was. I had a feeling he was talking or chanting. Then he raised his arms wide to each side, pointing upriver and down. After a minute or two he turned away and went back to his work down at the landing. Tears were running down my cheeks. I thought then, maybe my boy is drowned; maybe Bert knows.

THAT WOULD BE about the time our Bridie began to show. Oh dearie me, I thought, whatever are we going to do about this? We all loved her by now, and cared for her when we could. Her life was different but not unhappy. But Bridie with a baby was another matter altogether. We treated her like a child herself, for that was her nature now. She learned little things, sometimes a bit of a song. I tried to teach her the use of a spoon but she never was good at it. A cup she could manage. The Sisters taught her to bow her head and say a word before she ate anything, but I doubt she understood why or what she mumbled. She would sit still as a rabbit in church, smiling wide at the candles, looking this way and that at the Sisters and the priest in his fine vestments, and breathing the incense like the rest of us, but nothing of the words went in, any soul could see that.

The thing is, she is *not* a child but a grown young lady. Washed and brushed she would pass as a fine miss with prospects until you came close and saw the way her eyes wandered. Or watched her walk in that loose, dreamy way that is somehow different from a lady with her wits about her. At times she is downright beautiful. But for all that, I doubt any man at Pipiriki or the mission or at the village across the river would take advantage of her. The Sisters have taken her in and you can slide down to the fires of hell if the Sisters or Father Soulas put in a bad word. Anyroad, all us at Pipiriki House and those at the store and the settlers hereby, we all had a soft spot for our little wanderer. She belonged to us.

I knew there'd be trouble, though, when Angus McPhee found out. He was such a righteous man, all matters black or white to him with no space in between for grey — or even a splash of colour, it seemed to me. Did the man even know how to smile? Those Presbyterians are a dour lot; Father Soulas is right about that.

McPhee never heard that Bridie was with child from any a one of us. First I thought it was Hape Chase, the bullocky, got the news to McPhee, but he swore blue he never said a word. No, it was a group on a coach tour, we heard later, who came up on the *Waimarie* and stayed the night at Pipiriki House. It must have been a night when Bridie was around. I would let her in the kitchen for a bowl of soup with bread crumbled in it — she was never good at the chewing — and give her face a good wash if I had a spare minute. My guess is they saw her alone on the road with her belly all out in front, her feet bare and her pretty locks in a tangle. Those smart ladies would not turn a hair if they saw one of the Maori girls in such a state, but a white woman was different in their eyes.

So when the tourist coach brought them up to Pike's Hotel in Raetihi they reported her to the constable there — 'our duty to see the poor simpleton looked after', or some such pious nonsense. Then off they went next day in their coach to see the wonders of the mountains and Lake Taupo and the marvellous geysers at Rotorua, which none of us at Pipiriki have ever seen.

Nor would want to when we have the superior views of our own river every day of the year. Behind them they left a storm ready to break. In the shape of Angus McPhee.

Tim Naylor said later that it was his duty to report the matter to the father. 'When a complaint is laid,' he said, 'it must be followed up. That is the law.' But he said it shamefaced. A constable out on the wild edges, like he was, learns to bend the rules or he would have a riot on his hands.

Which is exactly what we all had once McPhee found out that his daughter — who he had not visited once in six months — was 'defiled', as he put it.

Down he came from Raetihi, his horse all in a lather, his little mouth writhing from that bristle of red beard.

'Why have I not been told?' he shouted, and flung his reins at Bert as if my husband had nothing to do but stand around waiting to serve his needs. 'Where is the man who has taken advantage of my daughter?'

He could not even wait to come inside or to make a civil greeting before he was shouting for all the tourists within earshot to hear him, casting slurs upon the good name of every man and boy in the settlement. Oh, I was mad as a hornet! If only Mr Hatrick had been on hand to cut him down to size.

'Where is she?' he bawled, looking around at the bushes as if she might crawl out.

'With the good Sisters,' said I, hoping it might be the truth, and that the mention of the blessed ladies might calm him. But not a bit of it. Mention of the mission seemed to throw him into an even greater rage.

'I trusted those people!' he shouted. 'That nest of Satan. Those foul Papists have defiled her. An innocent!'

He stood at the foot of the grand steps to the House, one hand on the urn with the potted fern, for all the world as if he were delivering some important oratory. The tourists, just back from their nice summer walk to the falls, stood listening with interest and beginning to gossip.

Proper or not, I had to stop it, so I gave Bert the nod. My good husband took the man by the arm, quite rough, as he would a drunken deckhand who might make a nuisance of himself in front of the guests, and led him away around to the kitchen door before he could protest. You could always count on a moment's peace while McPhee got over his surprise at being handled by a 'native'.

'Now,' said Bert to him, once McPhee was safely inside away from gawkers, 'first, we are mostly good Catholics here so we don't like any talk against our Sisters or the priest.'

Bert was as angry as me, that was plain. When he squares his shoulders and widens his eyes in that warrior way he can cast fear in even McPhee, I was pleased to see.

'You lay any accusations on the mission at Hiruharama,' he growled, 'and there will be no more supplies up to you from here. Any goods for McPhee might stay and rot in Mr Hatrick's shed for all any will care down this way.'

That was clever of Bert, for Angus McPhee does not like to be hit in the pocket. For a moment his face went still as he totted the risk, but his fury got the better even of his greed.

'They must face the consequences of their evil ways,' he cried. 'You are no better if you shelter such depravity!'

Depravity! The Sisters and Father Soulas! The man was beyond rational thought. Later, thinking about that unnatural fury, I wondered if it was the man's own guilt was fuelling his outburst. Maybe people up in Raetihi had heard the news too and were looking askance at a father who would abandon his poor sick daughter to lechers. Perhaps the wretched man's soiled reputation was more hurtful to him than his daughter's plight.

171

That might be closer to the bone.

Anyroad, I could see the man would not be appeased and was set to ride down to the mission with his wild ranting.

'Mr McPhee,' I said — the first words I had uttered aloud, though I had thought of plenty — 'your daughter is a wanderer. The Sisters, bless them, do what they can, but she is often seen hereabouts. And further upriver. Shame on you to think the good souls down at the mission are responsible. Who care for your daughter when you show no shred of interest yourself.'

That stopped the silly fellow. He eyed me sharply. He is not an attractive man to look at, his eyes like little pieces of ice, so pale and small, his freckled skin scaly and dry like a lizard. What two wives have seen in him I cannot imagine — the thought of being close to *that* makes me shudder.

'Well then, what do you know of it?' he demanded, stabbing his finger in my direction as if he would accuse *me*. 'If it is not the mission, then who?'

I was not about to lay blame, though I had my suspicions. There's a fellow in one of the river gangs . . . but I won't go into that. I told McPhee plain that his daughter had not the wit to recognise a lecher from a God-fearing man. That the father of the child could be a tourist, long gone, for all we knew. That Bridie had wandering ways and had been seen upriver as far as the hermit and Charlie Chee's place, and that there was no telling who might be responsible six months on.

Angus McPhee went silent at that. I thought he might have come to his senses and be ready to spare a thought for his daughter's plight. But when I looked at his face I realised different. There was such spite sitting there — and a kind of mad glee that would turn an angel to stone, let alone a poor mortal.

'The Chow did it,' he whispered. 'God in heaven, a Chow has touched my daughter.'

Bert and I exchanged a look. Charlie Chee might have strange ways and a stranger way of speaking, but he is so proper and good-mannered he would never hurt the least fly, let alone our Bridie, who is so fond of him. But before either of us could say a word that man was out the door and on his horse.

'Charlie would never,' I said to Bert.

Bert nodded. But the wretched man had put the thought in our heads and a grain of the dirt stuck, I suppose you could say. Was there more to Bridie's fondness for Charlie Chee? Perhaps the Chows have different ideas about women to us. I didn't want to think bad of Charlie but a little niggle of doubt crept in. That is the curse of men like Angus McPhee. They are worse than chickenpox the way their nasty ideas spread.

THE NEXT THING we know, two days later it would be, there is a notice posted on Hatrick's shed down by Pipiriki landing, and another up at our post office.

Too Little, Too Late!
Changes to the Chinese Restriction Act
Yellow Peril at our doorstep!
Meeting on Saturday 20th February 1908 at Hanson's house,
Pipiriki, 3 p.m.
Do your part to strengthen the arm of the law-makers.

IT WAS SIGNED *Anti Asiatic League*. Clear to see McPhee was behind it. Bert told me there was a notice posted on the *Wairua* for the upriver farmers' information. I thought no one would take notice and the meeting would come to naught, but I was wrong. Meetings are rare up our way and curiosity is a powerful influence. In the end I went too, I am ashamed to say.

TAX CERTIFICATE

**Under Section 7 of 'the Chinese Immigrants Act 1881'
and Section 2 of 'The Chinese Immigrants Act 1896'**

No. 1615.. £100
Date of Issue 16.11.04
Name ....Yee Nam
Born at..Canton
Apparent age.. 27
Former place of residence............................Canton
Arrived by ship ....Moeraki
From ....Sydney

Signed ....
Collector of Customs

A Chinese immigrant's Poll Tax certificate

ONCE A FORTNIGHT in the summer, Charlie Chee comes upriver on the *Wairua* to spend a day in the Houseboat vegetable garden. The Houseboat captain's wife, Mrs White, loves her roses and hydrangeas but leaves the veges to Charlie's expert ministrations. He has dug a patch on the bank above the crew's hut, lined it with ponga logs and levelled the slope so the water will not run off. Stella likes to visit him and watch as he coaxes the red-flowering string beans up dead sticks until they reach almost higher than she can pick them. His potatoes and carrots, cabbages and silverbeet keep the tourists fed all summer.

In a shady corner that Stella imagines would grow nothing, strong-hearted lettuces provide the crunch for the travellers' lunchtime sandwiches. Stella, who loves the crisp, summer taste of lettuce, has tried and failed with them in her own farm garden. Sometimes she will slip a few leaves into her pocket when she is washing vegetables in the Houseboat galley.

On this warm morning, early in the new year, she has cleaned the cabins and is free to walk back to the farm. Despite the worries on the farm and the exhausting work these days — the height of the tourist season — Stella is smiling. For some time after the accident it seemed she would lose her position. Mr Hatrick had sent a note, which Stella never read, but there was no mistaking the grim warning in Mrs White's eye. If any other maid could be found, said Mrs White, Stella would have to go. But the lack of suitable English-speaking applicants and Stella's cheerful, capable nature gradually wore down resistance. Stella stayed on. In this remote backwater the accident has never been of great consequence. Bridie is never up this way to remind them. The *Wairua*'s plates were so dented, even before the accident, that she was overdue for a trip to Hatrick's foundry down at Wanganui.

So Houseboat life continues and Stella still comes to work three days a week. She loves the time when the upriver and downriver steamers have departed with their chattering crowds and belching smoke. Peace spreads like expanding ripples in their wake, as the river settles back into its quiet flow. She can hear the dull roar of the Ohura Falls, and birdsong from the trees across the river. Nearby there is the odd crack of linen as her Mrs White shakes the crumbs from tablecloths over the green water.

Stella sings along with the birds. She is remembering last night, a grand evening. Two of the deckhands on the Taumarunui motor vessel, the *Ongarue*, brought their banjos down with them and entertained them all with the latest songs from the railhead. Young Douglas sat beside her on the riverbank following along on his own instrument, and then called for Stella to sing. She raised a round of applause with an Irish ditty Dannyboy had taught her and that Douglas also knew. If only Danny had stayed. Douglas said he had been down at the landing earlier but was in a mood and had left. Well, that's his loss. Danny is too often in a mood these days.

Stella climbs up to Charlie Chee's vegetable patch, hoping for a carrot or perhaps some lettuce to take home. Charlie straightens as she comes around behind the hut. He smiles widely, bobbing his head with enthusiasm.

'Good day, Stella,' he says carefully, proud to show off the phrases she has taught him. 'How are you today?'

'I'm well, Charlie,' she says, entering the game. 'How are you?'

'In good health too.' He grins and takes a letter from a pocket in his loose smock. 'A letter comes for Charlie,' he says. 'You help me read?' He claps his hands to shake off the clinging dirt. 'I think it about my new wife coming. I have all money saved now. He twenty pound for boat and he ten pound for government poll tax. All my saved.'

'*Her* twenty-pound boat fare and *her* poll tax,' corrects Stella, reaching for the envelope with its official stamp. Charlie has been talking about bringing a wife out from China ever since she has known him. Last year when Prime Minister Ward introduced the language requirement into the act restricting Chinese, Charlie sent some of his saved money back home to pay for an English teacher for the woman his village had chosen to be his wife. Charlie was angry at the time. 'Wife learn English here. Or I speak for her. No need she learn in China. Money wasted,' he had shouted, close to tears. Stella had felt sorry for him after all his hard work. But he had saved up again and finally all was prepared, the boat passage booked and the wife ready to come.

'You open it,' says Stella, seeing that the seal is still unbroken, 'and we'll read it together.'

Charlie holds out his dirt-caked hands. 'No no no. I dirty too much. You read, please.' He points to the wooden bench he has constructed and placed in the shade of a tall tree-fern. They both move into the cool shade. It is a beautiful spot, carefully chosen. Beyond the green rows of vegetables, Mrs White's flower gardens provide an exotic splash of colour. Below them the broad shape of the Houseboat, partly obscured by bush, sits on the glinting water. The small figure of the caretaker is fiddling with mooring ropes. On the other side of the river, smoke rises from whares that are otherwise hidden among trees. A child's shout carries across the water. Stella could watch it all day.

'The letter, please.' Charlie Chee taps the envelope in her hands. He removes his pointed straw hat as if he has entered a formal room. His dark, almond-shaped eyes watch every movement of her fingers as she unfolds the paper.

'Yes,' she says, smiling, 'it is from the government.'

Charlie bobs his head up and down, grinning. 'Read, read!'

'"To Hong Lip Yee, Chinese National,"' she reads. And stops to look at him. 'Have they sent to the wrong man?'

'No no no. Is me.'

'Your name is Hong?'

'My father name Hong. My self name Lip Yee. My brother name Hong Lip Sun.'

'So why do we call you Charlie Chee?'

Charlie frowns. 'One man call me that. Then every man.' He smiles at her. 'Lip Yee not hard to say? I learn English, you learn Lip Yee?'

Stella laughs. 'Lip Yee is easy. What do they call your brother up in Raetihi?'

'Sonny boy. He shop say Hong Lip Sun Groceries, but they call he Sonny boy. Make Lip Sun angry very much.'

'Oh dear. Well, Lip Yee, shall we read?'

'Yes, please read.'

'"In the matter of your immigration application for a Chinese national wife. It would seem that you are unaware of changes made some years back to the Immigration Act."' Stella stops reading aloud. Looks quickly up at Lip Yee. He is watching her face intently, has not understood a word, she thinks, but has sensed something in her voice. She reads on silently but cannot hold back a sharp intake of breath.

'Oh, Charlie!' she says. 'Oh, Lip Yee. This is bad, bad news.'

Lip Yee looks down at his earthy hands. 'Tell, please. Not understand.'

There is no way Stella can soften the terrible news. 'They have changed the rules for Chinese coming here. You must now pay one hundred pounds poll tax.'

Lip Yee stands. 'Not ten pounds?'

'Not ten.' Stella has not the heart to show him with her fingers. 'One hundred.'

Stella is outraged. Danny's uncle came out from Ireland the previous year and was not taxed. Her mother's family came out from England with no fee placed on their heads. Somebody in the government must hate the Chinese.

Lip Yee shouts at her, 'Brother pay ten pound for he wife! Brother friend pay ten pound!' He throws his hat to the ground. 'Why one hundred?'

Stella reads the paper again. 'Oh, Lip Yee. It has been one hundred pounds for years. No one told you. She must have one hundred words of English and one hundred pounds' tax.'

Lip Yee picks up his hat, turns away from her. 'Go, please,' he says. 'Go.'

Stella lays the letter on the bench. She speaks to his back. 'Perhaps your brother can help?'

'Aieee!' His cry startles birds from the trees. 'Not know where Lip Sun go. Maybe he go home. Not know anyone man here!' And then, quieter, 'Go, please.'

He will not turn around. Stella thinks he may be crying. There's nothing she can think to say. As she walks away down the slope she hears a shout of pure rage and looks back. He is grabbing handfuls of vegetables and soil, flinging them towards the river, his long pigtail flying from side to side, his screaming mouth a shocking slash in a face usually so calm.

Stella dodges a flying carrot. She wants to pick it up, take it home, but the thought seems disloyal somehow, in the face of such anguish. She leaves it to wither in the sun.

BACK HOME, STELLA finds she cannot interest Danny in Lip Yee's plight.

'Oh, Stell,' he says roughly, 'let the Chinese look after themselves. We have enough worries of our own.'

He stands at the gate, hatless in the hot sun, fiddling with a loose wire. He looks so forlorn. Stella takes his hand, pulls him down towards the river.

'Come on, sweetheart, it may never happen.'

'What may not?'

She laughs at his serious face. 'Whatever you fear. Where has my happy Dannyboy disappeared to? Eh?'

Danny sighs, shrugs.

But Stella doesn't wait for an answer. She slaps his arm. 'Race you to the water!'

Danny can't resist and with a whoop he sets off after her. Stella's flour-bag bonnet flies away and her dark hair streams

179

out. Her bare feet fly down the bank but his slapping boots are close behind. They arrive at the river together. With one expert shove Stella pushes him in, clothes and all. Laughing on the bank, she strips off her skirt and blouse, dances there naked and provocative before plunging in on top of him.

'Hey! Hey!' Danny splutters, but he is laughing too now. 'Wait till I catch you!'

Stella swims across to the big rock on the opposite bank, her body slippery as quicksilver in the dark water of the little river-hole. Lip Yee's anguish, the blistering dusty tramp up the track are washed downstream. She hangs on the rock, half in, half out of the cool river.

'Heaven! Oh, Danny this is heaven.'

He pulls her down off the rock, kisses her sweet wet mouth. They both laugh as he struggles to strip off his wet clothes. The wretched trouser buttons are too stiff to manage underwater. Finally she draws them down as he floats out, clinging to an overhanging branch. She flings the stubborn things up onto the bank. There, with the sun on their heads, the cool water flowing past them, they make love. Danny's toes curl into the gravel of the riverbed; Stella wraps her legs around his waist, lets her head fall onto his shoulder. Their twin shouts, as they come — amazingly, at the same moment — are echoed by a dog's bark. Finn, alerted by the commotion, is flying across the paddock, ready to protect them. Danny and Stella, oblivious, lie together in the cool water.

LATER, WHILE STELLA is milking Freda the house cow in the back paddock, she feels Danny's hand, gentle on her shoulder. She bobs her head without breaking the rhythm.

He doesn't speak; winds his fingers into the hair above her

180

ears, resting them there for a moment before he walks away over to the shed, trailing the horse's harness.

Stella smiles into Freda's flank. She draws the last drops from the wrinkled old teats, washes them in her bowl of clean rainwater, and sends the placid cow off with a slap to her rump. In the shed she dips a little of the warm creamy stuff for the cat, who has followed her in, then sets the lidded pail in a cool corner for the cream to rise.

Danny is rubbing mutton fat into the worn harness leather. He nods over at her and smiles, blows a kiss, his shock of wiry hair unruly after the swim. He is so beautiful. Stella skips her way back to the house, singing a clear, high song of her own design. Tonight she will make a pie; she'll set it on the fire in the lidded tin oven while they eat their mutton. Please, God, Danny will stay sweet.

As the pie cooks, and they drink their mugs of tea in the cool shadow of the verandah, Stella says, 'You were down at the landing yesterday?'

'Yes.'

'Why didn't you stay? There was singing.'

'I was in a hurry. Work to do back home.'

'At night? What work?'

'Farm work. Same as usual.'

'Douglas says you talked with him.'

Danny sets down his mug. 'Yes, I did.'

Stella tries to keep her voice light. 'You had time for that boy.'

'You were busy, Stell. Then it was dark and I had to get back.'

The rich smell of apple pie steals out through the open door, but the air between them has chilled.

'Danny, love, what is it?' says Stella. 'You are avoiding me. That's what it feels like.'

'What else did that boy say?'

'Why are you so interested? Because he is your precious Bridie's brother?'

'Oh, Jesus!' Danny stands suddenly; jumps down off the porch and strides off into the dark.

Stella could bite her tongue out. She goes into the house to see to the pie. It is perfect, golden crust, tender steam of cooking apples curling up through the diamond cuts she has made. She wills Danny to come back.

He does, the smell too rich to ignore.

'I'm sorry,' she says as she spoons Freda's thick cream onto their plates. They eat the fragrant marvel, sitting together at the table. 'But I worry about you,' she says. 'Are you unhappy with me over something?'

He shakes his head, mouth full of pie.

'With something else?'

Danny swallows. Winks and grins crookedly. 'Stella O'Dowd, that pie is a bloody miracle. I have fallen in love with you all over again.'

But he won't answer her question.

Samuel Blencoe

SHE GOT HEAVY with the babby, our Bridie, so was not up our neck of the river so often. I reckon the Sisters kept ahold of her more. But on a bright summer day she might come. And so she did that time. There she were sitting on my bank, feet cooling in the dark water. A pretty sight in the sunlight, that copper hair shining and her white smock clean washed. She'd been with the Sisters all right.

I went down to sit beside her and she give me that big wide smile. I do love that smile of hers — no cloud in it whatsoever. Some might say it showed an empty mind. I say Bridie's smile bestowed more blessing on them that received it than the Pope himself could manage in a year.

We sat there in that peace, the river smooth as glass, no soul upriver nor down. I made her a bite and we ate it together. I reckon she liked it with Charlie and me for the way we would let her be. The Sisters and them at Pipiriki would fuss at her to do this and that. Tidy herself maybe, or sit like a lady. That's how I reckoned. Otherwise why did she bother to make this walk all the long track up? Another way of looking is that she maybe liked to put one foot after another. Some need in her. Even that morning, her feet cooling in the river were moving back and forth, back and forth — nothing frantic about it, just back and forth, hardly stirring the green water.

But she were restless that day, poor soul, I could see the babby kick under her smock, something I never seen before. I put my hand on it and there it went. Some little tyke inside, all right. Bridie smiled and shifted a bit, then up she stood and off away upriver, as I knew she would. She would come back after seeing Charlie Chee. Like as not she would stay a day or two up his way, pull out a weed for him, then come back down. You had to trust the Sisters to put the brake on her when the babby was near to coming. I doubt Charlie nor I could help in that direction.

This time she did not stay any night with Charlie Chee but was soon back, lolloping along, first time I ever seen her run. Her sweet face all in a fright. She took my hand then and pulled, sounds coming out her mouth — not words, but any fool could tell what she wanted. So I come with her. Red and panting she were, but would not slow down or let this old feller favour his stiff joints. Something were up, that was clear.

Well, so it was. We come to Charlie's place, as neat as a pin like usual, every row of carrot and potato in order and the chooks pecking at nothing much in front of his hut. Bridie pulled me round behind Charlie's shed. Still I saw nothing till she pointed up. Jesus, Mary and Joseph, there he was.

Charlie Chee had gone and hanged himself. The bugger. His body hung high off a branch of the big beech, brown bush-flies zooming in and around him. His pointy straw hat hooked to a branch up there — trust Charlie to put it away neatly before he done the deed. His body so small and thin and that blessed pigtail hanging straight down his back.

Why did he have to do it so high? No way I could get up there, cut him down. Dear God. And Bridie standing there, holding her tummy and rocking, rocking, turning her face away from that horrible sight. Back and forth she shifted, one foot to the other and her eyes closed. Moaning sounds coming out of her like a young piglet looking for the sow.

What was Charlie Chee thinking of? With his wife soon coming out and his business doing well? And now giving poor Bridie the fright of her life. Nothing I could think to do to get the bugger down. I was right wild with him except he were dead.

Well, I took Bridie into his hut and sat her down. Pulled a carrot and give it to her. That seemed to calm the poor soul. Then I give the chooks a handful of corn like I do sometime when Charlie is away, and put an egg or two in my pocket. My hands trembling so I near dropped them. I seen hanged men before, plenty of them on Norfolk, but then you might envy the dead, that they were out of it for good. I never expected any hanging upriver here. I had to sit a while with Bridie and eat a carrot myself to stop the trembling.

Bridie seemed to forget about Charlie Chee after a bit. She went out and pulled a weed. Brought me a tomato and ate one herself. So then we left. Left Charlie hanging high off the beech like a dark banner, never stirring in the still afternoon. We went downriver again to where the river Maori were camped. I told them. They come up to see him but would not touch the body for some fear they had. Tapu, they said. Something to do with the tree he were on, or the colour of his skin, so there he hung inside his curtain of flies.

Bridie and me stayed in my hut. She's used to stopping here. No way I could shift her, nor did I care to. Poor soul was tired out. The both of us. She sat on my log and I cooked us the eggs with a potato or two from my own scruffy patch. We ate. I talked to her the while, as I do when she needs calming. Only person I find ease to talk with is Bridie. Her and the river. Neither the one of them will come back at me. Once I got fifty lashes for some word came out my mouth — I never learned what wrong word it was. Some warder in a foul mood. Back there you learned to distrust words. But here, some days, I might talk all morning to the river as she flows on past. The words drift away, no sense to them maybe, but some kind of ease unto myself.

I told Bridie some nonsense about Charlie and his Chow heaven and whatall. Did any words make sense inside that pretty head? I never seen any sign of it.

The Anti-Asiatic Meeting, Pipiriki

The Chinese were a race of people that should be kept out of a civilised community like the Dominion. They were the most immoral race under the canopy of heaven . . . What the League wanted was an increase of the poll tax to £500, also an amendment to the Factories Act to prevent Asiatics competing unfairly with Europeans . . . He concluded his address by expressing his admiration 'for those people of Ohakune who had consistently refused to let shops to Chows.'

Extract from a report in Waimarino County Call, *January 1908, of an address on the 'Yellow Peril' by Mr John Cameron, secretary of the New Zealand Anti-Asiatic League*

DOUGLAS IS SURPRISED at the number of people crammed into Hanson's big front parlour. He had expected a handful. The sashes on the bay window have been raised so that men on the verandah can lean their elbows on the sill and hear the speeches within. Captain Jamie Jamieson is there, and Bert Morrow, showing interest but not willing to make the commitment of a seat inside. Stella and Danny have come down on the steamer, not to support the meeting's purpose but to fight it. At least that is Stella's purpose. She has been on fire with indignation since her encounter with poor Charlie Chee.

Douglas watches as Stella and Danny approach the house. He sees her turn to point out something to Danny; sees him move away quickly in another direction; hears her angry shout. He smiles. Danny was ready enough to make the trip downriver, but as soon as they reached Pipiriki he is sniffing around, no interest at all in the meeting. Douglas is sure Danny must be interested in another woman, the wretch. Perhaps he is planning to leave Stella this very night. A thrilling thought.

'Stay out here with me,' Douglas whispers to Stella when someone shouts that there is room for the ladies inside. Stella looks at him, frowning. On the trip down she argued with Douglas and others aboard, fiery in her indignation. Douglas, who has been brought up to hate and fear the Chinese, argued against Stella's strange attitude. Surely she could see that if the way is made easy for the heathen Chinese they will swamp the country and make life even harder for the white farmers?

'Have you met Charlie?' she countered. 'Have you talked with any of them?'

Stella makes every issue personal; it means that arguing an abstract issue becomes difficult. Douglas prefers to steer clear of confrontation, and would not be at this meeting but for Stella.

He sees the tall figure of his father at the front of the room, by the fireplace, smart in a dark suit, his watch-chain glowing across the neat waistcoat, his red beard combed and trimmed. McPhee smiles and nods at something Hanson is saying, turns to address another man at the front. Almost all the audience is male. Douglas can count only three women, including lovely Stella.

He slaps at his neck. The sandflies are out in force this afternoon.

Stella laughs. 'I'm going inside. Come on. You'll be eaten alive. These tough old farmers have hides like eels. You'll be scratching all night if you stay here.'

Douglas allows himself to be manoeuvred into a corner. He stands hidden behind a big fellow while Stella slips into a vacant chair beside her mother. Despite the open windows the air is stuffy with pipe smoke and the smell of sweat. Douglas wants Stella to notice him, but is also afraid of attracting his father's attention. He leans against the wall, interested to discover why these people, so far from the world of politics, are disturbed about the Chinese.

Hanson bangs a ship's bell for attention, which earns him a cheer. He is a heavy man who farms in Pipiriki itself and has done well, they say, supplying meat and timber to the railway camps further inland.

'Welcome, ladies' — he winks at Mrs Morrow, Lily Feathers and Stella — 'and gentlemen. We will commence our Anti-Asiatic Meeting with a prayer and a song.'

Reverend Smith from Raetihi delivers a long rambling exhortation to the Lord to deliver these humble servants here present from the Yellow Peril — the heathen hordes from China. The audience becomes restless; one or two defiantly raise their heads. They are not used to wordy Protestant prayers. Douglas smiles. His father has miscalculated the Catholic fervour down this way.

Then comes a surprise. From the kitchen doorway steps his sister Gertie, dressed all in green satin with a purple silk flower in her hair. She waves at the audience and simpers. Douglas thinks she looks ridiculous, but the men cheer and clap. Mrs Hanson seats herself at the piano while Gertie folds her hands together and frowns to indicate the seriousness of her message.

'My song,' she says, 'is one of my own composition. It is titled "Clouds of Peril from the East".'

She sings intensely in a strong alto voice. The tune bears a striking resemblance to the hymn 'Those in Peril on the Sea', the sentiment similarly hopeful of rescue from disaster. The crowd cheers when it is over and calls for more. Gertie is willing but Mr McPhee steps up to lay a proud but stilling hand on his daughter's shoulder. Douglas has never before seen him show any sign of approval towards her. Gertie looks up at him with something akin to worship; Douglas finds her expression unbearable in a way he would not be able to explain.

Now Angus McPhee takes the floor. He stands upright, speaking without notes and from a deep conviction. Douglas has heard him make the speech before, several times, down in Wanganui. No doubt he has already spread the word up in Raetihi as well. McPhee hooks a thumb in the pocket of his waistcoat as if feeling the tick of the time-piece nestled there. Indeed, time — the urgency of it — is a theme of his speech.

'Every minute that we turn away from the problem, another Chinese crawls under the net and into our country! If we turn away our eyes, shrug our shoulders and murmur, "This is another's problem," we betray our children and our children's children.'

McPhee stabs the air with his forefinger, drills the audience with his fierce blue eyes. He is a compelling orator. Douglas is proud of his father, despite their differences.

'Friends,' says McPhee, his voice rising in indignation, 'the Yellow Peril threatens to engulf us. If the government allows, they will pour into our free land, overwhelm us with their heathen hordes, snatch work from our hands and food from our mouths.

'Recently the government passed a bill requiring a knowledge of one hundred English words from every Chow entering the country. We say: "Too little, too late!" Why not increase the poll tax to five hundred pounds? Why not ban that evil and depraved race from our shores entirely?

'Already, friends, there is a shop run by Chows set up in Raetihi! Yes, up the road in Raetihi! A store that should be sustaining a good British family. Already there is land in the hands of that yellow race here in our very midst! I have seen the title myself and despaired at the ignorant fellow who has sold the land.

'Now, friends, I have learned that a Chinese man has set up here on the river. If you buy vegetables from him — shame on you! You are encouraging the spread. He will use his ill-gotten profit to bring another of his race to our shores. And another, and another. Turn from him! We must stop the rot, chop at the roots before we are overrun.'

McPhee clears his throat. His eyes sweep the room. A silent expectation grows; something important is coming.

'And worse. Far worse. So despicable I can scarce find words to tell.' McPhee lowers his voice until all are craning forward. In fact he has no trouble at all finding the words.

'My own daughter Bridget, my poor lost daughter who near drowned and is ever since not right in her mind, has been defiled — yes, defiled, my friends — and I have good reason to believe that the Chow is the perpetrator . . .'

Ruvey Morrow has had enough. She rises to her feet, large and formidable, known and respected by most in the room.

'Mr McPhee,' she booms, her voice cutting through his whispered slander, 'this is not a fit message for the ladies present. I am leaving, and I urge others to do the same. Also,' here she turns to face the muttering audience, 'you all know Charlie Chee. He is a quiet and decent man, is he not? His vegetables are good and his prices fair. Have you not heard Father Soulas say that the Lord welcomes all humankind, whatever the colour of their skin?'

There is a murmur from the crowd at the mention of Father Soulas.

'Pipiriki House,' the formidable lady rolls on, 'will continue giving Charlie Chee its custom. It was he who rescued this man's daughter, and I do not believe he did any harm to her.' Ruvey Morrow turns back to McPhee. 'Shame on *you* for pointing a finger at your daughter's *saviour*! I will hear no more of this rubbish!'

As she turns to leave, there is a commotion at the back of the room. A big man is being pushed through the crowd at the door. It's Eru, deckhand on the *Wairua*, embarrassed by the attention he's receiving and cursing volubly in Maori. He struggles to stay back, but is shoved by friendly hands until he's in clear view.

'Listen to Eru!' shouts one of the men. 'He's got some news from his cousins upriver.'

McPhee frowns. The meeting is taking an unfortunate turn. The fellow Eru looks as if he's been drinking. He raises a calming hand.

'Friends, friends,' he says, 'let us keep to the point. My good man, sit if you want to join the meeting, but keep a civil tongue. We are speaking God's English in this room.'

'No, wait,' says another voice. 'He's got news of Charlie Chee. Hear him out.'

The room quietens at this announcement and all heads turn to Eru, who rolls his eyes and slaps at the restraining hands of his captors.

'Charlie Chee's dead,' he says. 'Hanged.'

The silence is complete. 'Strung himself up,' Eru adds. 'My cousins are feared to cut him down. He too tapu.' He shrugs. 'No point you buggers having a meeting. Send some white men up to cut him down.' He mutters something low at the standing men and they part to let him stumble out.

McPhee clears his throat. 'Well, indeed,' he says. Then, his voice gaining strength as the faces turn towards him, '*Indeed*.

If this is true, surely the hanging is a sign of guilt. A guilty conscience. A defiler of our women. This, friends, is what the Asiatic race is capable of!'

Stella stands now, tears in her eyes and shaking with rage. 'His name is Hong Lip Yee! If he has hanged himself it is because of people like you! You don't know anything about him. Why would you think Lip Yee . . . hurt . . . Bridie? Why? Anyone could have. You know what she's like. Ma's right. Lip Yee wouldn't do something like that. He was about to bring his wife out here and now he can't afford it after he has saved for so many years. Despair, not guilt, is what Charlie — Lip Yee — what drove him.' The tears are running down her face now. 'You people make me sick!'

Ruvey Morrow puts an arm around Stella's shoulders and leads her weeping daughter outside. Lily Feathers follows. There is general movement in the room — an uncertainty. Bill Anderson, downriver captain, rises and leaves with the women. A smartly dressed gentleman — one of the guests at the House, perhaps — also leaves, pushing his way through to the door. But Angus McPhee is speaking again, persuasive, needling. Douglas stays to listen, earning a furious look from Stella.

'They are women, friends, with a softer way of thinking. Their female minds do not see the hard truths — or the duty we men have to protect their sensibilities. If the Chow has indeed hanged himself, we are well rid of him. But we must be vigilant. Others will come. Others are in our midst.'

The growl of agreement swamps the more hesitant questions. Douglas hears Hatrick's store-master say, 'But would Charlie Chee do such a thing?' and the farmer next to him answer, 'Who knows what the Chows think is right? Maybe taking defenceless white girls is acceptable to them.'

'I do not suggest — as many might — taking punishment

into our own hands,' says McPhee, confident now that he has the crowd with him again, 'but we must send away these — I hesitate to call them members of the human race — *heathens* from our isolated community. This man has a brother in New Zealand, I hear, and perhaps another will take his place here. Spurn them. Neither sell them land nor buy their goods. They must learn that they are not welcome here.'

McPhee waits confidently for a response.

Hanson raises his beefy hand. 'Can we bring a dead man to justice? He should hang again. In public.'

McPhee smiles. 'I fear we cannot, Mr Hanson. He has cheated us from our rights. But in our hearts we know him for what he has done. And we revile him.'

The men rumble approval. McPhee brings the meeting to a close with another, shorter prayer. He is jovial with the group, shaking their hands, urging them to be vigilant. Mrs Hanson hands around hot, buttered date scones.

Douglas is torn. He wants to be part of this good-natured crowd, several of them riverboat men like himself. But he remembers the conversation with Stella's husband: Danny's story of finding Bridget. His anger with Pita. Could Stella's dead brother be the one? Or Danny himself possibly? He admitted to hitting Pita, maybe killing him. Perhaps he has done worse. Douglas remembers the dreamy way Danny spoke of Bridget. Stella's husband could well be both murderer and lecher.

He walks out of the meeting, his heart beating hard. Stella might be in danger! She should at least be warned. Alone up on the farm, who knows what Danny might do to her.

He finds Stella in the kitchen at Pipiriki House, clutching a mug of tea as if she would strangle it. Her face is red and swollen. Douglas stands in the doorway, uncertain of his welcome. Before he can utter a warning Stella turns on him, her dark eyes blazing.

'You agree with him, don't you? I saw you nodding.'

'No . . . Not really . . . I . . .'

Tears roll down Stella's face. She wipes them away furiously. 'Go away, you silly boy. You let him persuade you! You're just like all the others.'

Douglas is unmanned by her onslaught. He can't think of the right words.

'Why didn't you leave the meeting?' she shouts. 'If you — that man's own son — had walked out, *that* would have meant something.'

Douglas shrugs. Looks at the floor. 'I only listened. It doesn't mean . . .' But he cannot defend himself in the face of her fury. Miserable and silent, he leaves the room. Behind him, in the kitchen, Stella throws something that shatters.

Douglas stands outside for some time, hoping she will come to the door. He must warn her about Danny. He grows more and more certain. It is his duty. Perhaps he should seek out the constable and tell what he knows. Danny must be taken away — locked up before he can damage Stella.

Samuel Blencoe

AFTER CHARLIE DIED, Bridie slept in my hut, one, maybe two days. Next thing I heard the horsemen come upriver. Talking loud with that hard laughter a bunch of men will give out when up to no good. I saw them ride up the track, no sideways look to me nor my hut. They was heading for Charlie's all right. I reckon the river Maori give the word. But these men carried no respectful manner as you would coming to collect the dead. They had more a police look about them, those riders, so I let them be. That McPhee was with them.

Those damn men on their horses. Damn them all to hell, and

especially McPhee. They cut Charlie Chee down and buried him without no word to a soul. I heard it later from a river Maori. Buried him with no sign nor marker. Even on Norfolk the dead got a marker. I seen a lag work away on a headstone for his dead friend. A whole month he scraped away on that stone with a blunt knife — just his name, J. Scrivens, and birthplace, Devon — and then set it straight and proud. The dead were free men on Norfolk and afforded a marker if there were someone to care. But McPhee put Charlie Chee in a hole and went away. Never told no one. I heard later one man boasted that he peed on the dirt that covered Charlie Chee.

They came back our way, those black-hearted horsemen; stopped at my hut and spoke rough words that I cared not to answer. But the sound woke Bridie and she come out and her father cursed most foully, and struck me on the head with his whip. He dragged the silent girl up on his horse, she smiling at the horse and the ride, poor simple soul.

Away he took her up to Raetihi and locked her up in his cold house, so her belly would not shame him. Nothing I could do, damn them all to hell. Shut her up out of sight like some nasty thing. Our Bridie that needed open air around her and her feet to be moving over the land. Poor sad soul.

I never seen our Bridie again for a good long while.

Charlie Chee's brother, I never knew his name, come upriver later. He been chased up north a while back, he said, by angry white men, and was afeared to come down this way. Heard about Charlie from some Chow man in Raetihi. Respectful, he were, quiet in his dark suit and hat set straight and real leather shoes polished to a shine. He carried a bunch of yellow flowers and some other things in a bag. He stopped a bit and took a mug of tea with no milk nor sugar. His English is better than Charlie's. He said his brother was too shamed because of Charlie by not having money to bring a wife. He said he was shamed too but would not kill himself because he had a wife and sons to feed. And because he was a different man from Charlie Chee. He called his brother some other name but I guessed he meant Charlie. Some anger about him, I could feel it, but he never said any sharp word. A good polite man.

He stood and bowed to me, give me back my mug and went up to Charlie's.

When he come back he stopped again. Told me he had fixed the grave. He asked me to keep it nice and I said I would. He said he would come back in twelve month time to pick up Charlie's bones. I asked him why. Seemed a disrespectful thing to do. He said he would send the bones to China to rest in peace there. He said it cost too much to send a whole body so he would wait till the bones were clean in the ground and then send them. He said this country was not welcoming to Charlie, so his bones would rest more easy in ground that respect him.

He said all this in a quiet low voice but I heard the anger in it.

Charlie's grave is all clean dirt and a good yard all around it swept clean. A white stick with Chinese writing marks it, and a pretty box. I never open the box to see if something is in it.

I keep the place tidy and have a word to Charlie if I have a mind. To my way of thinking his bit of land here by the river is respectful enough for him to stay.

---- 〆 ----

Aboard the Wairua *upriver to the Houseboat*

We left Pipiriki on Monday 3rd at 10 a.m.
by the S.S. 'Wairua', (the water being 36½
inches below 'the mark') with 11 passengers
and about 2 tons weight of cargo for
Arawata. Considerable difficulty was
experienced in hauling over Paparoa 197
and 196 Paparoa . . . The reef on the R.B.
was completely dry and the rise on the
rapid estimated at 3 feet in 3 chains.

195 Good water
194 "   "
193 "   "

*Extract from Wanganui River Trust Tour of
Inspection, February 1908*

THE DAY AFTER the Anti-Asiatic Meeting Danny and
Stella return upriver aboard the *Wairua*. Today even the weather
is a traitor. In Stella's books there should at least be rain — a
fitting mourning for the hanged man — but the sky is clear and
the river tranquil as the *Wairua*, belching black smoke, chuffs
away from the landing. Stella's mood, though, is stormy. She has
not spoken to Danny since he arrived, dishevelled, haggard, just
before the steamer pulled away from the jetty. She ignored him
while he pleaded for passage: looked the other way as if they were
not related. Even now — months after the accident — Danny

must use every trick of guile, make earnest offers of assistance in poling up the rapids, to even be allowed aboard a Hatrick boat. He was grudgingly waved to a position in the bow while Stella frowned at her feet.

Stella is on duty in the saloon, as the usual steward is not well. This position is coveted, and normally Stella would be well pleased to hand around scones and sandwiches, pour tea and point out to the tourists the scenic wonders: the famous drop scene, where the bush-clad hills ahead seem to sink into the river, the waterfalls and caves. But for once she is silent. It is up to Mr Feathers, returning to his farm after the meeting, to point out the attractions.

In the bow, Danny stands frowning at the three-stepped rapid ahead. Ngaporo. This is where all his troubles began. He takes up the long, iron-shod pole, thrusts it into the shingle and heaves against the current. Eru and Rangi do the same. The deckhands are pleased to have his assistance, as the river is low and the rapid strong. Danny lifts and digs again. The *Wairua* inches forward, her plates rattling, engine pounding. They will manage the first of the triple without winching. But Danny takes no satisfaction. All night he has searched the road from Pipiriki to Jerusalem but found no trace of Bridie. People look askance now when he asks after her, so he is embarrassed to knock on doors. He has called her name, searched picnic spots by the river where she might sleep, but the night revealed nothing. When he plucked up courage to ask Ruvey Morrow, that lady was sharper than usual.

'Danny, you are going too far. Think, for heaven's sake, man, of her condition. What are people to think?'

Danny had no idea what she meant. 'It's my duty,' he replied doggedly. 'She needs me. I must see to her.'

Ruvey Morrow snorted. ' She wouldn't know you from Adam.

It's those of us down here who care for her. Now go and take your wife to the meeting. Have you not noticed the way young Douglas moons after her? You will lose her if you don't take more care.'

But Danny had walked away into the dark.

He thrusts again with his pole, his shoulder muscles cracking. Eru and Rangi exchange a look. They have noticed the silence between those two songbirds, Danny and Stella.

An hour later the *Wairua* enters the gorge. Here the water is deep and serene. In Hatrick's brochure the gorge is described as the most beautiful scenery in the whole Dominion — perhaps even the world. On either side green ferns, hanging from the high vertical walls, glisten in the morning sunlight. A bird watches them from one of the many holes that dot the walls. As children, Stella and Pita would travel upriver in their father's canoe, admiring the way he slotted his pole into these ancient holes to propel the craft forward against the current. Now many river Maori travel the long distances by steamer, and birds have taken residence in the abandoned poling holes. Stella misses Pita: his wicked laugh, his outrageous tricks. She would like to have him here by her side now. Pita would cheer her up.

But her mood lifts anyway. The day is so perfect, the gorge so peaceful. She walks out onto the deck, humming a tune in time with the beat of the engine.

Douglas crawls out of the engine-room hatch, sluices himself with a bucket of water. For stoker and engineer this is the one quiet time of the trip. After the long gorge there are many more rapids waiting to test their skill and the engine's fortitude. Douglas waves up to her and she smiles down. Douglas grins wider. He is forgiven, it seems. He is about to go up to the top deck but is disappointed to see that Danny is ahead of him.

Danny, too, has been affected by the serenity and beauty

surrounding them. Who can brood in this magical place? All the passengers have come out on deck, are standing silent and awed. Even the pounding engine seems quieter here. Danny walks back through the crowd to stand by Stella. He lays his arm gently across her shoulders, kisses her ear. 'Sorry,' he whispers.

There are tears in her eyes. 'It's not allowed to kiss the staff,' she murmurs. He can hear the love in her voice. With a gentle finger he catches her rolling tears.

'I'm all mixed up,' he says. 'I need to talk to you.'

She nods. They stand there, troubled but smiling, arm in arm, watching the ferny walls slide past.

Douglas frowns to see them so.

LATE IN THE morning the *Wairua* pulls in to the Feathers' landing. Betty and Rob Feathers are there with the cart, cheerful and garrulous as ever. Betty hands a freshly baked cake in a tin up to the captain.

'Give that to Vi White, will you, Jamie? The recipe's inside. She might like to try it for the Houseboat table.' She helps her sister ashore. 'Welcome home, Lily, my dear. Dinner's on the table back at the farm. I'm dying to hear all the gossip.'

While the men unload supplies for the River Trust block, Lily and Betty Feathers stand in the sun, chatting. Danny, who is giving a hand with a piece of heavy machinery, overhears Lily reporting to her sister on the Anti-Asiatic Meeting. But Bridie, not the Yellow Peril, is the topic of their gossip.

'Well, we all knew the poor child was in the family way, Bet, but that dreadful man had to shout it to all and sundry. He accused the Chinese man.'

'Charlie Chee?'

'In front of the whole meeting! Ruvey Morrow gave him the

edge of her tongue — it is a brave man who crosses Ruvey, as my Mack well knows. Well, I marched out with her. And then we heard that Charlie Chee has hanged himself!'

'He hasn't!'

'That's what they say. So maybe he is the one got her in the family way. Oh, Bet, you should have been there!'

Danny has to interrupt. 'Bridie is with child?'

The two women turn to stare at him. Their gaze is very cool. Without another word they turn and walk away out of earshot. Danny stands there dumbfounded. He scrambles aboard as the steam whistle sounds, still shaken by what he has heard. She will have a baby! For the rest of the journey he is busy as they grind their way up rapid after rapid. He feels no pain in his shoulders as he struggles with the long pole. Bridie's child!

STELLA IS NEEDED that evening at the Houseboat. She had hoped to go home with Danny, but Mrs White says she cannot manage to feed the large group of tourists on her own. Stella sighs and agrees to stay. The extra money will be welcome.

Danny is in a strange, distracted mood as they say goodbye on the landing. He picks up his bag, starts to go and then returns to kiss her in front of all the guests.

'It will be all right,' he whispers. 'Don't fret, sweetheart.'

She smiles at him but is puzzled by his dancing feet, the way he tugs at his cap; he is in some kind of ferment.

'What is it?' she asks. 'Tell me, Danny or I'll be in a stew all night.'

'You'll see — you'll see. We can make it all right.' He kisses her again and is off up the track, half running. A back-handed wave to her with his free arm and he is gone — past the big tree and out of sight.

Stella smiles as the dust settles. That is Danny all over. He has some new scheme and can't wait to get it under way. Like many of his ideas it is likely doomed, but at least it may help lift the cloud they have been living under. She climbs the plank and enters the steamy chaos of the Houseboat galley.

Later, dog-tired, she climbs the bank to the Whites' house, where a room is kept for her on these nights. Outside the crew's quarters the men are singing a last song in the soft dark.

The water is wide, I cannot get o'er
And neither have I wings to fly . . .

Most of the guests have retired to their cabins but a few of the younger couples still linger on the bank, lolling on the grass under a full moon. Stella can't resist the beautiful, sad song. Her clear soprano lifts above the deeper voices.

Build me a boat that can carry two
And both will row, my love and I.

The other singers fall silent, leaving the banjos to accompany her to the end.

. . . but love grows old and waxeth cold
And fades away, like the morning dew.

There is a moment of silence and then a pattering of quiet applause. Stella bobs a curtsey, smiling. She is suddenly awake again — could sing all night — but the party is breaking up. Captain White is strict with his rules. As she turns to walk up to the cottage, a hand pulls at her from the dark. It is Douglas.

'That was so beautiful it made me cry,' he says.

Stella smiles. 'Thank you.' He is so intense, this young lad, standing there, tall and bony, half hidden in the trees, his copper hair silvered in the moonlight, his damp eyes glowing.

'You could be on the stage,' he says. 'You could be famous.'

'Well, I am happy enough as I am.' Stella knows the boy is smitten with her. Sometimes she enjoys his attentions, but not tonight. She is ready for bed. She turns away but again his hand stays her. He is panting a little and his hand shakes.

'I must warn you,' he says. 'I must.'

'Warn me?'

'You are in danger. You mustn't go home.' Douglas whispers in her ear as if enemies might be hidden in the bushes. He pulls her closer. 'Your husband may harm you.'

'What!' Stella snorts. She's had enough of this nonsense. She pulls away but he grabs at her again.

'Wait! Please, Stella!' It's the first time he has used her name to her face. For a moment he is silenced by his own bravery. Then quickly, before she can tear away again, he tells her. Every word is clearly aimed. He has imagined this moment so often. 'You know how strange your husband has been recently? I heard you tell Mrs White.'

'You hear too much for your own good.' She is curious, though.

'No, listen! Listen, Stella. Your husband killed your brother!'

Stella laughs.

'I saw him leave the landing today. All jittery. He is planning something. You mustn't go home!'

A pair of tourists, walking arm in arm down to the Houseboat, turn at the urgency in his voice.

Stella lowers her voice but the words are cold. 'Douglas, you are a silly boy. Go to bed.'

He takes both her hands, forcing her to look at him. 'It's true. He told me himself. He told me right here — you know, that night you saw him with me. He said he hit Pita, smashed his face in a fury. Sent him senseless into the river. He is a murderer, Stella.'

Stella's heart is thumping. There could be some truth in this outpouring. She tries to keep an edge to her words. 'Why would he tell you such nonsense?'

'I think he forgot I was there. And then it all spilled out. He didn't mean me to hear.' Douglas is thrilled by a new thought. His voice becomes shrill. 'We may both be in danger. Now we both know.'

Another couple walk down past them. The man steps towards them. 'Are you all right, miss? Is this fellow bothering you?'

Stella makes use of the diversion to break away from Douglas's grasp. She mumbles something and runs away. The wretched boy stumbles after her. 'But wait! We must think what to do . . .'

She reaches the porch, rushes inside and slams the door in his face.

In her own room she sits on the edge of the bed, panting. She can see him standing still behind the hydrangeas, watching her window. She pulls the curtains, undresses quickly and slips under the blanket. But she can't blot out the picture of the boy's tense face, his urgent words. There is some kind of madness in the way Douglas speaks, and yet why would he make up such an extravagant story? Stella's problem is that she can imagine it happening. Danny's sudden rage at the ruined expedition. His moodiness in recent months. Perhaps the obsession with Bridie is because he is guilt-ridden? She remembers Danny's words on the landing as he left for the farm. 'It will be all right. I can make it right.' And suddenly she is dreadfully afraid of what he might do. Dear God, if only she were home with him.

In the end sheer exhaustion drags her down into sleep. She lies in the dark room, her arms flung wide, her bedclothes tangled.

Douglas sits outside all night, watching over her.

When Stella stumbles out into the early morning light he is there, eager to walk down to the Houseboat with her.

'We must think what to do,' he says.

'Douglas, please go away.'

'You mustn't go back to the farm. It's not safe.'

'My safety is not your business.'

'It is! It is!'

Stella clamps her lips and walks ahead of him. At least he cannot follow her onto the Houseboat. She escapes into the galley while he reluctantly climbs aboard the *Wairua*.

After breakfast the last guests leave the Houseboat and climb aboard the black-belching river steamer. Stella peers from behind the galley window, fearful that Douglas will abandon his duties and remain ashore. She sighs in frustration to see the lanky boy emerge from the engine-room. He goes to climb the rail. Dusty Miller has other ideas, though. His wiry arm grabs at Douglas's shirt and yanks hard. 'What d'yer think you're up to, lad? Get back in here — pressure's dropping!'

Stella breathes more freely. But his strange words last night chase around in her mind as she changes sheets and sweeps out the cabins. She is on fire to get back home.

AT THE FARM Stella finds that Freda is milked, the pail standing in the shed. The chooks are let out and the horse fed. Finn, surprisingly, is tied up on the porch. He yelps to see her — a high agitated sound, not his usual deep-throated warning. She unties him but he doesn't fly up to the high paddocks where Danny must be — there's no sign of him close to the house.

Inside Stella finds the note. It's written on a sheet torn from her notebook, with stumbling letters that read:

Brides baby I am father. Gon to bring her here. We can look after both. Will be alrite soon. lov Danny.

SPECIAL NOTE

Meals are supplied on the steamers at 2/- each
Meals and Beds on Houseboat at 2/6 each
Accommodation at Pipiriki House 12/6 a day
For visitors staying a week or more 8/- a day
Morning and Afternoon Tea in Dining Room
or Winter Garden Free
Afternoon Tea on Steamers Free

Illustrated and Desciptive Booklets

of the Wanganui River can be purchased from
Stewards on the Steamers, at the Houseboat, Pipiriki
House and from Messrs Hatrick and Co. Wanganui.

Hatrick & Co. promotional brochure

I WAS MAD as a bush-fly with him, even if he is my own son-in-law. 'Danny O'Dowd,' I said, 'you are the one so keen for the land and the farm work. Go back home in the name of heaven and get on with it.' I might have saved my breath. The boy was beyond reason.

He came pounding on our cottage door the one free hour in the day. My feet soaking in mustard water and a wet towel over my eyes. A woman in my position must keep herself in strong health or where would we be? Everyone at the House knows about my hour. 'Between two and three in the afternoon no one bothers Mrs Morrow or there'll be a cost to it.' Even Bert wouldn't dare. But Danny comes barging in, all in a lather and shouting.

At first I hardly recognised him. You would think him some crazed man come out of the bush, his hair every which way and his eyes shining in some kind of fervour. There's a holy picture I'm fond of — St John in the Wilderness. Danny had the same mad, wild look as that saint.

'Where is she?' he cried. 'Where is Bridie?'

Dear oh dear, the same old saw. 'Go back home,' I said. I covered my eyes with the towel again. 'She's not here. Nor will be.'

Danny is not one to take a hint. When his mind is on something he runs at it like a charging bull. I used to admire him for it. His energy. But oh dear, he does run wide of the mark sometimes.

'I must see her, Ma Morrow,' he said. 'She is with child.'

I would not come out from under my towel nor lift my feet from their little treat. 'Danny,' I said, 'All the world knows she is with child, nor is it any concern of yours.'

That cut him. He didn't like to think others knew more about his precious Bridie than he did himself. He was silent for a moment and I was foolish enough to lift my towel. He was staring at me, a little smile on his face, sheepish and proud — not at all what I expected. I began to fear what he would say next: a premonition of disaster. Laugh you may, but I am well known for my premonitions. We are in for trouble, I thought. And was right. 'Danny,' I said in a voice I hoped was firm, 'Bridie's father has the matter in hand. There is nothing we can do about it.'

'What matter?' he asked, gentler now, but still smiling in that odd, crooked way.

I told him how Mr McPhee had taken Bridie away up to

Raetihi. I suppose I let my anger at his treatment of her show — it was hard enough to forget the picture of the poor girl tied in the cart, twisting and crying for her freedom. 'But she is gone, Danny,' I said. 'He has the right; he is the father.'

Danny cried out then. 'But it is my right! My fault! I am the father of the baby, Ma Morrow!'

Well, that silenced me good and proper. Mooning over the girl is one thing, adultery another entirely. I sent him my sharpest look and waited for more, wet towel and sore feet forgotten.

He spread his hands towards me — he can be very appealing when he tries, can Dannyboy O'Dowd.

'Sorry, Ma,' he said, 'I did wrong. I was tempted — you know how she is — and I fell. But the baby is mine and now I must care for them both.'

There was something not right about the way he spoke. I couldn't put my finger on it. Too glib, perhaps. You'd expect a man confessing such a deed to be more abject. Pride was there, the silly chook, and his usual crazy determination, but no real sense of shame that I could tell. Nor any mention of my Stella, I noticed. What did Stella think about all this? I wondered.

It turned out he hadn't told her — just left a note, he said. What husband would walk out leaving her to find out through a letter? I stepped out of my nice mustard bath in quite a rage. Raised a hand to him, if I remember right.

'Danny O'Dowd,' I said, 'get on that boat and go straight back home to her. What are you thinking? Your wife will be in a right state, with no one to comfort her. You will be a lucky man if she does not walk away from you and the farm both.'

That gave him pause, I was pleased to see. And my slap. He is a dear boy but well overdue for taking his place in the adult world.

'No she won't,' he said at last. 'I said in my letter' (Danny smiling at me, cocky that he had written a letter, as we have all been on at him about learning his ABC) 'that I would bring Bridie back to the farm and we would look after her and the baby. I wrote it would be all right.'

Holy Mary. The man cannot think past his nose.

I tried to sit him down then, talk some sense into him. If only Bert had been there we might have made some progress. Bert can be a very straight talker when push comes to shove. And I am no slouch either, as any will tell you, but I could hammer no understanding into his silly head. The baby might not be his, I suggested: if he was tempted and fell others might have also. Danny was outraged by this, as if he owned the poor girl. Then I asked him how could he care for poor senseless Bridie, away upriver, with Stella at the Houseboat four days out of seven and him out on the farm all hours? Danny flicking his hand at my good points as if he were swatting flies. I could have been talking to the flowers of the field for all the progress I made.

'Bridie needs me. It's my duty,' was all he would say, over and over.

'Bridie needs you like I need the pox,' I snapped. 'You are little enough use as it is, to Stella or any of us.'

Well, he goaded me. I should not have been so harsh. He has not done too badly, and Stella seems to love him, but the upshot was that his face closed like a fist and he was out the door before I could say another word.

If only he had given Stella a baby. She is healthy enough. I have said to her that she is away from her husband too many nights. You cannot expect to get with child, I said, if you are away down at the Houseboat so often. But secretly I feared she was barren. I had the same fear myself years ago when no children came. Then my firstborn dead a week after birth, and the second, not a year old, dying before we could get him down to Mother

Aubert and the Sisters. It can be a heartbreak giving birth, another heartbreak if no children come. But we still pine for them. Children are our lot: our cross and our joy. After Danny went on his way I sat down and shed a tear for my poor barren Stella. What must she be going through, on her own up at the farm?

NEXT THING WE heard, Danny was arrested for disturbing the peace. Other charges to follow. Danny in the lock-up at Raetihi, due to be sent to the jail down at Wanganui, and Stella on our doorstep in tears. As if losing Pita wasn't enough.

Raetihi

```
'being lunatic and wandering at large'
'depositing waste matter in the gutter'
'was found drunk in charge of a horse'
'did introduce liquor, to wit whiskey into
Maori kainga'
'did play a certain game of chance to wit
two-up in a public place, to wit Raetihi
main road'
```

Extracts from police charge sheet, Raetihi, early 1900

TIM NAYLOR ADDS *Appropriating a horse* to the growing list on his charge sheet. McPhee watches while he writes, then turns on his heel without a word and leaves the station. The constable sighs. He likes Danny, finds him earnest and co-operative, unlike Angus McPhee, that officious sawmiller, who is in and out of the station six or more times a day with his complaints and accusations. McPhee has ferreted out the news that Danny did not ask the farmer down in Pipiriki if he could borrow his horse and has brought in the news with a triumphant smile.

'You need to sharpen up, lad. I have work enough at the mill without doing your job as well.'

Away then to your mill and out of my hair, thinks Naylor as he writes. He guessed the horse was not Danny's — has put it with his own in the police stable, waiting for someone to claim it. Danny is in enough trouble.

He saw Danny ride into town two days ago, his horse in a lather, dust caking the sweat on the poor beast's flanks, Danny himself a ghost man, masked in silvery dust. The grey papa clay, such a claggy curse in winter, was almost worse when it dried in summer, drifting with every stirring wind or footstep to coat the town and its inhabitants in its soft mantle. But Danny clearly had no thought to his appearance. The constable saw him lean from his horse and ask the postman for directions; saw Matt Hunter point in the direction of the McPhees' place. Off Danny rode, his mount snorting and pulling at the bit, reluctant to get going again. Naylor had imagined some emergency to do with milling orders, or perhaps the son, Douglas, was hurt.

Naylor considered riding up to McPhees' but then let matters be. He was not welcome there since he had married his dear Emily. Gertie McPhee had stormed into the station on the very day he came back from the wedding, screaming that he had betrayed her trust, that she and he had an 'understanding', that he had insulted her and would never be forgiven. 'How could you choose a native,' she bellowed, 'ahead of me?' All this in front of Emily. He had taken Gertie by her shoulders, shunted the wailing girl outside and closed the door. Emily, whose father's chiefly family owned most of the land around Raetihi, only laughed at the silly woman, thank goodness.

All in all, Tim Naylor was in no mood to ride up to the McPhee household to inquire about their well-being. Especially now that Bridget McPhee was back. The fate of that poor girl has gnawed at him these past few weeks. Several townspeople have asked him is it right? Can something be done? The Sommervilles next door to the McPhees say they hear moaning day and night. Even the Chinese vegetable man came into the station — his first visit, very polite and nervous — to say that the girl had been a friend of Charlie Chee down on the river and that she was harmless.

'Not right tie her up. I see her feet tie by rope when I go with veges to Sommervilles. Please make them free her.'

Tim Naylor had tried to explain that McPhee did have the right. That the daughter was troublesome and wandered. Jimmy Sun had listened carefully, his face unreadable, his black eyes fixed on Naylor's face.

'This is not free country,' the man said at last. 'Not better than my home country.'

He waited for an answer but Naylor could think of none.

Then foolish Danny came riding up to rescue her. While the whole town applauded his failed attempt, Tim Naylor has been forced to arrest him.

He looks down now at the charge sheet:

Disturbing the peace, to wit striking a man in his own home.

Trespass on private property.

Attempting to abduct a female.

Unlawful union with a female of unsound mind.

Adultery.

(Naylor is not sure McPhee can lay a complaint of adultery. Surely that would have to be Danny's wife?)

Abduction of private property, to wit a horse.

DANNY HAD APPROACHED the house properly enough, the Sommervilles reported. (They were on his side, naturally, and visited him in the lock-up with cakes and other delicacies, which the constable allowed.) Danny had knocked on the door and when one of the children answered — Mrs McPhee was in bed, unwell — had asked to see Bridie. The child had said, as she had been taught, that Bridget did not receive visitors. Danny stood on the porch, refusing to go, no doubt a strange sight, covered as he was in grey papa dust, his hair a wild bird's nest from the headlong gallop up through the gorge.

Then Gertie McPhee arrived at the door to stir up emotions, as was her habit. The Sommervilles had observed it all for later reporting.

'Didn't you hear what my sister said? Get off our property or I'll call my father!' said Gertie

'Fanning flames,' said Lucy Sommerville, her ample bosom rising and falling indignantly. 'The woman has clearly never been taught the gentler virtues.' Tim Naylor had to agree.

Danny's flame had indeed been fanned. He pushed past Gertie and strode though the house until he unlocked a door and found Bridie, tied by rope to a bolt in the floor, her ankles chafed, her hair matted, moaning and rocking from one foot to the other. Danny had gone to her gently, he insisted, untied the rope, taken her by the hand and was attempting to lead her outside when McPhee arrived, followed by a panting Gertie. Who struck first was a matter of opinion. This took place inside the house and the Sommervilles, for all their peering, couldn't make it out. Both men sustained blows and wore the bruises as proof. McPhee, a trained boxer and a good six inches taller, bloodied Danny's nose, while Danny winded the furious sawmiller.

The Sommervilles could hear the insults, though. 'By God, I'll have you for this!' shouted McPhee. 'Breaking into my house, stealing my daughter!'

'I am the father!' shouted foolish Danny. 'She must come with me!'

More blows, thud, crash.

'Trespasser! Thief!' from the father.

And again Danny shouted, 'It is my child! Bridie needs me!'

By the time they had taken breath from all their manly shouting, Bridie was out of the house and walking. The Sommervilles called to her but she paid no heed. Barefoot, in her petticoat and bodice, no skirt or bonnet, the bare skin of her big belly showing for all to see, she was off across the yard and over fences, ignoring the road, heading for Pipiriki.

A sorry sight. Sorrier still to see Gertie reach her and try to drag her home. Several townspeople had gathered by this time. Bridie would not budge while Gertie yanked and shoved and railed. Red as a beetroot she was, at all this public display of their shame. Then Bridie sat down suddenly, in the Hoddles' back yard, moaning — a sad, wordless hum, on and on. A few descending, heart-breaking notes, endlessly repeated. Tim Naylor was on the spot by then, with the Hoddles, wondering how to shift the poor soul when McPhee arrived, manhandling a bloody Danny and demanding his arrest. Danny had eyes only for Bridie, and no words except to insist that he was the father, which did him no good in the eyes of the law.

Tim Naylor had no choice but to arrest Danny O'Dowd. He led him away to the lock-up, away from the gossiping townspeople, while McPhee fetched a cart and heaved his daughter aboard. She was quieter then, gone into herself. Danny, too, dispirited, perhaps, at the sight of her, or too bruised.

HE IS STILL in low spirits, Danny, or at least much quieter. He talks very little; eats what is put in front of him. After all that fury two days ago he appears strangely at peace now. Almost as if he's pleased to be incarcerated. Naylor takes him the plate of stew his wife has prepared for the midday meal, unlocks the

217

heavy door and sits in the entrance, watching as the prisoner eats. Danny shows no inclination to escape.

'There is a complaint,' says Naylor, 'that you have stolen a horse on top of all the rest.'

Danny frowns. 'Did the farmer complain?'

'No. McPhee.' Naylor allows a sour smile to show.

Danny smiles back. The first for two days. 'Jock Haami is a friend of our family. He wouldn't complain. You can cross that one off.'

Naylor fingers the charge sheet. 'You're in plenty of trouble without that. Do you have to claim fatherhood so loud? That's the one will set judge and jury against you.'

Danny chews his meat. Takes a quick look at the constable and then back to his food.

'You have done the girl no favours, you know. She is locked up tighter than before.'

'I know.' Danny's voice is low. 'I should've done it better.'

'You shouldn't have done it at all! What about your wife? What will she be thinking?'

Danny takes another forkful. 'This is good stew. Please thank your wife.' Then, defensively, 'The people here think I did well to try and rescue her.'

'Some do. Others cry shame about fathering the child.'

Danny puts his plate on the floor. Holds his head in his hands. 'Oh, God, it is all a mess. Can't you do something about Bridie? That bloody McPhee doesn't want her.'

'He does, it seems.'

'Don't I have some rights? As father?'

'Danny. You have a wife. You have committed adultery, for one thing. Who knows whether you took the girl against her will . . .'

'I would never! Never!' Danny suddenly hides his hands in his pockets. An odd, furtive gesture. 'She is so loving! So sweet!'

The man seems to have no instinct for self-preservation. Naylor sighs. Danny will do poorly at trial if he goes on like this. And yet it is true that many in this town applaud his actions and condemn the police for allowing Bridie to be held so cruelly. His own Emily would happily lead an expedition to free her.

'Danny,' he says, 'she is a poor, mindless girl. If she was sweet to you, and you fell, perhaps others did? Can you be sure the baby will be yours? Eh? Why are you so bent on condemning yourself? It makes no sense at all. Think of your poor wife. Surely she is wretched?'

Danny rocks back and forth on his little bench, his hands still deep in his pockets. 'I am no use to Stella. She is better off if I am here.'

'That's nonsense.'

'I have done her such harm . . .' Danny looks up quickly at Naylor. Is about to say more but clearly decides against it. He stands. Shrugs. Peers out of the high slatted window of the lock-up. 'Could she be brought to see me?' he says at last.

'Stella?'

Danny nods. 'I need to talk to her.'

Naylor is sharp with him. 'I'm sure you do. But will she feel the same need?'

Danny doesn't answer.

Autumn 1908

꒰ꕤ꒱

Sly-grog

PITA MORROW WAS not dead, as feared by his parents and assumed by Danny, but had become a skilled and well-paid dropper for Mr Melville O'Leary's sly-grog trade. Twenty years earlier the government, in its blessed wisdom (according to Mel O'Leary) declared this whole district — the Rohe Potae or King Country — a 'No Licence' area. Settlements along the Whanganui River were included in the 'liquor desert', after representation (so the government said) from Maori elders upriver. In all this vast area not one hotel or shop or guesthouse might sell liquor. A private citizen (if he were Pakeha) might apply for one case of whisky a month for private consumption, but that meant filling in a form in triplicate, depositing one copy with the local police and sending money somehow to a licensed store outside the area — too much trouble for most of the railway workers and mill-hands.

Not everyone had the power to influence authority that Alexander Hatrick possessed. That worthy citizen applied to the licensing court in Wanganui for a packet licence for his boats. When the application was declined, Hatrick, lowering his brows, demanded to know the grounds.

'That is not required,' said Chairman Bassett firmly. Then he added that the meeting was adjourned so that the applicant might prepare arguments for an appeal.

'I have come down today, and am here now to argue my case,' raged Hatrick. 'I think it is very unfortunate and unsatisfactory that gentlemen should sit on this bench whose judgements are warped by their prejudices.'

The very next day his packet licence was granted.

The thirsty growls of the railway workers, building the new north–south main trunk line, carried no such clout. They were trapped in a dry area, months on end in their bush camps, and not a drop to be had — legally, that is — for miles.

Thank the good Lord for Mel O'Leary and his breed, who risked their lives and reputations bringing illegal liquor up the winding bridle tracks, along logging roads in the bush, travelling at night with their clinking succour, making their secret deliveries, using every trick in the trade to outwit the police.

By this time, 1908, the railway was almost finished. Sizeable milling towns now flourished along the tracks, all dry. Complaints from the citizens were numerous. 'Give us the chance to vote prohibition or not!' they pleaded. They would have voted 'Licence' to a man; forget about the ladies. But the authorities remained deaf. The King Country was dry for its own good. End of the matter.

At every election time in Wanganui, O'Leary voted with the prohibitionists: ticked 'No Licence' on his voting paper. His droppers were instructed to do the same. 'We don't want a good business ruined by legal liquor,' he boomed, his vast belly rolling under his watch-chain, 'so be careful where you make your pencil mark.' Mel O'Leary had even taken out membership with the Wanganui Band of Hope, though he never once attended a meeting, not him.

Railway towns and bush camps

'Another request I have to make is that the sale of spirits within our district shall be stopped absolutely. I do not want this great evil brought upon our people. I hope this House will be strong in preventing this evil coming upon us and upon our people.'

Wahanui, leading chief of the Rohe Potae (King Country), speaking to Parliament, 1884

'It is a feature of the arrangement that no liquor is to be sold if the territory is opened for the railway.'

Premier Robert Stout, speaking when he turned the first sod for the main trunk line

AFTER EIGHT MONTHS as a dropper, Pita owns six horses — two mounts and four pack animals, a good wool suit and a gold watch-chain with watch attached. He visits the bawdy house near Turakina once a week and drinks (proper imported Scotch whisky) at O'Leary's legal public house on the outskirts of town. He never goes near the river, though. Pita Morrow enjoys taking risks; will dodge around the law with the best of men. But the thought of being locked up in jail fills him with horror. It gnaws at him that he cannot go upriver, or even visit his parents and cousins, but the thought of the drowned girl, of Hatrick's powerful rage, keeps him distant from his beloved waterway. Too many people would recognise him. Meantime he takes great care to keep his identity and that of his customers secret.

The lucrative railway line is Pita's beat: Karioi his first drop, then Rangataua, Ohakune, Horopito and Erua — all rough railway towns. Further north he serves the line of rugged camps where men hack a route through the towering bush, digging out an even gradient and laying sleepers for the creeping iron rails that have almost joined north and south — Auckland and Wellington.

But eight months is a good long time for a dropper to stay clear of the law. The weekly runs have lost their edge of excitement. On this, his final long trek through the bush, Pita Morrow, alias Phillip Matthews, has a plan — involving greater risk, bigger profit, and a bit of fun. He pulls his new hat down over his eyes, against the low sun (and also against recognition), swaying easily in the saddle as his mount plods up the winding Field's track towards Karioi. The packhorses follow, labouring under their precious loads.

He reins his horse in under the shade of an old beech tree. There is grazing here, and a stream winding in and out of the dark bush. The three horses and Pita all drink noisily. The water, tasting sweetly of leafmould and rich earth, is running clear over stones in a westerly direction. Sooner or later it will find its way into a larger river and then down into the Whanganui itself. Pita finds a small dry beech leaf, shaped like a tiny boat. He places a drop of spit into its curved centre, then places the leaf gently onto the surface of the water where the current flows swiftly. It is an action he has performed many times.

'Ka kite,' he whispers, knowing himself foolish, but all the same eased to think the little craft may deliver part of himself back to his own river. Will it ever be safe for him to return?

Pita cannot be hopeful. They must all think him dead by now. Perhaps they were pleased to be rid of him, but still he would like — sometime when he is safely away — to reassure his mother.

Pita (Phillip) had come into Mel's business via one of that entrepreneur's illicit distilling operations in the bush upriver. Pita had brought in a consignment of evil-smelling raw alcohol and had been intrigued to watch Mel doctor it with his own secret concoction of herbs, sugar and water, adding a splash of genuine whisky until he judged it pleasant enough to fool his customers — enough raw spirit to inebriate, but well short of a lethal dose. Mel O'Leary was very firm on this.

'Those sly-groggers who sell raw poison! Mad, they are. Cutting off their own noses for the sake of a quick sale, boyo. Who needs a fine drinker poisoned by raw alcohol? Now, my good stuff will do the trick but keep the fellow alive to drink again. Isn't that the way, then?'

He would send his droppers north and west, upriver and inland, deep into the King Country, to men ('and women — let's not forget the ladies, my boyos') to the many secret destinations where money lay hidden along with an order for whisky. Mel O'Leary only dealt in the hard stuff. Not enough profit in beer and too heavy to pack in.

Prohibition was making Mel O'Leary a rich man. In the summer of 1908 his best dropper, Phillip Matthews, decided it was time to cut himself a bigger slice of the profit.

Back under the shade of the tree Pita sips from a hip-flask of the pure Scotch whisky he can now afford. He will not touch the bottles he is transporting — adulterated rubbish, as he well knows. As the liquor warms him, Pita dreams of a new life on some distant river — perhaps in Australia; he has heard they have mighty rivers there.

'What do you think?' he says aloud to Tawhi, his munching

horse. 'I could be river captain of my own boat up some wide foreign river. That'd be something, eh?' But the river he imagines is his own: his bush and his rapids and his own people admiring his prowess.

Pita has money hidden in a secret 'drop' of his own, and soon will have more. He grins to think of his plan. O'Leary considers his system faultless and his droppers beyond reproach, but in an illegal trade all manner of fiddles are possible. Pita has been shaving a little more than his half share of the sales for months. Easy to explain — a bottle smashed here, a drop short-changed there. But on the return journey from this run he will risk much more, and have a good laugh too.

He stands as he hears barking. Someone whistles his dog, below on the track. Quickly Pita leads the packhorses deeper into the bush and ties them there, out of sight. No point in hiding altogether — the dog would know. Pita pulls his hat lower and waits under the tree with Tawhi. It's unusual for a traveller to be on this part of the track so late in the day.

A tall fellow rides up, the dog at his heels. Pita calls to the dog. Pets it and offers a piece of the bread and mutton he's eating. Anything to keep the dog from wandering, for Pita is dismayed — and a little excited — to note that this man is in police uniform. The tall man leans out of the saddle, offering a hand.

'Tim Naylor, constable at Raetihi,' he says, smiling in an easy way, though his eyes are sharp.

'Ko Tawhi, au,' he mumbles, taking his horse's name. 'Kia Ora. E pehea ana koe?' He ruffles the dog's ears, lets him lick his greasy hand.

'Kia Ora,' replies the constable. But he can go no further with the Maori language — a relief to Pita. 'Heading up to Karioi?' he asks.

Pita shrugs and lets out a stream in his own tongue. Naylor persists. He points up the track, indicating that they might travel together. Pita gives what he hopes is a foolish grin and indicates that he is tired, will sleep under the tree. It would spell disaster if the constable decided to stay too, but surely he will have business up in the town? Probably, Pita thinks — enjoying the danger of it — he has come to keep an eye out for droppers.

'I'll be on my way, then,' says Naylor. His manner is light, unsuspecting.

Pita grins again. 'Ka kite.' He releases the dog as the policeman whistles him to follow. Man and dog head on up the track and out of sight.

Pita waits, sipping on his whisky, until he's sure the law is a good distance away. While he's on a run he can keep to the fine and lovely line between drunk and sober. Back home in his one-room hut, hidden in a quiet stretch of bush behind O'Leary's Public House, he will often lie for hours in a drunken daze, and then, next day, sick and gloomy, hate himself for the fool he is. But now the danger and the thought of his plan keep him sober enough.

As the shadows reach into his sunny corner and light begins to fade, he brings the packhorses back to the stream. He unloads the patient beasts, then tethers them to graze while he sees to his cargo. There are three dozen green glass bottles in each pannier, six dozen to a horse, hidden under bags of flour. All are stoppered with a glass ball and wire spring contraption. Easy to re-use. Pita unpacks them all, lines them up on the grass by the stream. Now, from the bottom of the panniers, he takes two large glass preserving jars. Carefully he uncaps each bottle and pours a small cupful into his jar. A same small cupful of riverwater refills the bottle. When he has finished, his two jars, brimming with O'Leary's liquor, are back in the panniers, under the twelve dozen slightly less potent bottles of 'O'Leary whisky'.

Pita strikes a match to re-read his paper noting tonight's orders. Mostly he can remember them, but every time there are one or two new places.

Karioi, he reads. Three fenceposts past the signpost bend — 3 bottles.

That's a familiar drop. As are the next two — Big rock by white stone in stream — 1 bottle. Hole in old stump by single totara tree 3 chain before town — 4 bottles.

Then there's a new one on the other side of the little township: 5 chain on Rangataua road. Two small bushes then a big one. Under the big one — 4 bottles.

Droppers do not usually deliver inside the town boundary, and Pita is no exception. Not tonight, anyway. A few days' hence, we'll see! He heads up to Karioi, leading the horses on the edge of the track so the grass will conceal the hoofprints. It's a good black night, the Milky Way tracing a bright cloud across the sky, a little breeze shifting the branches. A perfect dropper's night.

Before he reaches the first drop Pita dismounts, ties Tawhi and one of the packhorses off the track, hidden from sight. He leads the other horse quietly forward, counting the fenceposts. At the third past the signpost he reaches into a hollow, covered by small branches, pulls out three empty bottles, a leather pouch tied to the neck of one and jinking with coin. Pita counts the money — 36 shillings — pockets the order for two weeks' hence and places three full bottles in the hollow, re-covering them with the branches. The big rock near the river is close by, though neither recipient knows it. Drop addresses are jealously guarded. One bottle (why does the man bother?) goes into the carefully disguised hole beneath the rock.

Pita doesn't like the tree-stump drop — too close to town. He leaves his horse back a bit, walks quietly through the shadows, makes the drop and is away again before any silly dog gets a whiff of him.

Back with the other horses, he makes a wide circle around the town, using sawmillers' tracks through the bush. Rangataua next, and then Ohakune. That's all he can do in one night. He'll camp in the bush during the day and ride to Horopito at dusk.

Near Rangataua he is almost caught. Some kind of celebration is going on — a party and bonfire on the edge of town. He can hear the singing and laughter, see the shooting flames. This is a regular and a big drop — a dozen and a half bottles for a buried kerosene tin marked by three river stones in a row. Pita can't simply ignore the drop — a disappointed drinker is a dangerous man — but the revellers are too close. He wraps the bottles in sacking and walks alone towards the marked spot. The flames of the bonfire will make the men blind to the wider surrounding, or so he hopes. Quietly he lowers his bundle and removes the cleverly disguised lid. Perhaps he clinks the glass as he exchanges full and empty bottles, or perhaps the breeze carries his scent. Suddenly there is a furious barking and a big dog hurtles towards him out of the dark. Pita freezes, tucks his head down, waits for the attack. The dog approaches on stiff legs, silent now. Pita sneaks a look, tries a quiet word. The tip of the dog's erect tail begins to wag. A good sign. He will not be attacked. But a friendly dog is almost as dangerous to him as an angry one.

Someone at the bonfire calls out, 'Rags! Get over here!' The voice is coming closer.

'Go on,' whispers Pita, hoping his command sounds fierce. 'Go home! Get! Haere atu!'

'Rags, you bastard!' Pita can see the shape of the man against the flames.

'Leave him be,' shouts another voice. 'He'll be right.'

One command or another makes sense to Rags. He turns and

trots back to the fire. Pita completes the drop without waiting to count the coin, runs back to his horse, his heart pumping. But he is grinning. This is fun! Perhaps the second voice was the owner of the drop, waiting anxiously for replenishments and fearful that his hiding place might be discovered. At any rate he is away again, through the maze of logging tracks, his load growing lighter as the night progresses.

TWO DAYS LATER Pita is ready with his bold plan. He has sold his two packhorses to a sawmiller near Erua for a handy sum. He won't need them again. Now, ready to move at speed, he packs up his bush camp. Half the empty bottles he hides in the scrub, the others, wrapped and carefully stacked in the panniers, he loads onto his own mount. These all contain a golden liquid — one-quarter O'Leary sly-grog, three-quarters cold tea. Anyone taking a pull would soon know — less kick than a newborn babe — but the look is good. Pita chuckles. His money pouch is full and will soon be crammed. O'Leary will set no eye on this stash — or his dropper. After today's run Pita will take off for new lands and new adventures.

He feeds his horse the last of the oats. Today he must ride quickly, in broad daylight, along the new railway line, from one work gang to the next.

He starts well north of Horopito, near Erua, where the last section of the line is almost complete. The work gangs have finished the heavy work, felling and levelling, and are now shovelling ballast around the newly laid rails. Thirsty work. As far as Pita knows, the bush camp gangs do not have regular drops. They are always moving. No time to set up regular supply routes. They will be easy meat.

He is in high spirits as Tawhi picks his way alongside the

railway line. On one side the bush towers; no logging tracks here in Tongariro National Park. To his right the land is more open: pale toetoe tassels droop in the still morning air like dipped flags at a funeral. But Pita's mood is far from funereal. Ahead he hears the shouts of a railway gang and then he sees them, five wiry men stripped to their singlets, pipes clamped between teeth, shovelling stone. The man standing atop the railway hopper leans on his shovel and shouts a welcome. The rest stop and look towards Pita, pleased at the interruption. Pita rides up easily, gives them a cheeky grin, though his heart is pumping. It would be just his luck to hit a wowser first time up. They exchange names. Pita calls himself Phillip — the last time he'll use it. If word gets back to O'Leary, Pita likes the idea that the fat bastard will know who cheated him.

The leader of the gang, Slim Fitchett, asks if Pita is lost. 'The coach trail between railheads is off to the right. You won't find travellers up this way, not till the rail opens.'

Pita winks. 'Suits me, gentlemen. I have an offer for you and don't fancy running into the law. You know?'

They look at him, unsmiling.

'Have I made a mistake, then?' says Pita, grinning, but the sweat prickles under his thatch of hair. 'No drinkers among you?'

Slim clears his throat. Spits. 'You a sly-grogger?' His interest is obvious.

'I was,' says Pita, 'Getting out while I'm ahead. But there's stock here I'm selling off cheap. Interested?'

One of the men, Hapi, a big fellow, laughs. 'Boy, I haven't tasted a drop in five weeks. Interested? My tongue's hanging out, man.'

Slim is more careful. 'Seems strange, coming in broad daylight. Your stuff good?'

Pita produces a bottle of pure O'Leary, pours a small shot. Offers it. 'I'll be honest with you — it's not as good as Scotch, but it'll do the trick.'

Slim knocks it back. Inhales sharply and grins. 'It will do that!'

'Hey! Me too,' growls Hapi, already belligerent.

Pita pours him a shot. Hapi whoops with joy.

'Ten shillings a bottle,' says Pita, 'and there's a condition. A serious condition.'

'Well, then?' Slim is hooked. Hapi too. The other three are definitely interested.

'You get the liquor cheap. It's fifteen shillings anywhere else. But I've got a run of bush camps to do and don't want word getting out till I'm well down the line.'

Slim smiles wryly. 'I can understand that. You're taking a risk, letting us see you.'

'I am. But by tomorrow I'll be out of the business and away.'

'So the condition?'

'You don't touch the liquor till sundown.'

'What?' Hapi is clearly ready to get stuck in.

Pita frowns at Slim. 'If anyone is found drunk on the job they'll find me before I'm away. Can you keep him under control till nightfall? Otherwise the deal's off. I'll take the goods down the line.'

He heels his horse, moves a step or two away. One of the others speaks up. 'We'll stay off till night. There's a job to be done here and the boss is due sooner or later.'

'From the north?' Pita is suddenly anxious.

'North, yes.'

'Well, gentlemen? I'll need to keep ahead of him. Are you in? No more than two bottles apiece. Plenty of thirsts where I'm headed.' Pita has timed the run for the day after payday. He knows they will have coin in their pockets.

Slim looks at his gang. They all nod. Quickly Pita dismounts, exchanges his rotten liquor for good shillings and mounts again. He grins at them. 'Stay sober, friends. If I'm caught, your mates down the line will miss out on the deal and I'll be sure to let them know who blew the whistle.'

Slim grunts. 'You can trust us. Good luck, then, with whatever you're off to.'

Pita waves and sets Tawhi off at a gallop. The run is on! They won't catch him. He doesn't even think about taking a drink. By night-time he'll be a rich man and on his way. He shouts in triumph to a hawk hovering high above. Yes, friend, we are both good hunters! See if you can make as good a catch!

By late afternoon he has sold all but the last six bottles. He has thundered down the railway line, through five gangs, veering away only at the towering Makatote Viaduct, just completed, which the horse will not cross. Here Pita is forced to take the coach route, winding steeply down to the great Makatote River and crossing at the ford there. For such a river, heading as it does straight towards his own beloved Whanganui, spit is not enough. Pita nicks his finger, lets his red blood drip onto a broad rangiora leaf and sends the glistening offering downriver. Tears gather and threaten to fall at the thought of all he had lost. 'Whanga-nui-e!' he calls, high and drawn out, and hears the echo come off the high ferny walls of the ravine. Then he is off again, dashing up the slope before a coach full of tourists might notice and describe the solitary rider. They say there is one more gang just north of Horopito. After that, Pita will disappear into the bush.

HE HAS MISCALCULATED, though. He discounted the risk of some drinker discovering the trick before he is properly away, reckoning that a man buying illegal liquor in a dry area will not complain. He is wrong on that count. Slim Fitchett is not one to laugh off a clever trick. When Hapi takes a secret glug in the bush and comes out roaring, Slim doesn't hesitate to slip a quiet word to his boss. 'Don't say who complained, boss, but the wretch is headed down the line, set to cheat the whole gang of us. Can you get word out?'

The boss can indeed. Another error, though Pita could not have been expected to plan for this one. Down on his river, the only way to send a quick message is by pigeon, and that's never going to work with shifting railway gangs. But strung alongside the railway track is a brand new telegraph line. The boss rides his jigger back to tiny Erua, telegraphs through to Horopito, and when Pita rides up to the last gang he's shocked to see a couple of policemen on the line, blocking his way forward.

Desperately he wheels Tawhi, heading for the nearest patch of bush. But there are no tracks here except the railway line and the coach road beside it. Tawhi is soon brought to a halt by clinging undergrowth. The policemen's horses, fresher, more used to the territory, close in on each side of the sweating Tawhi. Pita is caught with the money and the adulterated liquor. In a rare moment of despair, he feels the walls of a cell crowding in. He howls for his mother.

Horopito lock-up is an old railway wagon set on blocks and going nowhere. It is full — with drunks, as it happens, the result of Pita's latest drop. The constable telegraphs to Ohakune and Raetihi: 'Lock-up full up. Any space?'

As it happens, Tim Naylor has just sent his prisoner, the strange fellow who claims to have molested the McPhee girl, downriver for trial in Wanganui. He offers to lock up Phillip Matthews in the Raetihi jail until he's due for sentencing.

Commercial Hotel

Est. 1903 George Pike prop.
Seddon St, Raetihi

*E*xcellent accommodation.
*F*irst class meals.

14 rooms; 8 bedrooms
12-stalled stable with secure padlocks for
travelling stock
Staging post for Crowther and McCauley's coach:
Tokaanu – Pipiriki via Raetihi

Advertisement, Waimarino Argus

MY POOR STELLA. I fancied she'd live a charmed life, with her clever ways and her good looks. Could have been anything, even famous like Mother Aubert — wouldn't that be a turn-up — but instead she lands a criminal for a husband, a childless womb and worthless land for a farm.

'Come and stay with us a while,' I said to her when she came down to the House. 'You can't be on your own up there.' But she wouldn't. Her sweet face swollen with tears, the hiccups still wracking her, but still she swore she'd go back on the next boat. That's Bert's strong blood won't let her give in. In my opinion a bit softer, a touch more of a woman's gentleness wouldn't go amiss. Danny needs to feel in charge now and then.

'At least go up to Raetihi and talk to him,' I said. 'Have it out. He's a foolish lad, has made his mistake, but he's not really bad, Stell. He won't like being locked up and all alone.'

To tell the truth, I had an idea that if Danny and Stella adopted Bridie's baby, that might ease things. They needed a family. And what's more, Bert and I could do with grandchildren. So I stuck out for Danny. 'He wants to take responsibility,' I said. 'That's something at least.'

'He wants to take on the girl, too,' said my daughter hotly. 'Did he tell you that?'

'He did, and that is his foolish side. He's a dreamer, Stell, you know that. You can talk him out of it.'

'Oh, Ma!' Stella wailed like a lost child — it wrung my heart to see her like this. My strong girl. 'Ma! It's more than that. Douglas said . . . he said . . . awful things about Danny.'

I am not generally one for cuddles but I took her in my arms then. Rocked her as if she were still my baby. 'I am not interested in any views from Douglas,' said I firmly. 'That silly boy is smitten with you, anyone can see that, and will try to poison you against Danny if he can.'

Stella saw the sense in my words. She nodded against my shoulder and sniffed a bit.

'I wish Pita was here,' she mumbled.

'We all do,' I said, pleased that she had changed the subject. 'I cannot help feeling he will walk in some day, grinning as if nothing has happened.'

'He's dead.' She said it flat, as if she knew.

'Dear oh dear,' I said, 'you are down in the dumps. We'll have a cup of tea. Where's my chirpy girl gone?'

But she would not be cheered up. Caught the morning boat

upriver, her face white and set. With the farm and the Houseboat, she said, she couldn't be wasting time trekking up to Raetihi.

She loved him still, though; any fool could see that.

WHEN BRIDIE'S BABY was born the news spread like a bush-fire. Pigeons couldn't have done better. Stella was back down to Pipiriki, eyes full of hope, not more than a day after I heard from Jock, who runs the Crowther and McCauley coach down from Raetihi. He had stayed the night at Pike's Hotel in Raetihi and heard it all as it happened.

Poor Bridie was in a bad way, he said, with the birthing, Mrs McPhee and that Gertie no use at all, so they sent for Mrs Hoddle, the butcher's wife, who is a good sensible soul and experienced, goodness only knows. Even she had to send for her sister-in-law, and then one of the lady tourists at Pike's gave advice, so there were plenty of witnesses and no lack of wagging tongues. A breech birth, as if the girl hadn't enough to deal with. Angus McPhee was down at Pike's, evidently, for a hot meal, showing no care for his daughter. Jock heard him say that it would be a blessing if the poor girl died. Said it out loud to George Pike! The man has a lump of lead where his heart should be.

At last, with Bridie moaning and writhing — she wouldn't understand it at all, and no friend to hold her hand: I might have calmed her, or the Sisters — the babe was born, a little boy of a good size. But Chinese! No mistaking it. They were all shocked into silence, the lady tourist told me. His little head covered in long black hair and his slits of eyes. I could tell that lady was no friend of the Chows. The only good thing, she said, was that the mother seemed to like him. Held the mucky bundle while they tidied her up, and whimpered to hold him again when they washed and wrapped him.

If the ladies were silent at the birth, Angus McPhee was anything but. Jock said that when the news came down to Pike's that his grandson was Chinese you could have heard his fury miles away.

'Get her out!' he shouted. 'Out of my house! I'll not set foot there till she has gone.'

Mrs Hoddle, who had been sent with the news because she is a powerfully built woman and can stand up to most, tried to reason with him. 'He is your grandson, when all is said and done, Angus, and may be a useful hand in the mill for the future.'

'No grandson of mine!' the fellow ranted. I can just imagine his pale skin turning raspberry and those icy eyes searching for anyone to blame. 'He will not be a McPhee! Get her out. Get them both out!'

So the Hoddles took Bridie and the baby in until she stopped her bleeding, and then they were both sent back to the Sisters at Jerusalem, thank the Blessed Virgin.

STELLA WAS WITH me when Hatrick's cart brought them down. McPhee wouldn't pay for the coach. Lucky brought the cart right to the back entrance of Pipiriki House, Bridie bouncing around among the empty sacks, smiling and holding the baby. That same empty smile. My heart in my mouth that she would drop the babe. How could they allow her to hold such a precious bundle over all the ruts and pot-holes between here and Raetihi? Lucky is a good carter, but has no thought except for his horses and his cart. I reached up to take the babe, for surely he would need changing, but Bridie frowned and clutched at her baby. Here's trouble, I thought. Even then I could see it. The Sisters were going to have their hands full. So I called to Stella to fetch fresh napkins and a big mug of sweet cocoa — Bridie's favourite.

Well, there was no getting her down, and anyway Lucky would

take her on down to Jerusalem, so up I climbed — no easy feat for me — and sat with them both. Bridie was neat and clean, the Hoddles had seen to that, but I was shocked to see how pale and thin she was, and terrible raw patches on both ankles. They had tied her up like some animal! Bridie smiled, though, and showed the babe. Wouldn't let me hold him, mind. The best we could do, when Stell arrived, was to change the poor mite on Bridie's lap while she gulped at her cocoa.

'Oh, the sweetheart,' cried my Stell. 'Look at all that hair! Look at his button nose! He's so like . . .' And then stopped. No doubt remembering Charlie Chee and his sad end.

We got his little black head latched on to her breast. At least we were at the back of the House and no guests in sight — Bridie has no idea of modesty. But the little fellow sucked away and Bridie let him. I fancy she liked it, for she went into some quiet dreamy world and sat still for once. It was strange, though. The babe so Chinese. My babies were half Maori, so you'd think I'd be used to a mixture, but I have to admit it was an uneasy sight to me, that foreign head latched on to Bridie's pale breast. I could see Stella had no qualms, smiling and clucking at the sight. She is more modern than me.

So it was Charlie Chee all along, that poor lonely man. We none of us understood one thing about him.

Then Lucky hupped his horses and took the two of them down to the Sisters. They would know how to manage. I suppose it was the news that Danny wasn't the father, but my Stella was transformed that day. I hardly recognised her from the tearful wreck who went upriver a few weeks ago. Glowing is the word that came to mind. You'd think she was the one with the baby.

'I'm heading downriver,' she said, giving me that wonderful smile. 'Dannyboy and I need to talk.'

'But why on earth,' I said — I couldn't stop myself asking the question — 'would Danny claim fatherhood?'

Secretly I thought that if Charlie Chee had lain with her, Danny might well have done the same, and a good many others I could name.

'I need to talk to him,' was all she would say. Stella knew something. Some bee in her bonnet. But it was a tonic to see her so alive again, so I let the matter lie.

'They can't hold him now,' I said. 'Or not for anything more serious than hitting that wretched McPhee, and he's done lock-up time for that already.'

'Yes,' she said, very determined. 'I'll bring him back.'

'And if you're down in Wanganui, ask around about your brother,' I said. 'I have a feeling . . .'

For some reason this sobered her up. 'No, Ma, he's gone. We would have heard by now. Pita's gone.'

Next morning she gave me a quick hug and was running down to the landing where the *Waimarie* was belching and whooping, pressured up and ready for the run downriver. Douglas McPhee was down there, seeing to the *Wairua's* coal bunker. I saw him come across to Stella. Pleading, it looked like. Saw Stella push him away so he stumbled. They had an argument; I could hear the shouts even up at the House, Stella's hands flying at him.

That boy is becoming a nuisance. The other day he told Tim Naylor some cock-and-bull story about Danny killing our Pita. As if Douglas would have any idea. When the constable came to me, worried about the silly tale, I told him how Douglas had taken a shine to Stella. Probably thought he was in with a chance while Danny was locked up. Perhaps, I suggested, now that Danny was off the hook in the fatherhood department, Douglas had dreamed up another tale to keep him out of the way. I laughed at the time, but the constable didn't see fit to crack his face.

Bert must have a word to Douglas.

Hatrick's Landing, Wanganui

Approximate time occupied on trips: Travellers must understand that these vary according to the state of the river.

Wanganui – Pipiriki: 9 hours up stream.
Pipiriki – Wanganui: 5 hours down stream
Pipiriki – Houseboat: 10 hours up stream.
Houseboat – Taumarunui: 8 hours up stream
Taumarunui – Houseboat: 3½ hours down stream
Houseboat – Pipiriki: 6 hours downstream

Taumarunui to Wanganui is 150 miles

FARES

Do not at any time exceed 3d. per mile. Return Tickets are issued at a large reduction. Fares are subject to alteration; it would therefore be misleading to quote a fixed rate between any two points, but the above will be a sufficient guide.

Note. A telegram from any telegraph station to **HATRICK & CO.,** Wanganui will receive prompt attention. Tourists can arrange for transit of horses and carriages on the steamers

Advertisement in a tourist booklet, c.1906

STELLA CAN'T KEEP her eyes off Danny; can't stop smiling. They sit side by side on the grass in the early morning sun. In front of them the river flows, green and placid, curving past houses and wharves, in no hurry to lose itself in the sea beyond. Close by, on Hatrick's landing, men are loading sacks of flour and sugar, tins of kerosene, a pair of cart-wheels, a long piece of shining metal that could be a blade for a ploughshare, the mail sack emblazoned with official stamps, wooden boxes — the heavy ones would be nails; those that are tossed from shore to boat are tea — and finally, lifted aboard with great care, a beautiful carved harmonium, bound for one of the missions upriver. Already smoke is pouring out of the paddle-steamer's funnel, but it is a good hour before the passengers will embark. Stella and Danny still have time to talk.

At first light Danny was released from jail. He found Stella waiting. Now they sit hand in hand. Stella wants to talk about safe things first — the farm, news from upriver — but Danny places a gentle finger on her mouth.

'Stell, I have to tell you something. If I wait I might lose the courage.'

Stella watches him. He's breathing fast. His face is pale from his weeks in jail, thinner, but she senses something different there. A determination. But the words won't come.

'It's all right,' she murmurs, stroking his dear, bony hand. 'Say it, Danny.'

He looks at her clearly then. 'Stella, I killed your brother. I didn't mean to, but I was angry. I hit him — hard — and he drowned in the river.'

Stella nods. 'Yes.' She sighs. It's out now. They can start again.

Danny's eyes are still on her. 'I'm so sorry. I should have said something straight away but I was frightened . . .'

'. . . that they would take you away from me. The farm.' She smiles at him.

Danny nods helplessly. 'You knew?'

'Only a few weeks ago. Someone told me.'

Danny growls. 'Douglas?'

'Yes, Douglas. He's a silly mixed-up boy, don't worry about him. At first I didn't believe him — no one does, the fool. But then I thought about it all, back at the farm, and suddenly it all made sense.' She holds both his hands. This is important. 'Danny?'

'Yes?'

'You didn't sleep with that poor girl, did you?'

Danny shifts uncomfortably. Looks away. 'No.' He laughs shortly. 'There were times I could have . . . she would rub up so close . . .'

'All this . . . this carry-on about Bridie. You were trying to make up, weren't you? For Pita.'

Danny shifts impatiently, but Stella is with him, holding on to him, heedless of who might be watching.

'No, Danny, listen. Please! Oh, Dannyboy, I want you back home. I need you. We have to sort it out!' She won't tell him her news until Bridie is out of the way.

Danny twists in her arms. He pulls away from her, walks off down the riverbank, but she comes after him. Holds on to an arm. He stops then, hanging his head hopelessly. She sees the tears in his eyes, knows he's in pain but will not give in.

'Danny? You're not in love with her? With Bridie? You're just mixed up about Pita. Guilty. Isn't that it?'

'Leave it, Stell,' he mumbles, shaking his head as if to rid it of her words. 'You're making it all wrong.'

'What?'

'I don't know,' he mumbles. 'Maybe you see it more clearly than I do, Stell. Or maybe too black and white. We're different. With me it's all mixed up. Bridie is important. A good thing, not some explanation. I wanted to save her! I still do.'

He looks at her now, steadier, though the tears still drip off his chin. She catches one on her finger. Licks it and smiles at him. 'Sweetheart.'

Danny groans. 'I'm not clever like you, Stell. I can't explain what goes on in my head. Maybe you're right. After the accident I helped Bridie when I should have gone to save Pita.' He looks at her defensively. 'At least I did help her. It's a sort of promise, I suppose. If I go on taking care of her, that makes . . . makes leaving Pita better.' He rubs at the tears impatiently. 'Don't ask me to explain. I can't be fitted into any neat box, Stell. Don't try. I wish I'd saved Pita but I didn't and now this is something . . .' His words dry up.

Stella kisses his wet cheek. 'I can understand that. It makes sense.'

'I thought you would hate me. For Pita.'

She smiles at him. 'Maybe I should.'

'I still want to look after Bridie. It's a good thing I can do.'

Stella sighs. 'If it is so important to you. But not at the farm. We can't.'

He frowns at her, that same set determination that she noticed earlier. But says nothing. They stand side by side, watching the water.

The steam whistle makes them both jump and they laugh together.

'Oh, Stell, Stella,' he says. 'My beauty.'

WHEN THEY ARE well upriver, the bend before Pipiriki, back in the country they both love, he tells her his plans, his mouth close to her ear so she can hear above the chuffing engine. He has talked to someone while he was in prison. A place has been found for him on a road-building gang. He will work for six months. Earn enough to buy good seed and stock for the farm. Spend one more year getting it into good enough shape to sell.

'Then we'll move downriver a bit, start up a business. You're clever enough for anything and I'm not really a farmer. We could start up a shop. Take over the post office at Pipiriki! We could be the entertainment at the House! Old Arthur is past it — I've heard your mother say it often enough!'

Stella laughs. It's so good to see him like this again. 'Yes! Yes!'

she says. Her own news must be spoken in a quieter place.

'But first,' says Danny, suddenly serious, 'I have to tell your Ma and Pa about Pita.'

Stella is proud to hear him say this. Her parents need to know. It will be a terrible blow to Ma. She has been so sure he will turn up. Danny obviously thinks they will not turn him back to the law. But is he right on that count? Suddenly she's afraid for him.

Danny is still planning. 'And I'll ask Bert to send one of his nephews from the kainga up to help on the farm while I'm gone. And to protect you. We're going to be all right, Stell.'

It's as if he knows.

LATER, SHOUTS AND cries from the Morrows' cottage travel on the still evening air. Several inhabitants of Pipiriki happen to be about, curious to watch as the subdued young couple creep down the hill to the crew's quarters. They beg a cabin and escape inside before questions are asked.

Both are trembling as they lie squeezed together on the single bed. Breaking the news to Stella's parents has shaken them both badly. Bert came close to striking Danny. 'Get out of my house,' he said, his eyes popping with anger. 'You can't be here. How can you think it? Killing my son.' He stood, unbending, by the kitchen door, waiting for Danny to go.

Ma wept and scolded. But for her secret hope that Pita still lived, she might well have gone to the police. 'All these months,' she cried. 'All these months and you said no word! Shame on you, Dannyboy O'Dowd!'

'He's sorry,' wept Stella. 'Can't you see how racked he is?'

Danny's head hung lower and lower. He had no words in the face of their anger and scorn. Finally Stella led him away.

Beyond the tiny window, somewhere in the hills above the little settlement, the comforting whoo-whoo of a ruru sounds. A dog barks. The dark river makes no sound but they can smell its fresh closeness. Stella strokes the curly hair on Danny's chest. 'They will accept it in time. It's the shock.'

Danny holds her tight. His body is slick with a cold sweat. 'I killed their son.' It's as if he has only now fully realised it.

Stella's breath catches in her throat. She had imagined it would all be easier. 'We will give them a grandson,' she says, 'or grand-daughter. We have a child growing, Danny.'

For several minutes he says nothing. She can sense the change in him, though. He stops shaking. Her fingers find his face, trace the smile. She smiles with him and then feels the silent chuckle — or is he crying again?

'Not some Chinese baby?'

'Danny!'

'Or red-head Scot?'

She laughs with him, outraged and delighted. 'Get away with you! He . . . she . . . will be pure-blooded Dannyboy. Remember the time in the river, when we swam?'

Danny laughs out loud now. 'Oho! A water-baby! Oh, Stella.'

Later he asks, 'But will they want a grandson with my blood?'

'I don't know.' Yesterday she would have been sure. 'But I will, my darling.'

IN THE MORNING, before Danny heads downriver to his road gang and Stella goes back up to the farm, Danny tells her of the great world-champion rowing race due to take place on the river later in the year.

'Everyone down in Wanganui is full of it. In jail they were

taking bets already! Our own Billy Webb beat the Australian last
year and now will be defending his title. It'll be a grand day, Stell.
Every boat on the river will be crammed. We'll go too, eh? We'll
meet there. Let's make that the start of our new life.'

There is something hectic about his high spirits. Stella worries
about the time they will spend apart. She wants to hold him,
steady him, but also feels that it is somehow right for him to go.
He needs to find his own way. She smiles and agrees that they
will meet at the great race.

Stella kisses him quickly and runs to board the *Wairua*. He
waves from the landing. She expects him to board the downriver
steamer, which is already pluming black smoke into the still
morning air. But later she is told — by Douglas — that her
husband instead walked down to Jerusalem and asked to see
Bridie.

Jerusalem (Hiruharama)

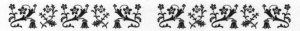

The Celebrated Herbalist

Mother Mary Joseph Aubert Of the Mission at Jerusalem, Wanganui River. Her remedies bear the imprimatur of men like Lord Onslow, ex Governor of New Zealand, Archbishop Redwood, the late C.M. Crombie, Chief Commissioner of Taxes . . .

Influenza, whooping cough, Lung Disease, Asthma are cured by *MARUPA*

Liver Complaints, Rheumatism, Heart Burn, Indigestion, Pains in the Stomach vanish by the use of *PARAMO*

Diarrhœa, Dysentry, General Debility cease by using *NATANATA* and *KARAUA*

The best tonics and invigorating agents yet known. **SCROFULA** yields to *NATANATA*

Distributing Agents
SHARLAND & CO., LTD, WELLINGTON

Advertisement (abridged) from a tourist guide, 1893

DANNY IS STILL waving to Stella as the *Wairua* disappears around the bend. He stands on the landing for a moment and then walks away towards the narrow bridle track that leads downriver. He swings his arms, enjoying the clear sweet air, the curve of the river, the steady left right of his feet on the soft earth. Enjoying the freedom. He has not set out on foot with the purpose of seeing Bridie, as Douglas later reported, but simply for the pleasure of walking free. Six weeks of clanging doors, cramped spaces and noisy inmates has been more than enough to convince Dannyboy that freedom is too precious to be taken

251

lightly. If the Morrows decide to report him over Pita's death, then at least he will have walked this day alongside the river, alone. Sooner or later he will find a track, heading north through the bush to the Parapara road, where there is work for him. If it takes him two or three days to walk it, well and good. He raises his hand as the *Waimarie* rattles downriver, and Bill Henderson, standing at the wheel, waves back. In the deeper silence that always follows the passing of the riverboats, Danny whistles a jaunty tune he learned in jail.

As he nears the settlement of Jerusalem, a wind rises and drives upriver. The ruffled water appears to be moving upstream against the current. Danny thinks of the log raft, the way it bucked in the rapids. His life was so much simpler then. But Stella and he will work it all out. Dark clouds follow behind the blustering wind. Rain is on the way. Danny stops to pull his jacket from his swag. It's then that he thinks of Bridie and decides to visit her. To see if she is in need of anything — nothing more, nothing sinister. The first heavy drops fall as he walks past the row of Maori whares. This is the prettiest of the river settlements, according to Father Soulas, rising gently above the river, which curves around it like a protecting arm. Dogs bark as Danny hurries, head down, against the wind. He doesn't look up to where the beautiful spire of St Joseph's points a finger to God, but stops at the door of the white-painted convent. Here the Sisters sleep and here, on the ground floor, they conduct their school. Perhaps Bridie will be with them.

He knocks, hunching his shoulders against the rain which is driving now, and when a Sister beckons him in he enters and stands, dripping, in the tiny entranceway. The Sister is in no hurry, it seems, to greet him.

She closes the door to the classroom firmly behind her so she and Danny are cramped together in the narrow space. Danny thinks again of the tiny dark lock-up at Raetihi. Sister Carmel frowns. Danny had hoped for Sister Anne, who is young and gentle.

'So, Danny O'Dowd, they have let you out of prison?'

Danny tries a bright smile and a nod. 'They have, Sister.'

His charm seems to have no effect on this tall nun. She keeps her hands firmly tucked into her sleeves, her eyes unsmiling. Danny can hear the starched wimple creak as she moves her head to look through the glass at the quiet children, then back at Danny.

'And so?'

This has been a bad idea. Danny feels his good intentions slide, like the rainwater, away from him. His smile, also, slips. 'I wondered,' he says, looking at the floor, 'how Bridie is? Does she need anything?' He looks up for a moment, hopeful, but Sister Carmel remains stony.

'Danny,' she says, 'you have done enough harm already. Have you come for confession?'

'Not . . . not really. I was passing, and thought . . .'

'You claimed, I believe, to have had carrrr-nal knowledge of our poor Bridie?'

Danny blushes to hear her French accent relish the words. 'Not really,' he stammers. 'It was just . . .'

'Lying is also a sin. What malade have you caused your wife? Her parents?'

'I just want to see her!' shouts Danny suddenly. This is intolerable. 'Is she all right?'

Sister Carmel waits in silence.

'She might need a friend. A friend!'

'The Sisters of Compassion have befriended her. And she has the comfort of the Blessed Virgin. Most certainly she does not need you. Good day. God bless and instruct you, Danny

O'Dowd.' Sister Carmel nods stiffly and re-enters the classroom, leaving him alone.

Outside the rain is pelting now. Danny is glad of it. The sheeting water seems more of a blessing than Sister's onslaught. He shelters under a tree, shaking. Is everyone going to condemn him like this? Surely he has shown only kindness to Bridie? Surely they don't think . . . He drives a fist into the rough bark of the trunk, embarrassed by his own muddled thoughts. But of course they do. Everyone will think he lay with Bridie and is simply lucky the baby is not his. Everyone will feel sorry for Stella and the Morrows to have such an idiot — or worse — in the family.

The rain stops. Danny stands there steaming in the sudden warmth. He looks up at the church. The windows are reflecting watery sunlight. Even they seem to be flashing scorn. He is still standing there, half hidden by the tree, when the children come out to eat their lunch.

There is no sign of Bridie or the baby.

Danny walks away.

IN FACT BRIDIE can see him but makes no sign. She is standing by the window of the little cottage next to the mission school. She rocks her baby. Sister Anne is sitting with her, busy with needle and thread. She sings a few notes of a lullaby and stops. Bridie smiles and repeats it. But when Sister Anne tries to string two lines together, Bridie cannot match her. Two or three notes of a song, two or three words. Nothing more. Little John begins to cry and Sister Anne sighs. This is where the battles begin. Bridie may be under the protection of the Sisters and the Blessed Virgin, as Sister Carmel has asserted, but all is not well with mother and baby.

Sister Anne walks gently towards Bridie and her baby, singing as she comes. Sometimes the music will calm little John and he will fall asleep again. But not this time. Bridie backs away as Sister Anne holds out her hands for the baby. Cornered behind the bed, Bridie turns to the wall, whimpering, while the baby's cries grow louder. Gently, singing still, Sister Anne takes Bridie by the shoulders and pushes her down until she is sitting on the bed. Bridie looks terrified. Slowly, slowly, Sister Anne lifts the mother's smock and guides little John's mouth to the breast. The baby snuffles and wriggles but finally begins to suck. This will always calm Bridie, and is the only way the Sisters can change and wash the little mite.

The trouble is, he will not take the bottle. The little fellow is as wilful as his mother. With no breastfeeding woman in Jerusalem at the moment, there is no alternative to Bridie herself. Her milk is plentiful but the baby is not well, it seems. He cries often. Bridie cries with him. They sleep together in the same bed. Twice the Sisters have forced a separation, hoping that Bridie will forget and little John learn to take milk from a bottle, but mother and baby both became so agitated that the experiment was quickly abandoned.

Sister Anne sighs in exasperation as she fiddles with the napkin. Bridie, her face vacant, lets the baby suck but seems unaware of what else is going on; will not shift or help in any way. It's a messy business.

The Sisters have made inquiries downriver, but it seems that possible wet-nurses are reluctant to feed a Chinese baby. Sister Carmel thinks they will have to send the babe to the convent downriver at Ranana, or even to Mother Aubert's orphanage in Wellington. Which will not solve the problem of Bridie. Sister Carmel is of the opinion that Bridie will forget the baby if they send him away. Sister Anne is not so sure. Some things fly out of

Bridie's head the minute you place them there, but others seem fixed and unchanging. Her desire to walk freely, for example. Bridie has never given up her wandering ways; would walk out with her baby right now if the door were unlocked. Surely her feeling for the baby will be the same; the need — the love? — is fixed. Yet it is clear to them all that it can't go on. John will have to grow up normally, away from Bridie's smothering.

And yet, when the baby is feeding happily they are such a pair! Bridie is thinner now, but is not allowed to wander and so always appears at her best — washed and brushed and properly dressed. A truly beautiful young woman. Her shining copper hair and the delicate freckles on her pale skin give her a look, at moments like these, of great sweetness. An innocent. And John, with his fine straight dark hair and pale creamy skin seems too fragile — those almondy black eyes fringed with perfect delicate lashes make him look somehow wise. He's very different from the robust Maori babies in the village. Sister Anne would love to cuddle the little fellow, but as long as Bridie is awake she will not allow it. Will not allow anyone else to love him. Sister Anne fears Bridie will damage little John, not intentionally, but perhaps by holding him too close, or forgetting what she is doing. Something will have to be done.

Samuel Blencoe

I HEARD HER babby was Charlie Chee's, the old bugger. I
never believed it till I seen that Chow babby myself. It were his
all right.

I remember the way she would hold close to Charlie sometime,
a handful of his tunic, or his hand, as if he were the one steady
thing in a world adrift. I seen the look on Charlie's face then — a
shadowy smile, something tender in it. That little smile made him
look young. Maybe he *were* young: just a boy maybe. A lonely
boy who gave in to her poor innocent tempting of him. They will
think, now, that he hanged himself out of shame. More likely the

despair of the proper wife not coming. No sense wondering: he is hanged and dead.

Bridie come upriver with the little tyke. Terrible mess, the both of them. Bridie, I said to her, Bridie, we can't have this. She just smiled away and walked down to the river to dangle her feet like she used to. Blood running away from the cuts on them. Her smock torn. The little babe crying. She held him in a gentle manner, I'll say that for her, but he were not at all clean. Nor her. She were doing her rocking, like she used to when things got too much. Not the gentle kind of rocking a mother does to a babby, but back and forth, back and forth; urgent, it seemed. And Charlie Chee's son crying the while.

I feared she might drop him in, so I sat with her. Then when she seemed more settled and the rocking not so fierce, I got my billy and dipped clean riverwater and washed the two of them as they sat there. The sun being up and warm, neither a one of them seemed to mind the cool of it. Then somehow Charlie's boy got his little mouth latched onto her breast and we had a bit of peace.

Dear God.

What were the Sisters thinking of, letting her loose with the babe? I heard our Bridie were back with them, away from that cold bugger McPhee. That were a great piece of news, I thought, and thanked the Maori feller down at the pa that come up and told me. He knew I were fond of her. Now she'll be right, I thought. Then she turns up, scratched and torn and the baby's mess all down her front and stinking. We can't have that at all. My hands were shaking as I washed the two of them, and then my legs caught the shakes and I had to sit beside her till I could catch my breath.

My poor Bridie. Dear God.

It would be some months since I seen her. She gone right

downhill. Thin. That sweet smile gone. Any soul could tell she were not at peace with herself. Some kind of flickering between her eyes, like a small frown, on off, on off. I put out a hand to smooth it away, stroked her like you might a sick dog. But that twitch kept on till I was mad thinking how I might bring some peace to her. I could not.

Bridie was one thing. She were a free spirit and I thought it good for her to come and go. And Charlie alive and on the same beat as it were, up and down river, to keep an eye. But the babby were another thing altogether. I could not think of how to go on. Deadly afeared, I was, to leave the two of them and find help. What if she dropped Charlie's boy in the river? Or hugged the life out of him?

Then I thought, sure to God those Sisters would be searching and sure they would know to look up here. That thought calmed me a mite and my legs stopped their trembling. The three of us could wait. I washed out his bit of cloth and spread it on a bush and then he peed again, a shining curve up into the air — a real beauty to see. I laughed and Bridie laughed too, her first. But then he shat all down Bridie's front again and no one was laughing. I washed them both clean. But now Charlie's boy cried. I reckon he were cold so I give them both my old coat.

We waited. I started my trembling again. She would not come up to the hut but stayed with her feet in the river. Those feet turning blue.

'Some good soul please come!' I said it out loud and she echoed me.

'Come.'

But no idea in her head what it might mean or how afeared I were. We was all shaking with the cold.

Then thank the good Lord or the gods of the bush or whoever, up come Bert Morrow in his motor-waka, chugging slow, looking at the bank. I stood and waved and he come in, drifting the last feet, sweet and gentle as featherdown, to touch the bank right at our feet, giving Bridie no cause to startle. That sight of the big man standing in his craft, a smile on his face, was better than a vision from heaven itself. Bert knowing to be quiet, taking my hand and guiding it so I might hold the waka in to the bank, but no word spoken, so her and the babby might stay calm. I thought how that damn McPhee carried her off without any shred of gentleness and in my head I blessed Bert Morrow for his knowledge and his wise ways.

Bridie stood with the babby and allowed Bert to guide her into the waka. I don't know how he did that — some Maori trick, for I had no luck getting her to shift. Bert had a good blanket which he wrapped around her and the boy and then he signed me to get in too, to guard her and make sure she would not jump out.

I do not take pleasure in leaving my spot. I cleared my throat once or twice and spat, but in the end I come, out of care for Bridie and respect for Bert Morrow. He would bring me back, I reckon.

We went down direct to the Sisters, where I never been since I come upriver. And we handed Bridie to them. Bert Morrow knit his brows and spoke most sternly.

'You must take the baby away from her, Sister.'

The tall sister, in her white and black like a magpie, said, 'We know that, thank you, but it is more difficult than you think, Mr Morrow.'

Bert said, 'Difficult or not, you must think of the boy first. We none of us would want his death on our hands.'

The sister sighed and frowned. I reckon she had no taste for being told a few home truths by Bert Morrow.

Bridie was not happy. It took three of the Sisters to lead her away. She screamed when they forced her arms open and took Charlie Chee's son from her. A small sound — thin and sharp as glass. I never heard her scream yet, not once, not even when Charlie hanged himself.

Bert Morrow and myself watched her go up with the Sisters, struggling every step and groaning for her babby. We neither of us spoke. It were the saddest sight.

Then Bert took me back home, up the rapids in the dark; he knows every ripple and bend blindfold, I reckon. When he put me in to the bank he spoke the first time since Jerusalem.

'You did a good thing to save her and the baby. It was good she came to you, Sam.'

I said nothing but climbed up to my hut and lay down under my blanket. I should be glad to be back in the quiet and the soft night, and listen to the motor-waka fade off downriver, but those words Bert Morrow spoke kept churning in my head. Were it good I saved her? Would she be moaning and crying still? I had to hope the Sisters would let her roam again when the babe was safely away from her. But I reckon they would keep her locked for fear of some other man taking advantage of her. I could think of no good path for my Bridie.

Dear God, she seemed so lost, poor soul.

15 December 1908

⁓

The World-Champion Rowing Race

ON 15TH DECEMBER 1908 no Hatrick steamer was seen upriver. Pipiriki House was deserted except for the gardener and his two dogs. A caretaker was left in charge of the empty Houseboat at Maraekowhai. Captain White, his wife, Stella and many of the farming families had crowded the deck of the *Wairua* two days earlier and steamed downriver to be in time for the great race. Father Soulas had suggested the Sisters take the convent children down to view this historic event. Naturally he was interested himself; wasn't the pride of Wanganui at stake here? Mr Hatrick, that great man, was in the thick of it (and making money hand over fist), with his whole fleet recalled for duty down at the race.

One year earlier William 'Wiri' Webb, citizen of Wanganui (no one liked to remember that he was born in Christchurch) and a brilliant sculler, had crossed the Tasman to row against world champion Charles Towns on the Parramatta River. And beat him! Who would have dreamed the Australians could be beaten — or for that matter the English, who considered themselves the rightful owners of sculling skills? Not only did our Wiri bring back the world champion cup but he defended it, in February of this very year, against that Tressider of England. Beat him, too! On the Whanganui.

Hatrick, usually not one to miss an opportunity if there was money in it, realised he had slipped up over the Webb vs Tressider match. Several hundred citizens were there to watch but it should have been thousands! Now, in December, with some fellow from the South Island challenging our Wiri, Hatrick was pouring all his resources into the event. Since dawn his fleet, pluming coal smoke into the blessedly calm air, had been churning up the five miles of calm water to Upokongaro, where the race would be held. Every inch of every deck was crowded. Up and down the steamers chugged, until the banks were crowded with spectators: the ladies dressed to kill in their widest hats and most colourful scarves, the gentlemen as smart as Sunday. Picnic baskets overflowed with sandwiches, tarts and flasks of tea. If you took the boat early in the morning the fare was three shillings. Each hour later the fare rose by a shilling. Wealthy citizens have paid one pound for a place on the steamers that would follow the race, or even two pounds (think of that!) if they could afford to be a friend of Mr Hatrick and ride with him in the umpire's boat, the *Waione* — one of the Hatrick fleet, of course.

On the Hatrick boats you could buy souvenirs of the event,

picturing our Wiri, so handsome with his flashing dark eyes and his curving moustache, on one side of the postcard and Richard Arnst, smaller and surely no match for Wiri, on the other. Between them a tranquil scene of the beautiful Whanganui. Silver teaspoons sporting enamelled images of Wiri sold well, as did the mugs painted with a spray of manuka flower and a man sculling into the petals, *Wanganui 1908* painted below in gold. The tote was taking official bets, but if you looked along the banks there were plenty of unofficial bookies would take your wager.

Naturally, the odds favoured Wiri Webb. Hadn't he beaten the best that Australia and England could throw up? And wasn't he rowing on his own river? Captain Bill Henderson had taken spectators up to Webb's training camp on two occasions (another of Hatrick's money-making ideas) and said that our champion was in top form. In Captain Henderson's opinion Webb could not be beaten. Bert Morrow took his advice and laid a careful two shillings on Webb to win and another shilling for him to break his own record.

The Morrows and O'Dowds were there on the bank, a few chains below the finishing line, Bert's motor-waka moored close by so he could keep an eye on it. Every craft on the river was here, even the *Togo* and the *Mascot*, the Harbour Board tugs. Had world shipping come to a standstill for this race? Bert spotted Hepi Samuel's worm-ridden flattie wallowing under a load of his family and predicted (accurately, as it turned out) that it would sink before the race began.

And, unknown to any of his family, Pita was there too. Even the jail was more or less empty, prisoners near the end of their sentence having been let out early to view this famous event and perhaps develop a little civic pride along the way. Constable Tim Naylor had spotted Pita and was following him through the crowd. Word was that he had a cache of illegal money hidden somewhere, apart from the sum confiscated from him on arrest. Naylor wanted to catch him red-handed.

Angus McPhee had come down 'on business' with his daughter, Gertie. Evangeline McPhee declined, with a pale sigh, the arduous river trip. None of McPhee's workers was given leave to travel. 'Wanganui is no concern of ours,' he growled to his sulking men. 'Raetihi is the future of this area. Mark my words, the branch railway will come through here and we will be sitting pretty — citizens of a town, nay, a city — to put Wanganui in the shade.' The future would prove Angus McPhee's prediction to be nowhere near as accurate as Bert Morrow's. The sawmiller was losing his touch — and his business — though he didn't yet know that. McPhee was on a sharp lookout for his wastrel son, Douglas. It was high time the boy returned to the sawmilling business.

Douglas McPhee was expected at the race — expected to be shovelling coal along with all the other stokers in the fleet — but he had taken advantage of the general mayhem of the day to slip off the *Wairua* as it drew in to Jerusalem to pick up a chattering load of Sisters and convent girls. Douglas was on a mission of his own.

No one expected Sam Blencoe or Bridie to be interested in the great event. Nor were they.

Danny and Stella

THE WORLD CHAMPIONSHIP!
BILLY WEBB
TRAINED ON . . .

ferro-Stout

Advertisement, Wanganui Herald, *December 1908*

AT FIRST STELLA can't see Danny among the milling crowds at Hatrick's wharf. For a moment she fears the worst but there he is, hopping from one foot to the other, shouting and waving.

'Stella! Stell! Over here!'

After the quiet despair of the farm at Maraekowhai, the noise and activity at the landing is almost overwhelming. So many people! Stella has travelled down to Wanganui on the day before the race, but already the whole town seems to be on the move. Tents and makeshift whares dot the banks of the river; hawkers invite sightseers to buy souvenir postcards showing W. Webb in every pose imaginable — always against a background of luxuriant bush and peaceful river. An enterprising couple have set up a plank on which bottles of home-made lemonade are selling well. Another fellow shouts and cajoles customers into buying his muscle-building tonic — 'guaranteed to give you the strength of Wiri Webb, gentlemen! You will notice the difference in one week. And all for only two pence!' A photographer has set up a life-sized portrait of Wiri Webb standing beside a fashionably dressed lady with a hole where her head should be. Women are lining up to be photographed, smiling and posing through the hole. At the Hatrick's office people clamour for steamer tickets. The hesitation Stella feels in the face of this cheerful pandemonium is unusual for her. Usually she loves new sights. But the dragging weight of the baby and her uncertainty at meeting Danny after all these months have made her nervous. She lifts a hand to wave to her husband but then holds back as the other passengers surge off the boat ahead of her.

THE PAST SIX months have been difficult. More than difficult. From the moment when her cousin Hone came upriver to lend a hand, her feeling for the farm changed. Hone was pleasant enough, but no farmer. He came up expecting an easy time; that his task was to protect his cousin and in return be fed and housed. When Stella pointed out that the sheep needed shifting, the meagre crop of hay cut, he became sulky. He demanded that she leave cooked food for him on the nights she spent at the Houseboat. They quarrelled over who should milk the cow.

'You're too bossy, girl,' shouted Hone. 'Milking is woman's work.'

Stella shouted back that she couldn't milk on Houseboat days; that Danny milked Freda and so should he; that Hone should be grateful for the food she cooked and earned. Looking back, Stella could see she had indeed been too bossy. Exhaustion was her excuse: walking back and forth to work became a chore as the baby grew heavier; cooking a meal at the end of a long day almost more than she could manage. Hone's surly manner spoiled any pleasure at homecoming. Stella began to resent the dead weight of the farm.

Then Mrs White took her aside for a quiet word.

'My dear, we can't keep you on after next week. You'll understand, I'm sure.'

Stella had been dreading this, but had to argue. 'Hasn't my work been good? Have I slipped up at all? You know I have completed all my tasks well.'

Mrs White had frowned at her bold words. 'I don't need to tell you. You are showing, my dear, and we can't have you serving the guests in this state. There have been complaints.'

'Who? Who?' shouted Stella in a rage. 'They all love me!'

A foolish statement. Mrs White tightened her lips, turned away. Later the captain told her that a new girl would be coming upriver at the beginning of the week to replace her. He gave Stella a half guinea and a pat on the shoulder and that was that.

Stella walked back to the farm, still raging. She found Hone lying in the sun and Freda bellowing with the pain of a full udder.

'Go, then!' she yelled. 'I'm home now and can take care of everything. I don't need a useless extra mouth to feed.'

For two months now she has been alone on the farm, watching the weeds grow and the sheep lose condition. On good days she would still sing at her work; would praise the chickens when they produced eggs and ruffle Finn's ears as he sat with her in the sun. Other days she dragged around the house, the chores exhausting her, hardly bothering to make bread or wash her clothes. The thought of Danny working hard to earn money for the farm sometimes encouraged her, but more and more often it filled her with dread. They were stuck here.

Her mother begged her to give up, to come down to the comfort of Pipiriki. But Stella had never failed at anything before; she didn't know how to give in.

Twice she received a letter from Danny. They were full of hope and pride. He was learning to read and write; he had been given a banjo just like his old one and was playing with his friends; he was saving good money; he sent his love to his darling and to the baby. Stella sat alone in the dark farmhouse, envying his happiness and freedom.

When Freda and her new calf both died inexplicably, Stella, in despair, asked a neighbour to look after the horse and the sheep, opened the chicken coop door and walked away with Finn, down to Pipiriki. Her mother welcomed her, railed against Danny for leaving her alone, fussed about with special meals and new clothes for the baby. But Stella felt her failure keenly.

NOW SHE HANGS back on the boat, uncertain. Her heart lifts to see Danny, but something holds her to her seat. Danny, shouting and hallooing, jumps the railing and comes aboard. His grin, when he sees his wife's belly, splits his face. 'Will you look at this!' he yells. 'Oho! See what my darling has been cooking for me!'

'Danny, for goodness sake!' But Stella is suddenly laughing, happy now that his arm is around her, steering her off the boat and through the crowd. He chatters away — some plan she doesn't quite catch.

'Let me sit a while, somewhere quiet,' she says. 'I'm not used to all this, Danny.'

272

'No time, no time, sweetheart. We have an appointment!' But he finds a bench and they sit a moment, arm in arm.

She can see how on edge he is. A sheen of sweat beads his face, and his hands are trembling. 'Is something the matter, Danny? Tell me now or I'll be fearing heaven knows what.'

'No sweetheart; I'm nervous is all. How is your voice?'

'My voice? You can hear me, can't you? What a question, Danny, when we have only just set eyes on each other.'

He grins. 'Sure, I'm sorry. You weren't listening just now, were you, poor darling, in all the crowd and the fuss. We are about to give a little concert. You are going to sing to Mr Hatrick himself!'

'What?'

But Danny has her on her feet again and is steering her across the road to Hatrick's offices. Outside the door three men are waiting with instruments. They are dressed in green waistcoats and bow ties identical to Danny's. Stella wants to walk away. This will be another of Danny's madcap ideas, doomed to failure. But his hand is steadier now and his mood quieter as he introduces the men.

'We have formed a band,' he says proudly. 'All of us were together on the road gang and found we could make a grand sound. So listen, Stell, I have spoken to Mr Hatrick this morning and he is willing to give us his ear!'

This seems unlikely, but Danny's evident pride is infectious. Stella smiles at Danny's friends and they grin back, clearly as nervous as he is. The tall grey-headed man, Fitz, carries a fiddle; dumpy Harry sits on a stool beside his side drum and tambourine. A freckled young lad, Ginger, hands a banjo to Danny and then unhooks his own accordion. Danny talks non-stop while they are tuning up. Goodness knows how he catches the note.

'We are mainly Irish, Stell, so that's what we play. A bit of

Scottish. We've got one Yankee song too. And even a dance bracket! Wait till you hear! But he wants songs, Stell. He wants a lady singer for evenings at Pipiriki House. I told him I knew all the songs and he nodded away but then demanded a lady singer as well. A lovely sweet voice for the gentlemen tourists, he said. And a band on the steamers for the weekend excursions. We would play on board and then present an entertainment up at the picnic ground. The excursion parties want music, he said, so he's in the market if we're good enough. We thought we'd play him an instrumental — "Yankee Girls", maybe, eh, lads? And then you could sing "Rose of Tralee" or "Teddy O'Neill". Which would you like? We can do either just grand, sweetheart.'

A crowd is beginning to gather outside the Hatrick offices, attracted by the sound of Fitz's fiddle. Once the instrument is under his chin, it seems he can stop neither fingers nor bow. The lively tune has them all tapping.

'Wait, man, wait!' shouts Danny. 'We got to do this right.'

'Get the boss out there, then,' says Fitz, jigging and nodding away in time to some tune in his head. 'I can't hold back the music all day!'

Stella's head is reeling with it all. She has come downriver, full of anxiety about her husband, dreading having to tell him how badly the farm is doing, wondering how he will take the news that she has lost her work at the Houseboat, and here he is, chirpy as a cricket, none of the old cares and anxieties. She fears a sudden descent.

'Button your coat, love, so he can't see the baby just yet,' whispers Danny. Then he's off inside to bring out the big man, walking proudly, banjo tucked under his arm.

'You've a good'un there,' says grey-headed Fitz to her. 'He'll do the business all right.'

No one has ever said this to her about Danny.

'I hope your voice is as good as he says,' he adds. 'I need this job right bad.'

'We all do.' Ginger is strapped up and ready, his fingers poised over the buttons of his accordion. Stella guesses that he is not quite so confident as the older two. 'I'd be pleased if you chose "Rose of Tralee",' he whispers. 'The chords are easier.'

'"Rose of Tralee" then.' Stella clears her throat. 'I like to sing it high.' Ginger pulls a chord out of his squeeze-box. She hums a note or two and nods. 'That'll do.' She smoothes the creases in her worn old coat; wishes she had something smart to wear like the others. Fitz notices and remembers something. He pulls from a bag at his feet a long green scarf.

'Danny bought this for you. The idiot forgot to give it to you. On with it smartly!'

She wraps the bright material around her neck, letting it flow loose down over the mound of the baby, then pulls out the ribbon tying back her hair. It falls long and dark over her shoulders. She turns to the men. 'How do I look?'

'A bloody vision of loveliness, madam. Welcome to Danny's Irish band!' says Fitz, laughing and bowing low.

And here, surprisingly, is the great man himself, out on the pavement to listen. Something Danny has said has put him in a good mood, for he is laughing, his bushy moustache leaping around like a small animal and his big paw clamped on Danny's shoulder.

'Let's hear you then, Mr Cheeky O'Dowd, and we'll see.' He stands, feet apart, hands on his hips, every inch the successful entrepreneur, with no minute to waste on inferior matters.

Danny counts them in and they are off at a lively pace. They're good. Someone in the crowd knows the words and joins in at the chorus: '. . . *Yankee girls, can't you dance the polka?*' Others clap. Mr Hatrick likes that, you can tell. He's watching the crowd, noting their reactions. Stella watches him. Does he realise the connection? The logging accident? Her parents at Pipiriki House? Then the slower introduction to 'Rose of Tralee' brings her back to the moment and she sings. The band stick with her when she draws out a note, the fiddle playing a counter-tune. It's such a pleasure to sing with them! Stella turns towards Mr Hatrick and sings just to him for a line or two, then turns back, smiling, to the crowd. Danny beams at her.

'Should we play another?' asks Danny when the applause fades.

'Not today, sir, or we'll all be behind schedule,' booms Hatrick. He turns to the listening crowd. 'What do you think? Shall we hire them?'

'Yes! Give them a go!' the calls come back. Mr Hatrick can work a crowd better than any entertainer.

Hatrick bestows on Stella what might pass for a smile. 'You have an enterprising husband,' he says.

Stella smiles back, light-headed with it all. 'I have.'

'Can you manage the singing *and* a baby, though?'

So he's noticed. She might have known. 'The excursions might be tricky,' she answers. Best to be truthful with this man. 'But at Pipiriki House it would be fine. My parents work there and could help.'

'The Morrows, yes. Your man here has confessed who he is.' He watches her face closely and then turns to Danny, growling. 'See how pale she's gone. As well she might, you rascal. One single hint of adventuring downriver again with logs and you're out that very day.'

Danny dares to grin. 'Ah sir, that was a youthful indiscretion. I was led astray.'

Hatrick is not minded to join in the fun. 'An ill day for your wife's family, I believe. And for a girl's lost mind.'

Stella moves to take Danny's arm. For a moment it seems he will argue, then all the light goes from his face. He swallows, looks to the ground. The members of the band watch on, clearly not understanding.

Hatrick pulls out his watch. 'Well, enough of that. I am trusting that your "youthful indiscretions" are a thing of the past. I like a man with enterprise and will give you the chance. Come back this afternoon, then, and we'll settle the terms.' On his way back inside he turns. 'There's a new Australian song, "Waltzing Matilda". Can you play it?'

'No, sir.'

'Learn it.' And he's gone inside.

'I know the tune,' says Fitz. 'A bit common — no style to it at all. We'll have to educate him.'

But Danny is not laughing with the others. He mumbles something to Fitz and walks away, across the road to the river, leaving Stella to make excuses.

'He's upset by something Mr Hatrick said. Don't worry, he'll be there to sign.' Stella arranges a meeting time and shakes them each by the hand before hurrying after Danny. The little exchange with the men, the new plans give her pleasure after the months of failure on the farm.

She sees Danny immediately — a dear sight: his green waistcoat, his jacket slung over his shoulder, hat tipped at a jaunty angle. Though he is anything but jaunty now, standing still, head down, among all the bustle at the river's edge. She takes his arm, stands silent with him, watching the water flow past. A crowded waka with a barking dog in the prow paddles upriver. Stella wishes she had thought to bring Finn down. He would push his wet nose into Danny's hand, give him comfort.

'Ah dear,' he sighs. 'I had managed to forget, for a while there.'

277

'Pita?'

'Pita.'

'We will both have to learn how.'

'We will.' He looks at her, such a rueful, complicated smile. 'Dear God, it is wonderful to see you, Stell. And the baby.'

Suddenly Stella begins to shake. 'Oh Danny, I needed you so badly up there. I think the farm is gone, sweetheart. I couldn't manage.' Tears run down her cheeks: exhaustion perhaps, or shame. 'I did things all wrong, upset everyone. I'm no good without you. You mustn't go away again like that.'

Danny leads her to along the bank to where the weeping branches of a willow make a private place. They sit there, hidden, not caring whether their tears are sorrow or joy.

'That damn farm,' says Danny, smiling. 'It has a will of its own, eh, sweetheart? It wants its bush back. The tall trees and the ferns. Shall we walk away? Let it grow wild again?'

'It's already doing that, willy-nilly.' Stella sniffs. 'This band thing: can it work, then?'

Now it's Danny's turn to show doubt. 'I think so. We're good. We can do better, too. Fitz is a bloody genius. But we would need to live at Pipiriki. Would your parents have me there?'

Stella frowns. 'I don't know. Pa is still angry. The baby will help, maybe.'

Douglas McPhee

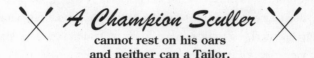

A Champion Sculler
cannot rest on his oars
and neither can a Tailor.

He must be
PUSHING AND VIGOROUS in Business,
give the **FINEST QUALITY OF MATERIAL,**
the **BEST of WORKMANSHIP**
& **REASONABLE PRICES**

This is what has gained the excellent reputation for
CARRAD & HOWE Merchant Tailors
125 the Avenue, Wanganui

Advertisement, Wanganui Herald, *December 1908*

WHEN DOUGLAS REALISES that Sister Anne is not among those embarking with the other Sisters at the Jerusalem landing, he speaks urgently to his engineer.

'Could you do without me for the last leg? Please, Dusty, please? It's easy going now. I'll make it up to you. Just don't tell Captain. It's my sick sister. She's in need up at the convent.'

He has no intention of visiting Bridie, but Douglas is on a desperate mission, which in his mind excuses the shaving of the truth a little. Dusty opens his mouth to grumble, but before the words are out, Douglas is over the side and into the river, quick as a fish. All eyes are on the excited convent girls and the perfectly starched Sisters; the captain doesn't spot his grimy stoker swimming away from the steamer, then drifting, with scarce a ripple, under the drooping branches of a willow. Douglas clings there, hidden among the green reflections, until the *Wairua* has steamed downriver, leaving behind the usual pale signature of its presence — a smudge of coal smoke hanging in the still air and the dying echoes of its pounding engine.

Douglas climbs out onto the bank. The little settlement seems deserted, but surely Sister Anne will be here if she is not aboard the steamer? His heart beats to think of her pretty young face, cruelly imprisoned inside the stiff folds of the wimple and heavy black veil. He is convinced she is being held against her will, and will come away if offered a way out. He washes the soot from his face and clothes and stands a while on the bank, letting the morning sun dry him. Even the dogs must have gone down to the race — or are asleep. He watches the settlement, looking for signs of Sister Anne.

WHEN STELLA'S BABY became obvious under her Hatrick uniform, Douglas soon forgot his great love for her.

'Whose is it?' he had whispered to her one night outside the crew's quarters. 'Did one of the tourists take advantage of you?' He was ready at first to forgive, to knock the blackguard down, even to save her reputation by accepting mother and child.

When Stella laughed and said of course it was Danny's he had stared at her, outraged. 'How could you?' he cried. 'How could you lie with a murderer and a lecher?' The poisonous words slid off his tongue, as satisfying as a warm bath.

Stella was very short with him. 'He is my husband. Whatever he's done is no business of yours, Douglas McPhee. I'll hear no more of your nasty little lies.'

The thought that she could be happy to carry that man's child made her repugnant — no better than a slut. She continued to work on the Houseboat and at the farm, often singing and smiling, even though her husband — the evil father of her child — had abandoned her, it seemed. It cut Douglas deeply that no one took seriously his report that Danny had murdered Pita. Stella had laughed at him. The policeman dropped the case, citing insufficient evidence, and then asked several sharp questions about his pestering Stella. Pestering! She was in danger of her life. Well, he doesn't care any longer. When Stella was dismissed from the Houseboat and disappeared up the Ohura River to her farm, Douglas felt no regrets.

AT JERUSALEM THE church bell tolls and the dogs join in furiously. There must be life here after all. Douglas climbs up to the convent on the hill. She'll be there. He's still thinking of Sister Anne, not his blood sister. He came down once to see Bridie after they took the baby away. It was so shocking he could not visit her again. She had torn the skin of her face and arms with her fingernails. The wounds were healing — the Sisters kept her nails closely pared now — but the sight of the scars and her angry staring eyes frightened him. She had been so gentle before. Sister Anne had been with her then, patiently feeding the demented girl. Douglas no longer thought of Bridie as his sister.

'This is a terrible task for you,' he had said. 'My sister gives you no thanks for your care.'

Sister Anne had sighed. 'It's very painful for her, poor soul. She cannot forget her baby, but searches all day for him.'

Douglas thought she looked so sad, the Sister — so beautiful, captured inside her dark clothes and sighing.

'Is this what you do all day?' he had asked. 'Sit with Bridie all day?'

'Goodness, no. I care for the other children, and clean their rooms and milk the cows and work in the garden. And pray to God for His guidance.'

Douglas, always ready to seek out those in need of rescue, could see only sadness in her face. 'Aren't you sorry?' he asked.

The Sister had sighed again. 'I am out of my mind with worry,' she said. 'There is nothing to be done that I can think of.'

Douglas had vowed then and there to devote his life to saving Sister Anne.

HE FINDS HER praying with another Sister in the church. He stands in the doorway watching her. The sun comes through the beautiful arched windows, illuminating her bowed face. She looks like a painting, Douglas thinks — so calm, so stoic, even though her life is so unbearable. He waits there, worshipping her.

As the two Sisters come from the church into the sunlight, Sister Anne smiles to see him.

'Hello, Douglas,' she says. 'While all the world has gone to the champion race, you have come to visit your sister. I am pleased to see you so caring.'

Douglas has practised the words he will say, but now they will not emerge. He stands silent before her, blocking her way forward. The other Sister waits, looking downward modestly.

Sister Anne tucks her hands into her wide black sleeves. 'I am on my way to see to her now. Shall we go together?' she says, stepping around him. 'Perhaps the sight of you can bring her some cheer. She has not smiled or said a word in all these weeks.'

The last thing Douglas wants is to see Bridie again. He is

forced, now, to follow behind the two Sisters as they pace in their quiet way over to the cottage where Bridie is locked.

'Sister Anne,' he says to her terrible black back. 'Please, Sister, I would like to talk to you.'

She stops, turns to face him. The other Sister pauses too; turns and stands very close to Sister Anne. Are they keeping her prisoner?

'Alone,' he says, but his voice trembles. He curses his flaming cheeks.

Sister Anne bestows on him her lovely gentle smile. 'Sister Agatha is my companion today,' she says quietly. 'Whatever you would like to say to me must be for her ears also.'

This is not working out as he planned at all. He clears his throat.

'I have come to realise,' he begins, then takes a deep breath and tries again. 'Sister Anne, I know in my heart you are not happy here. I would like to offer . . .' but he falters as his lady frowns.

Both the Sisters look at him in stern silence. 'Are they holding you here against your will?' he cries, desperate to hear her say the words. 'You cannot want to stay shut up here — inside those dark clothes! Surely you want to be free?'

Sister Anne smiles. She laughs! Oh, she looks so young and sweet. But why would she laugh?

'Douglas McPhee,' she says, and the words are broken by little bursts of laughter, which she is trying to smother, 'I am perfectly happy here. I am not locked up, nor forced in any way. I love dearly my clothes, which I wear proudly as a sign that I have chosen the way of the Sisters of Compassion.'

Sister Agatha is smiling too, and shaking her head. Douglas realises they are both laughing at him: trying to hide it but failing. It is worse than a physical blow.

'How could you lead me on, then?' he shouts. 'You lied to me — you said you were unhappy!'

Sister Agatha looks at her companion, her eyebrows lifted.

'Douglas,' says Sister Anne in a voice full of pity, 'I am unhappy about your *sister*, not my chosen path. It is all in your mind, any other thought you may have. All in your mind.'

Douglas watches her, searching for a crack. Sister Anne is serious now, her laughter under control.

'If you have a need to rescue someone, try your sister. Poor Bridie.'

'She's not my sister any more, she's one of you! Of your church. I never want to see her again.' Douglas can feel tears beginning to choke him. He turns away from the two black crows.

Sister Agatha's voice follows him. 'Or ask your family to take in your little nephew, John. That would be a lovely rescue, now.'

He can hear the accusation behind her words. But who, in his family, would take in a Chinese baby? He walks away from her words, back towards the river. When he dares to look back they are gone.

But later, as he stands by the slow-moving river, wondering whether to walk up to Pipiriki or to wait for any craft that might still be travelling down, Sister Anne comes running down the hill, her veil flying.

'Douglas!' she shouts. 'Oh Douglas, wait!'

His heart lifts and he runs to meet her.

'Your sister has gone,' cries Sister Anne. 'Holy Mother, while we were wasting our time, there with you, she has smashed a window and climbed out and away. She will be bleeding and frantic. Come quickly and help us search. The others are all downriver.'

Douglas stands rooted to the spot. He is panting, and closes his mouth against what words might emerge. It is all too much.

Sister Anne is already running up the river path, her veil flying behind her like black wings. She turns to beckon. 'Come! Come and search!'

Douglas looks after her. 'I am needed on my boat,' he calls. Suddenly he longs desperately for the sweaty, back-breaking work, the roaring furnace, his beloved crowded engine-room. The easy, uncomplicated friendship of the riverboat men.

He walks away down the river path, watching for passing craft. When the Morrows' motor-waka comes churning around the bend, heading downriver, Douglas steps into a clear patch and hails it. Bert brings the craft in to the bank, but frowns when he sees who it is.

'Where is your boat, sir? Has something happened to the *Wairua?*'

'No, I . . . I was left behind at Jerusalem.'

Ruvey Morrow, who has not favoured Douglas since he spread tales about Danny, melts a little. 'You're a good boy, Douglas, to stop and see to your sister. How is poor Bridie?'

'Not well,' says Douglas, trying to smile. 'Not well at all, Mrs Morrow. Can you give me a lift back to my boat?'

The waka is not crowded: Bert, expecting to bring Danny and Stella back upriver, has left space for them. He grudgingly allows Douglas aboard.

Douglas sits in the prow, watching the green water slide past. The memory of Sister Anne's laughter torments him. What an idiot he is. What a fool to think that pretty women will want him. He leaves a limp hand to trail in the water. Behind him, the Morrows chat with Mere and Eru. He knows he should have said something to them about Bridie's escape. But stronger is his own need to escape — from that cruel Catholic place; from the terrible, unsolvable complication of Bridie.

For a while the putter of the motor, the familiar twists of the river, the exhilarating rush down the rapids bring some kind of peace to his tangled feelings, his shame. But images of Bridie invade: a bleeding, desperate madwoman running through the bush. Sister Anne's plea to help find her haunts him. The beat of the motor strikes a pulse in his head. Bridie, Bridie, Bridie. He should have stayed to help. Douglas shifts restlessly against the rough wood of the waka. He can't be expected to look after her. Or her Chinese baby. How could he? Those black Catholic crows are mad to suggest it. Bridie is past anything Douglas can do. He blames his father, who should not have abandoned her in the first place. It's his fault. And so his thoughts twist, around and around, his anger mounting.

By the time the waka noses alongside the *Wairua* near the quiet settlement of Upokongaro, Douglas has worked himself up into a righteous rage against the entire unjust world. He climbs aboard to the whispered complaints of Dusty Miller.

'I am fed up trying to keep pressure *and* shovel coal single-handed. Captain noticed, of course. You're for it when we dock. Get in here, lad; we are not done yet and pressure is down.'

The familiarity of the abuse is somehow comforting. Douglas is about to climb down into the fug of the engine-room when a hand clamps his shoulder. He turns to hear his father's rasping voice.

'Well, son, I am come to bring you back home. You are needed in the family business and I will stand no more of this lazing about on the river.'

Douglas loses control. The past hours' shame and confusion rise like bile in his throat. He wrenches away from his father's grasp. 'I am a river man!' he shouts, 'and will be engineer in time! Go away! You have harmed enough people in our family. I will not be another!'

In a white rage he pushes wildly at his father's chest. The tall man windmills his arms but cannot maintain his balance. Over he goes, into the river, with a mighty splash. The crowd on the bank, waiting for the spectacle of the race, cheer at this curtain-raiser. The crew aboard the *Wairua* laugh and punch Douglas on the shoulder, his absence forgiven. Angus McPhee is not a popular man upriver. Meanwhile McPhee, panicked, thrashes and cries for assistance.

Douglas grins back at his friends, then, easily, all his rage evaporated, takes up a pole and offers it to his sodden father. McPhee seizes it and is hauled, dishevelled and complaining, to the deck. Douglas feels the stoker's strength in his arms and is deeply satisfied.

One of the Maori on the bank jumps into the water and wades over to the steamer, demonstrating to all that the sawmiller was never in danger: the water would never have reached past his chest had he but planted his feet calmly in the mud. This raises another round of applause. McPhee, dazed and humiliated, turns his dripping back on them all.

A tall and elegant woman brings a rug from the saloon, drapes it over McPhee's shoulders. 'There you are,' she says. 'That'll keep you warm till we get back ashore.' She leads McPhee to a vacant seat, then returns to Douglas. 'A childish act,' she says, her voice detached, as if speaking from a distance to someone of little note. 'Surely unnecessary?'

Douglas realises with a start that this fashionable lady is his sister Gertie. He stares at her, his jaw hanging open. How has she managed this transformation? Gertie's lumpy figure is now trimly corseted inside a green silk dress with darker trimmings and gleaming buttons. Her once lanky hair is pulled high on her head and tied artfully so that little ringlets cascade around her forehead. A deep amber shawl drapes around her shoulders, pinned at her breast with a golden brooch. This simple, elegant manner of dress is change enough, but more startling is her manner. Gone are the drooping shoulders and the pouting, sulky mouth. This Gertie stands proudly, her back straight, her eye clear, a faint smile on her lips as if she finds the doings of the world mildly amusing.

She watches Douglas, enjoying, perhaps, his amazement. When he remains silent she repeats her question. 'Surely unnecessary?' Like a kindly schoolteacher waiting for a reply from a reluctant pupil.

Douglas shifts his feet on the deck, lays a hand on the rail, reassured to feel its smooth wood under his fingers. 'Gertie,' he says at last. 'You've changed.'

'Yes.'

'You look . . . like a lady.'

'Yes. I hope so. And you do *not* look like a gentleman.'

Douglas laughs. 'What stoker aims to dress like a gentleman?'

'Exactly my point.' Gertie smiles at him, not with pity or scorn: simply not caring. 'Don't take any notice of Father,' she says. 'You are not needed in the business. I see to everything now.'

'Oh?' Douglas is irritated by her calm, wants to dent it.

'Father is a little old-fashioned in his business views. I think we will move out of sawmilling shortly. Raetihi is not the future for us. I have several ideas.' She smiles again. 'Which he will accept.'

Douglas finds it hard to believe that his stern father would let a woman run his business. Is Gertie mad, perhaps? But she seems so confident — almost beautiful, standing there so easy and elegant.

'So stay here in your dirty boat with your rough friends,' she says pleasantly. 'I am the one Father needs.' Without changing the even tone she adds, 'And if you ever do something like that to Father again, you will regret it. Deeply.'

Douglas breathes in sharply. 'You are hardly one to threaten. You who threw our sister overboard — to her ruin.' His voice rises. 'In this same river. With far worse consequences!'

Gertie raises her eyebrows. 'Surely it's beneath even you to bring that up. Bridget's fall was a simple accident. If anything, she brought it on herself. It was a sad, sad accident, no one to blame, well in the past now.'

Douglas, watching her closely for signs of discomfort or distress, is disappointed. Her calm grey eyes are steady on his.

'You, however,' she continues, 'pushed Father deliberately. He could have drowned.'

'Bridie lost her mind! She is out in the bush even now, alone and desperate . . .' Douglas feels a stab of guilt at his own words.

But Gertie is clearly impervious. She cuts in on him firmly. 'Bridget is not our concern. We cannot be held to account for anything in that direction. We did what we could when needed and are surely not expected to act further in the circumstances. She is no longer a member of the family. Father has crossed her name from the family Bible.'

Douglas can picture his father taking down the heavy, leather-bound volume that came out with him from Scotland; can imagine the black strokes of the pen drawn through Bridget's name and her date of birth. Perhaps his will be next. He goes to turn away but Gertie lays a gentle hand on his shoulder.

'It's all right, Douglas. Don't frown so. It's all right. Can't you see that?'

He brushes her hand away — a sharp, angry movement. 'It's not! It's not all right!'

She will not give way. Shows no sign of distress or anger. 'You are not thinking clearly. We have chosen different paths. You the river, I . . . other directions. That's good.'

'And Bridie?'

Gertie flicks at a speck of coal dust with an immaculately gloved hand. 'Douglas, our sister does not exist any more. Has not for many months. You know that.'

'I don't!'

'You do. Accept it.'

'She needs help!'

Her grey eyes are steady on his. 'Whose help, Douglas? Not mine. Yours?' She goes to her father, places a gentle hand on his drooping, blanketed shoulder. Without looking back, she guides him carefully towards the saloon.

'I'm needed in the engine-room,' mutters Douglas, but she's not listening. He escapes down to the busy throbbing heat and the welcome, forthright abuse of Dusty Miller.

Pita Morrow

What Oh!

THE PREMIER CATERER has been engaged to Cater
REFRESHMENTS and LUNCHEON at the

SCULLING CHAMPIONSHIP OF THE WORLD

W.S. DUSTIN begs to notify the Public that having
secured the privileges from Mr R. EARLE and the
WAITOTARA COUNTY COUNCIL for the erection of
LARGE MARQUEES, he intends to put on

Luncheon and Refreshments

IN FIRST CLASS STYLE

This should be a great convenience to those attending the race

Advertisement, Wanganui Herald, *December 1908*

FOR WEEKS, NOW, Pita has planned this day — the day
of his release. He will go straight to the tree stump behind
O'Leary's pub, where his cash is hidden, dig up the little bag and
head away — to the South Island or maybe Australia — where
no one knows him and no one will have reason to set the hand
of the law on him. Never, ever, will he be locked up again. The
days and weeks inside four blank and grubby walls have been
pure torture to Pita. He has tried every trick of imagination to
turn his prison cell into a dark and leafy refuge in the bush or
an empty stretch of river. Nothing worked. The heavy weight of

bricks and timber enclosing him won out every time.

He feared to find Danny O'Dowd in prison for the death of the girl; feared that he would be recognised by someone and tried, too, for that death. Or the ruined steamer. But not even the long-serving lags knew of Danny or any trial concerning a drowned girl. Pita didn't like to ask too many questions. Perhaps such a crime went down to Wellington for trial. At any rate no one questioned his identity. Phillip Matthews he remained.

But now, with the money in his hand and the blessed sun warming his back, the excitement of the day suddenly overshadows all his plans. Pita pulls his cap lower over his eyes and saunters, with everyone else, to the river. In prison, all the talk has been of Wiri Webb and the sculling race. Pita boasted that if the race were with paddles he himself might well stand a chance of beating the champion, but the older lags laughed him down.

'Our Wiri trains day and night.'

'He has arm muscles harder than pure solid timber.'

'Not a man in the world can come close to him. God himself would lay odds on Wiri Webb.'

Pita has to see it. The river itself, as much as the race. It hasn't occurred to him that his own people from upriver might be down here. He walks quietly along the bank, heading with the crowds towards Upokongaro. After a while he forgets to keep his head down and his shoulders hunched. He walks with his old swing, grinning to see the crowded cartloads of spectators, the mounted gentlemen trotting ahead, the dozens of waka poling up against the current, loaded with passengers. He whistles a favourite tune. The air is calm; the surface of the river green and smooth. A perfect day for sculling.

He asks an old fellow where the finishing line will be. The man points further upriver. 'But this will be as good a viewing place as any,' he says. 'Wiri will have tired the other fellow out well before the finish line. I reckon the race will be won about here.'

Pita nods and looks about him. Plenty of people have had the same idea. The riverbank is already two or three deep. He climbs a little higher, until he can see the stretch of water up and down. This will do. He sits with his back against a willow trunk and breathes in the earthy richness. His river. Below are several waka, seemingly untended. For a moment Pita is tempted to slip one away from its mooring and head upriver. His arms twitch to be thrusting the pole deep; he longs to stand, bracing his bare feet against the rough wood, shifting his weight slightly this way and that to keep the balance. But then he remembers the horror of the prison cell and looks away.

A little to one side a bookie is taking bets. Pita watches as, one after another, spectators go up to him, hand over the money and come away with their slips of paper. The odds would not be high but at least he could increase his capital if he bet it all. He scans the crowd. No one he knows. And anyway, the incident with the dead girl and the logs would surely be forgotten by now. Pita walks casually down the bank, waits for a moment when the bookie is alone and approaches him.

'Twenty-five pounds on Webb to win,' he says quietly.

The little fellow looks at him sharply. 'Twenty-five pounds? You trying to break me?'

Pita repeats the bet.

'Come off it.' The bookie is pleading with him. 'I'm going to make little enough as it is. If you want to bet big, take it to the Tote.'

'I'll make it thirty, then,' says Pita, enjoying the argument, forgetting to keep his voice down.

The bookie looks at him fearfully. 'Please,' he says, 'go somewhere else.'

Pita steps closer. Shows him the bag of coin. 'You're obliged to take my bet, mister. You want me to make a fuss?'

It's an empty threat but the bookie doesn't know that. Sulkily he fills in the slip, takes Pita's money.

'I dunno why I do this,' he mutters. 'Not one punter has bet on Arnst. Someone could take a risk, at least.'

Pita turns away without seeing the next man coming to lay his bet. He would know him, though — Danny O'Dowd. The bookie sighs to hear that Danny also wants to lay a large sum on Webb. Twenty pounds, for God's sake. This new punter is edgy, looking this way and that, shifting his feet and grinning at nothing. The bookie decides to take a risk.

'Twenty on Arnst then,' he mutters, filling in the slip, 'at four to one.'

Danny nods, oblivious. Pockets the slip. The bookie tips him a wink. 'Good luck,' he says as the fool walks away.

Pita is sauntering back to his vantage point when Sergeant Tim Naylor calls out loudly to him. 'Phillip Matthews! You've come into money, then?'

Pita freezes. Thinks about running. But surely he has committed no crime? He turns with a smile. 'Can't a fellow lay a bet on a great day like this?' he says.

'A fellow fresh out of jail doesn't generally carry large sums about his person.'

Pita shouts at him, desperate that he might be locked away again. 'It is *earned* money! I worked for it — every penny!'

'Doing what, I wonder?'

Pita, alarmed at the questioning, is about to make a run for it when he is slammed to the ground from another direction. Then hauled to his feet, his cap ripped from his head. Danny takes a bunch of Pita's shirt in his fist and hauls him close. He seems to have gone mad — laughing, swearing, shaking Pita back and forth like a dog with a piece of rag. The constable is forgotten.

'Pita Morrow!' shouts Danny for all to hear. 'It's Pita bloody Morrow come back from the dead!'

Pita tries to pull away. He can't make out Danny's reaction. Why would Danny shout his name — call attention — when the policeman is not two paces away?

'Keep your voice down,' he mutters, 'or we'll both be caught.'

'Is it really you?' shouts Danny. He turns to the gathering crowd 'It is! It's Pita Morrow! We thought him dead.' The spectators laugh with Danny, sharing his delight, offering congratulations. Tim Naylor watches closely.

Danny traces a finger over Pita's broken nose and scarred cheek. 'Oh God, did I do that damage? I'm true and sorry for it, brother, and have cursed myself every day since.'

Pita tries to shake free from this laughing madman. The constable will surely pounce any moment. 'The police is right behind you,' he mutters in Danny's ear. 'You run that way and I'll go the other.'

But Danny holds him tighter. Pita can feel the noose already about his neck. Tim Naylor steps forward and the crowd parts to let his uniform through. Pita despairs.

'Are you Pita Morrow?' asks Naylor.

Pita is about to deny any knowledge of the name but Danny gets in first.

'He is! My brother-in-law! It's him, all right!'

The constable speaks sternly. 'Pita Morrow, I should have you in for giving a false identity. Not to mention ill-gotten gains.'

Pita notices that the dead girl does not seem to be on the list. He decides to keep his mouth shut until matters become clearer.

'But,' continues Naylor, 'for one thing, your parents would dearly appreciate a sight of the son they think gone. And for another' — the constable is actually smiling! — 'for another, this is a day of celebration for Wanganui, and you are just out of jail. Shall we keep it that way?' He offers his hand and the startled Pita shakes it. The crowd cheers.

'Now off with you,' says Naylor, grinning. 'I am sick of the sight of both of you.'

Danny will not leave hold of Pita but steers him away through the crowd. Pita thinks he must have lost his mind, the way he is hopping and shouting. Then both turn, startled, as a shot rings out. But it is only the umpire's starting pistol. Wiri Webb is about to defend his world sculling title.

Ruvey Morrow

ARTISTIC
Photography

at the **TELSA STUDIOS** Opposite
the Post Office Wanganui
SCULLING WEEK —— photographs taken at special
concession prices during this
week!

Wanganui Herald, *15 December 1908*

BERT HAD US a good spot on the bank where we could see up
and down river. A grand day, everyone in their Sunday clothes,
strangers exchanging news and views as if they'd known each
other since birth. I'd never seen such a crowd! Every citizen of
Wanganui must have been there and more. A very friendly lady
next to me said she and her husband and her three sisters had
come up all the way from Foxton to watch the race! She was very
interested when I told her I was cook at Pipiriki House.

'Oh,' she cried, 'we have booked to visit there after Christmas.
They say the scenery is outstanding.' I told her all the fine

appointments of the House. She had read about the electricity and hot and cold running water and up-to-date sanitation, but didn't know about our croquet lawn and the beautiful winter-garden room.

Everyone wants to visit Pipiriki!' she said. 'You are lucky to live there.' So much for the doom-sayers who predict Mr Hatrick's steamer service will wither away when the railway goes through. Whanganui River and Pipiriki House will always be jewels in New Zealand's tourist route, mark my words.

A brass band marched up the road, very smart in their red caps and blue jackets, playing lively tunes and earning cheers as they passed. Bert said my mouth was hanging open like a child's. Living in our quiet little backwater, we forget how many people there are in the Dominion now — not that I'd say a word against Pipiriki: it is very modern, but in its own way.

Then Eru, who has sharp eyes, pointed to a little puff of smoke away downriver. 'They're away!' he shouted, and at that second we all heard the crack of the pistol. I could see nothing but two dots in the distance but our Wiri would soon be rowing up in our reach; we were all ready to cheer him on and wave the flag that Mere and I had stitched, which said 'WEBB AND WANGANUI — 1ST IN THE WORLD' in green letters on an old white sheet.

Beyond the two dots was a great black mass of smoke from the stacks of every one of Mr Hatrick's fleet, following behind the rowers. I had to hope the umpire would keep them back a respectful distance. It would be a fearful thing to hear those great churning steamers advancing side by side up behind you. Then as they came a bit closer the people around us raised a great cheer, for you could see our man was pulling ahead, and see his long oars flashing in and out at a great rate, the other fellow struggling to match his speed. Oh, I was that excited! 'Wiri! Wiri Webb!'

we all shouted. A tall fellow in a fancy uniform stood above us on the hill with some kind of trumpet or horn, which he pointed to the sky and blew long, high notes of triumph. It was like the King himself arriving. Mere and I waved our flag and shouted till we were hoarse. I am not ashamed to say that the tears were rolling down my cheeks. Definitely Wiri was pulling ahead now by a couple of boat lengths.

But then the strangest change. The crowd downriver quietened. We could see their waving arms go slack by their sides and hear their cheers wavering. I said to Bert later it was like the dark stillness of storm approaching, the way all the shouting and the ferment died away.

Eru was the first to see it. He turned to Bert, his face a picture of misery. 'It's not Wiri that's leading; it's the other fellow.' Then we all saw it. That Arnst from the South Island was well ahead and still pulling away! The trumpeter on the hill put down his instrument; Mere and I let our flag flap to our feet; Bert muttered that his two shillings were dead and gone. Somehow you could tell that our Wiri was beaten, even though the race was not done. His strokes were steady, but the other man pulled harder and faster. No doubt he was the better man, the wretch.

Well, he won and that was that.

The best of the day was yet to come, though. The two scullers proceeded up the river to the finishing line, the crowd all about us silent and stunned. Then came the Hatrick fleet — the three paddle-steamers in a row, followed by a boil of the upriver boats, even little *Ongarue*, so we gave the parade a cheer to keep our spirits up. And in all that burst of noise and black smoke we didn't notice Danny and Stella till they were almost on us, shouting and cheering as if we had won the world championship, not lost it to that silly little Avon River in the south.

My son Pita with them.

I could speak no word. You could have offered me a thousand pounds to say something but I would not have been able. There he was. His same sheepish grin, shifting his feet, expecting a scolding — as well he might — but whole and well. His nose twisted and a scar down one cheek — that would be the blow Danny gave him. I felt all along he was not dead. Didn't I say so? Didn't I tell Bert? My Pita.

It was Bert found his voice first. 'And where have you been, lad?' His tone ominous.

'In jail, Pa. A stupid thing. Just a mistaken identity.'

All charm and apology: he was always good at excuses, which today cut no ice at all with his Pa. Bert gave him a good tongue-lashing in both languages, telling him how sick with worry I had been all these months, how he owed to his whanau to keep in touch, how Bert would personally scrag him if he had shamed the family name with wrong-doings. What he said in his own language I can't say but the tone was blazing hot.

Bert did not mention his own heart-sickness but I had seen it — saw now the pleasure that he could not hide behind all those stern words. At last I found my voice, which came out shaking with tears. 'Pita Morrow,' I cried, 'you could have got word to us even from jail. We have had no word for an entire year! Wretched boy!' But my heart was not in the scolding. I had to hold that scrawny son of mine to make sure he was real and solid and not some ghost.

'Sorry, Ma,' he muttered into my shoulder. 'I thought . . .'

Whatever he was going to say was drowned then by a great blasting and hooting of steam whistles and ships' bells. The race was over.

Pita looked up, frowning. 'Why are you not all cheering? All these people? You'd think we'd lost the race.'

'We have, son,' growled Bert, 'and I've lost two shillings that could have been put to better use.'

Pita's mouth dropped open. He looked from one to other of us as if he didn't believe what he'd heard. Well then, I thought. That stupid boy has bet a large sum and lost it. You could read it all, clear as a book, in his face. That will do him no harm, I thought. Perhaps he will come home and take on a decent trade. But Pita just laughed. Then pointed at Danny and laughed louder, slapped him on the back. Poor Danny was in misery.

'Danny, you didn't,' said Stella, unbelieving. 'You leave me alone all these months to earn money and then you risk it all on a *race*?'

'Not all of it,' said Danny. 'Not all of it, Stell. Only half.'

'Half!' cried Stella. 'Let me see!'

Dear oh dear. Danny is born unlucky, or foolish, but at least Stella loves him and at least he had not the strength to lay our Pita out for good.

Poor Danny, head hanging, handed her his betting slip.

'Twenty pound!' she shouted. And then stopped, peered at the slip, then back at Danny. 'Is this some joke?'

Danny could not look at her for shame. 'I'm sorry, Stell,' he whispered. 'Sweetheart.'

But our Stell was laughing, her big belly heaving up and down till I thought she might have the baby on the spot, tears running down her cheeks.

'Look at it — look, Danny!' She waved the slip in front of his nose. Gave him a laughing great hug.

A blessing for once that our Danny never learned his letters too well. He had bet on Arnst at four to one!

Well, it was all too much for me. What with Pita and then this nice little nest-egg for the new baby and all the laughter, I had to sit down and catch my breath. Stella sat beside me on the grass.

'Oh Ma, are you all right? You're as pale as a ghost.'

My heart was going like a train but I said nothing. Tried to smile through all the tears.

'Ma,' she said, her dear, pretty face anxious, 'rest here a bit while Pa brings the waka. There's been enough excitement today to last the year.' She smiled, proud as a lady. 'And the baby not born yet!'

'Not today, please the Blessed Virgin,' I said, giving her a little pat. 'I could not stand another thing.'

'Is Danny forgiven, Ma? He makes mistakes sometimes . . .'

'Mistakes!' I said. 'That is a kind way of putting it.'

'But I love him, Ma, that's all there is to it. We fit.'

They do — they are a proper pair, for all their differences, so I gave them my blessing. Bert will no doubt come around to it in a while, now that he has his son back.

AS IT HAPPENED, there was more news that day. Father Soulas had a word with Bert as we crowded into the waka for the long journey home. He said that poor Bridie had run off. She was in a bad state, he said, and would Bert run up to the hermit's place when we got to Pipiriki. Father said it was not likely she had the strength to get that far but he would be grateful if we checked. He is very humble and polite for a great priest who, in my opinion, should be cardinal at the very least, though goodness knows I would be sad to see him leave our mission. Bert agreed to go when he could, but said we would not be home till the next day, as we had to stop for the night someplace upriver. Father Soulas said Bridie's baby was safe at the convent at Ranana, so the concern this time was not so great.

'Not so great?' said Danny as soon as the priest had gone. 'Is Bridie not one of God's poor creatures too?'

That outburst of his had me frowning. Stella too, I noted. Surely the boy was over his silly obsession with Bridie? Mind you, Danny had a point. But the sad thing was, we had all given up on Bridie. There is only so much a body can manage. Bridie had become too difficult and too strange. Only the previous Sunday Sister Carmel had said Bridie had slipped away beyond their ability to help her. She would have to go down to the lunatic asylum in Wanganui.

Danny and Stella

While we sympathise with Webb on his defeat — the more so because of the fateful circumstances known only to the few, which prevented him from rowing as his many friends and supporters believed, and rightly so, that he could row — we must express our heartiest satisfaction that the championship is retained in New Zealand . . .

Arnst is a man of magnificent muscular development, added to which he seems to have a natural aptitude for rowing otherwise he could not possibly have achieved success in so short a time . . .

While again sympathising with Webb we must congratulate him on the plucky fight he put up against such odds — odds which would have disheartened most men. He fought against fate and fought bravely to the finish. All honour to him.

Extracts from the report of the race,
Wanganui Herald, *16 December 1908*

AS THE LADEN motor-waka approaches Ranana, Bert says they must stop for the night. He won't risk the last few rapids in the dark, he says, not with such precious cargo. Stella smiles and cradles her belly. Pa is thinking of his two children and his unborn grandchild all together here. What a day! Stella is dog-tired, though, and ready enough to settle. There are no lights showing at the little settlement, but they can see the dark shape of the convent standing against the moonlit sky. There will be a bed for them somewhere. Stella would happily put her head down on the grass of the bank and sleep in the open, but Danny has other ideas. He takes her hand, easing her onto the landing as Bert holds the waka steady. Carefully he supports her with one arm, guiding her up the path to the wharenui. She leans on his shoulder, happy for once to let him make the decisions.

Sure enough, there are people awake and ready to welcome them onto the marae. The beautiful whare is already crowded with travellers returning home after the big day, but there is space still for the family. Stella groans with pleasure as she lies down on the mattress of straw, her mother beside her. Danny has stayed outside talking to some of the men, but now he comes inside and kneels to kiss her, to stroke her hair. His hand rests on the taut skin of her belly. She smiles in the dark to feel the baby shift under his hand.

Danny laughs quietly. 'As active as his mother!'

'Oh, it's a boy is it?'

'Boy or girl. Oh Stell, it's so good to be with you again.'

She can tell he is about to say something difficult. The baby shifts again. She waits for the twinge of pain to pass.

'Sweetheart,' he says. Then, 'I have arranged a horse. I want to ride up to the hermit tonight.'

Stella breathes in sharply. She wishes she could see his face but it is too dark. She would like to cry out — No! — but her mother is already asleep beside her.

'It's all right, Stell,' he says. She can hear the smile in his voice, and feels that it is, indeed, all right. He whispers in her ear. 'She is in need of help. She will have gone to the hermit, but he will not be able to manage her. It must be me.'

She is fearful that the old obsession may reawaken. What she hears now in his voice is simple concern, but will he change? 'Ride carefully,' she whispers, and when he tries to rise she holds him back. 'Bridie has changed. She is very difficult.'

'I know.'

'All she cares about is to have her baby back.'

'Yes. I know.'

'You may have to force her. To come with you.'

'I will be gentle.'

He touches her cheek and slips away.

IN THE EARLY morning Stella walks up to the convent. Back at the marae a few kuia are up preparing food, but the Morrows are still sleeping. Stella noticed as she crept out of the wharenui that Pa had a bunch of his son's shirt held firmly in his sleeping hand. Pita would not slip away without Pa knowing it!

A smiling Sister answers her knock. They have been up for hours, she says — no worry about disturbing them. She is happy enough to lead Stella around to the nursery. They have several orphan children, she says, more's the pity, but surely Stella is not thinking to adopt with one of her own so close? The Sister sighs over the many mothers who have died this last year — tuberculosis, in most cases. It is a crying shame.

Stella asks to see the Chinese baby, John. The Sister raises her eyebrows but leads the way. There he is, quiet in his cot, so small, so beautiful.

'Would there be a problem to adopt him?' asks Stella.

'My dear, no one seems to want to claim him.'

'There was someone — a brother to his dead father.'

'We have tried to trace him, with no success. The whole family has disappeared. He was not welcome, I believe, up at Ohakune and was moved on — forcibly, they say.' The Sister tut tuts. 'A Chinese baby will not be easy to place. He is doing well at last, but we have had a struggle.'

'Is Bridie allowed to see him?'

'Bless you, no! She was smothering him to death, poor mite.

We will certainly not be going through all that again. Dear Lord.'

Stella looks down at the sleeping John. She has a sudden memory of Charlie Chee. Of him tearing his carrots out of the ground and hurling them away in his despair.

'I'll come back,' she says to the Sister. 'Maybe we can take him.'

AT ABOUT THE same time, early that morning, Danny comes finally to the hermit's hut. He knows she will be here. Before he leaves the bush, before he comes to the little clearing, he dismounts quietly and tethers his horse. As he walks into the open the whole scene is laid out, every shocking detail.

The river is calm and dark, the morning mist just beginning to rise, pearly in places where the shafts of sunlight strike. Danny sees the little sandy beach, the bank rising up to the hut in the clearing. No smoke rises from the hermit's fire. The morning is still. Birdsong echoes back and forth across the river. The hermit sits, hunched under a blanket near the water's edge. Beside him lies Bridie, white and still, her hands folded across her chest, her copper hair smooth and wet each side of her face.

Even at a distance Danny can see she is dead. He remembers the violence of the earlier time, when she lay a short distance away upriver. He hears again the crack of his fist when he struck Pita, the rasping coughs as Bridie spewed up the river. But this scene is peaceful. The descending notes of the bellbirds tolling her death sweetly, the river sliding past without comment.

He walks forward slowly, not wanting to break the moment.

The old man looks up. His long grey hair is tangled, his face haggard. The hands that hold the blanket tight around his old shoulders shake, but he smiles to see Danny.

'Good lad,' he says.

Danny sits the other side of Bridie. He strokes her hair. Both men sit a while, watching the river.

'She drowned,' says the hermit at last.

Danny nods. Tears run down his cheeks. 'The poor darling,' he whispers. 'Poor sweet Bridie.'

Later Sam Blencoe says, 'You are the right one to bury her. Put her up with Charlie Chee.'

He will say no more, nor will Danny question him. It feels the right thing to do. If others rail against it, let them. Danny lights the fire and makes them both a mug of tea. He does not want to leave the quietness of that place, the sight of Bridie lying there, so peaceful. But at last he goes up the track and finds a place near the marked grave where Charlie Chee lies, and digs into the rich earth of the bush. The strike of the spade and the ache in his shoulders satisfy a need; he digs the hole deep and generous.

He walks back, eager to see her again. Nothing has changed. The hermit. Bridie. He lifts the light weight of her in his arms and carries her up gently to her grave. Sam follows, staggering a little from the stiffness in his limbs.

When it is done they stand together beside the mound of dark sweet earth. Sam pulls two carrots from the overgrown garden and lays them, side by side, on the grave. When Danny smiles at the odd gesture, Sam only shrugs.

Later they sit quietly together on Charlie Chee's bench, looking down at the river.

'Their boy should know this place,' says Sam Blencoe. 'You keep it clear when I am gone.'

Danny nods, glad to be given the task. 'I will bring him here. I will tell him.'

He watches as the old man stands stiffly, takes the broom of twigs that is propped against the hut and slowly sweeps the fallen leaves from Charlie's grave, stroking away from the mound until the earth is evenly scored and clear. Then the two take their leave, walking back through the bush in silence.

At Sam's clearing, Danny stops and turns to face the hermit. He holds Sam's bony shoulders for a moment, would like to draw him close but feels the resistance.

'You're a good man,' he says.

Sam snorts, shoots him a strange, wide look and walks away.

For a moment Danny watches as the old fellow makes his way down through the clearing. His breath catches in his throat to see again the place where she lay; his tears flow afresh. Then he turns to his horse, mounts and rides downriver, back to Stella.

Samuel Blencoe

SHE COME UP into my clearing just before dawn. First I thought it were that wild boar come again to root in my patch. I took up my stick and went out. The saddest sight there, in the early light, the poor demented girl, scratching the dirt like some animal, pulling up clods of moss, holding them close to her nose.

When she seen me she come stumbling, holding out her empty arms, clear as day to see she were showing me the lack of her babby. The sounds coming from her would break your heart.

Dear God.

She lifted my old shirt and thrust her face inside, searching my own old skin for some sign. Then went up to the hut. I could hear her pulling my few things about up there. Maybe there was some thought in her fogged-up mind that since I were with her that day they took her babby, I might have him here.

She would not give up. Up and down she went, searching and groaning. One arm had a long cut, the dried blood all down her dress, both legs scratched and her feet also cut, the black dirt on them mixed with blood. I thought to wash her but had not the strength to bring her to the water. Up and down, here and there she scrabbled, restless as a kiwi in the night, searching for its food. I had to let her be. Wait till she might calm.

She did not calm but at last slowed from the exhaustion. Suddenly her legs gave way and she sat on the grass there, still groaning. I went to her. She turned her face up to me. It was worse than when she found Charlie Chee. The deep misery there, and her eyes begging me to help.

I took her poor mashed arm, then, helped her up and she come down to the water. We walked in, the two of us, where the sand is soft and the slope gentle, up to our knees. Poor Bridie still moaning, but quieter now, the cool of the water taking her breath. Slowly I pushed her down till she sat, the rags of her dress floating out, her head leaning upon my arm. It were heavy work but I washed her clean: her cuts, her blackened feet, her dress. The slow movements of my washing calming her a little but those beseeching eyes still locked on to me.

Then I prayed for strength and pushed her sweet face under. One kind thing I could do for her. She struggled a while but I breathed deep for the strength and held her under till she found her peace at last.

Afterwards I could pull her no further than the sandy bank, so there we both stayed. The bright shafts of sun found the river; the mist rose. I told her what I saw.

Some historical dates relevant to Landings

1884   Snagging punts operated on the Whanganui River, to clear rapids of debris.

1891   The Wanganui River Trust was established by government grant to create navigable channels through rapids. Surveyor John T. Stewart headed the trust.

Alexander Hatrick's first paddle-steamer, the *Wairere*, made its maiden voyage from Wanganui township to Pipiriki. It took eleven hours.

1894	A road between Pipiriki and Raetihi was opened to wheeled traffic.
1899	Hatrick bought Pipiriki House from Huddle and modernised it. The house described in this novel burned down in 1909 and was immediately rebuilt by Hatrick, opening in 1910 with all modern conveniences. This Pipiriki House also burned down in 1959. In the 1990s an attempt was made to rebuild on the old foundations but the venture ran out of steam. The unfinished shell remains.
1903	Steamer trips above Pipiriki began: a weekly service to Taumarunui, then the terminus of the main trunk line. Carrier pigeon communication between stages was established.
1903–08	Clashes between loggers on the river and Hatrick's steamer service.
1903–13	Heyday for the tourist river service. Fourteen boats in the Hatrick fleet. Three-day tours between Taumarunui and Wanganui, via Houseboat and Pipiriki House. Service operated three times a week.
1904	The Houseboat (*Makere*) was built in Taumarunui and floated down to Maraekowhai. It was moved to Retaruke in 1927 and destroyed by fire in 1933.
1905	The Colonial Drink Bill stipulated that no liquor should be dispatched or delivered within the Rohe

Potae (King Country) and upper Whanganui River.

1907   Joseph Ward successfully proposed a legislative amendment extending the English-language requirement for prospective immigrants.

1907   A branch of the Anti-Asiatic League flourished in the Ruapehu district.

1907–08   A coach service connected the north and south railheads of the main trunk line between Raurimu and Ohakune. This tourist service also connected with Pipiriki House via Raetihi.

1909   Main trunk express train service between Wellington and Auckland opened.

1928   Wanganui River Services Ltd took over A. Hatrick Co Ltd (then owned by Hatrick's heirs). The service dwindled from then on, and the company failed in 1964.

NOTE: Two of the steamers named in this novel — the paddle-steamer *Waimarie* and screw-steamer *Wairua* — have been dug from the mud where they sank and have since been faithfully restored by volunteers of the Whanganui Riverboat Centre. These now run regular trips out of Wanganui. A third steamer — the greyhound of the fleet, *Ongarue* — is under reconstruction. The rapids, however, are no longer maintained in a navigable state for these craft. Hatrick's tourist route, 'The Rhine of Maoriland', which flourished in the first part of the twentieth century, can now be enjoyed only by canoe, kayak or jetboat.

Reproductions of John Stewart's superb hand-drawn map of the river, its rapids and the surrounding area, dated 1903, are available from the Whanganui Riverboat Centre.

JENNY PATTRICK'S BEST-SELLING historical novel *The Denniston Rose* tells the story of the bleak coal-mining settlement of Denniston on the South Island's West Coast — a place that makes or breaks all those who live there. Into this chaotic community comes five-year-old Rose and her mother, riding up the infamous Incline at night, in a storm. No one knows what has driven them there, but most agree they must be desperate to choose the isolated community.

Since its publication in 2003 *The Denniston Rose* has sold more than 45,000 copies and regularly appears on the bestseller lists.

EIGHTEEN YEARS HAVE passed since Rose arrived in Denniston, and she is now an unconventional young woman with a zest for life. Rose is expected to marry her childhood friend Michael Hanratty, but when dark and stubborn Brennan Scobie comes back to Denniston after a seven-year absence, conflict is inevitable.

The turn of the century has brought new challenges and opportunities to the inhabitants of Denniston in this fascinating sequel to the bestselling *The Denniston Rose*.

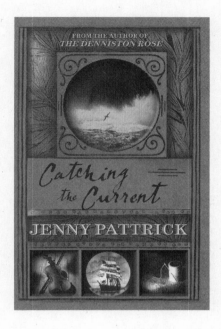

CON THE BRAKE from Jenny Pattrick's popular Denniston novels gets his own story in *Catching the Current*, which traces Conrad Rasmussen's emigration from the Faroe Islands to Manawatu in the 1860s. It is a tale of new lands and old songs, of seafaring and war and the search for love, and the early connections between Denmark and New Zealand.